WHO IF I CRY OUT

The Texas Pan American Series

Who if I cry out

BY GUSTAVO CORÇÃO

Translated by CLOTILDE WILSON

"If I cry out, who will hear me among the ranks of the angels?"

RAINER MARIA RILKE

UNIVERSITY OF TEXAS PRESS • AUSTIN

The Texas Pan American Series is published with the assistance of a revolving publication fund established by the Pan American Sulphur Company and other friends of Latin America in Texas. Publication of this book was also assisted by a grant from the Rockefeller Foundation through the Latin American translation program of the Association of American University Presses.

Library of Congress Catalog Card Number 67–64317

Printed by the University of Texas Printing Division, Austin
Bound by Universal Bookbindery, Inc., San Antonio

ISBN 978-0-292-71252-2

TRANSLATOR'S PREFACE

This philosophical Brazilian novel of our time by one of Rio de Janeiro's leading Catholic intellectuals is an elaboration in fictional form of a theme to be found in one of the author's earlier works. In the book that recounts his conversion to Catholicism, *A Descoberta do Outro* (translated under the title *My Neighbor as Myself*) Senhor Corção divides man's life span into two periods, childhood and adolescence. "In childhood," he says, "we live *ludus*, the germ of eternity, in adolescence, we live a pseudo-*ludus*, vertigo, and the first shuddering notion of mortality. . . . After the first plunge into adolescence life continues to leap and sway; now erect, now fallen in the depths of abysses; now pregnant with eternity, now poisoned by the awareness of death. . . . and all that is left of our hope of eternity is despair. . . . And all this because of the constant nearness of death."

"Here is material for another book," the writer observed, and thus suggested what might be the subject of a subsequent work. This work was indeed to appear some time later as the thoughtful novel, *Lições de Abismo* (Abysmal Lessons), whose title we have changed, since a literal rendition is not felicitous in English.

The novel's protagonist, José Maria, dying of leukemia, does indeed fall into an abyss of despair and bewilderment. His awareness heightened by the imminence of death, he communes with his soul (it too an abyss, an "abyss of subjectivity") and strives to enlighten his spirit in its gropings through the darkness toward the Absolute. Here, as in so many instances, is evinced the Brazilian writer's close affinity with the German poet, Rainer Maria Rilke, who, in a letter written in his youth, asserted: "I believe it is the duty of every artist to penetrate the fog of arid materialism and attain that lucidity of soul which throws out a golden bridge into limitless eternities." It is precisely such an enlightenment of soul that José Maria is seeking.

Man's perplexity and anguish in the face of death is but one of many of this deeply sensitive novel's Existentialist themes. The solitude of the individual, his anonymity, the impermanence of life and its apparent absurdity, all are poignantly expressed with a beauty of style that is often lyrical.

"Who if I cry out will hear me from among the ranks of the angels?" wonders José Maria, as he identifies with the poet, and, peering into the depths of a "dream Adriatic," repeats that passionate cry of the first of Rilke's *Duinese Elegies*, proclaiming the loneliness of the soul and questioning the enigma of life and death.

CONTENTS

PART THREE: JOURNEY TO THE CENTER OF THE EARTH

"Thou shalt find true repose only in the Blood . . ."

SAINT CATHERINE OF SIENA

part 1 KUNDRY

November 11th

The Announced Visitor

Now that the first moment of shock is over, I am beginning to experience a strange exultation in this waiting. For the first time in my life I feel as though I have achieved some coherence with myself, some order. The proportion between the present result and the long preparation—long, confused, disordered—will appear absurd. But is it not always so? Who could list the ridiculous number of trials and errors, the wasted days and futile suffering that precede the composing of a sonata? Yet in half an hour it comes before us and has its say, and it dies more quickly than the rose.

They tell that after Rilke wrote those first verses dictated by the wind of Duino's lofty cliffs he kept the germ alive for twelve years, years of wandering, conflict, and dissipated effort until that moment when in four days, as one who is dying, he realized his perfect elegies.[1] Is it probably not always so? May not life itself be no more than a long, confused bustling about in the wings, preparatory to a fleeting apotheosis?

I am alone. Two or three months pass quickly, and at this season of the year, if my absence is noticed, people will suppose that I have gone to take the waters. Eunice, I believe, is in São Paulo. Raul has not written to me for a long time, and from what he said in his last letter he is not planning to leave Belo Horizonte. He will get the news.

But I do not wish to linger over what my ex-wife and ex-son will think and feel. I am alone now. The house is too large, of course, but that will allow me more complete isolation. I am occupying

[1] Memories of Rainer Maria Rilke recur throughout the book. Indeed numerous parallels are apparent between its hypersensitive protagonist and the German poet (trans.).

Raul's room. I have brought an armchair into it, a few book cases, my work table, and the small opaline vase in which three or four roses will always keep me company.

The maid whom Dona Alice got for me will bring my coffee and my meals. She is discreet and preoccupied. She knows nothing, I believe, about our life. Nor do I know anything about hers. It is better that way; and, as two months pass quickly, there will not be time for us to become acquainted and have a falling out. Mornings I shall go out for a little while so that she may put the room in order, and then I shall return. As yet I have not decided whether or not I shall buy a paper. I think not. I must put every agitation, every accessory as far from me as possible, since the plan I am gradually maturing is to capture that rhythm that has so far escaped me. That is what is supremely important: the harmony, the precise composition, the counterpoint of time, and now it lies within my grasp.

I arranged the books that I had selected, adjusted the roses in the vase, and tidied my wardrobe, experiencing the pleasure of a bachelor who is establishing his quarters and a little that of the traveler who is taking inventory of his stateroom. And then, looking about to see if there was still some discordant note, I sat down in the armchair to await in decent and orderly fashion the visitor announced by Dr. Aquiles.

That was how I used to wait for Eunice in the house on Ipiranga Street, the only one that I was able to find for the urgency of our love. At that time there were few apartments. That house, also, was too large, and we had to close three bedrooms and two drawing rooms, which were not needed for our rendezvous. Love and death require little space. A house is superfluous. A house is necessary when life is extraordinarily active and undisciplined, when there are children who will not be quiet, maid servants who run vacuum cleaners, telephones that ring, and visitors who arrive unexpectedly. But love and death are alike in that they do not need all that abundance of parasitic details, utensils and compartments that make a house an effervescent and noisy microcosm.

And so it was that in a house thus simplified and in a quiet and stillness thus organized I used to wait for Eunice twenty-six years ago, during the adventurous weeks that preceded our marriage in Uruguay.

She was always late. Something unforeseen always came along to upset her plans, which would be perfect were it not for the existence of chance. One day it would be a streetcar that collided with a truck, the next an aunt that she found ailing—Eunice would come in breathless, full of explanations and events; and while she was taking off her gloves and hat—a hat was *de rigueur* in those days—I would follow the motions that she made in front of the mirror. What did the reasons for her lateness matter to me then? What matter the feverish and resentful impatience that had goaded me for an hour and a half? She had come.

"Wait, dear, let me remove my lipstick—"

She had come. She had been late, to be sure, because it seems part of her nature, her very essence, part of her feminine mysteriousness to keep others waiting.

From the time I was a small boy, I have seen that secret struggle between man who waits and woman who is late. My father and mother used to go out every evening, and every evening I witnessed the same scene: my father, pacing up and down the drawing room, snapping his fingers.

"Woman, we're going to be late!"

"Just a minute, for heaven's sake! You make me nervous!"

And upstairs Mama's high heels beat a hurried tattoo. From the bedroom to the dressing room, from the dressing room to the bathroom, from the bathroom to the bedroom again. Clack! Clack! Clack! And my father, back and fourth, snapping his fingers.

They always went out arguing. My father was sarcastic. He used to say that women turn everything into a ballet and have the knack of not being able to put on five garments without executing ten thousand graceful gestures. My mother, however, paid no attention to those sarcastic remarks; it was I who heard them. And it was I, too, who would wait far into the night for their return, straining my ears, following the street sounds and the striking of the big drawing-room clock, my eyes fastened upon the narrow strip of light under the door. When they came in I would pretend to be asleep, but I could not always maintain the pretense. More than once my anguish was so intense that I could not conceal it. Then Mama would find me bathed in tears, exhausted from crying.

"Silly, you're a big man—"

Later I would hear their muted conversation.

"That child's getting nervous—"

"All children of that age are nervous."

"Perhaps we should consult Dr. Beltrão?"

One day Eunice did not return home. Raul was twelve years old. I waited. I waited ten years in an absurd, improbable, irrational fashion, as one who imagines that he has won in the lottery without even having a ticket, as one who expects a miracle.

I said just now that the need to keep others waiting is of woman's very essence, part of her profound mystery. Yet, on the other hand, I am forced to recognize that the problem is complex and paradoxical. If it is true that woman is fickle, it is evident likewise—and one has but to observe the mother of a large family and the cloistered nun—that woman is a colossus of stability. Generally it is she who waits. In the majority of situations, it is she who suffers a cruel waiting that surpasses our masculine capacity and eludes our imagination.

Yes, it is she who waits; but when she faces the desired adversary in a love affair, though she knows that her role is to wait and that her nature is essentially passive, she finds herself compelled at times to take a certain initiative in order to excite him. Then in order to be seen, she moves about—she dances. Consider, for example, Machedo de Assis' "good Conceição" in his *Missa do Galo.*[2] First standing, then sitting; now hovering about and solicitous, and then distant and disdainful; gay of a sudden and of a sudden sad— it would seem that she is really dancing (my father was right), or that she is whirling about an axis. When she examines the hang of a dress before a mirror woman executes her essential gyroscopic gesture, that gesture that achieves the union of mobility and a marvelous fixity. People may speak of her passivity if they will, but let them add that it is an active, most active passivity, like that of things that rotate and attract.

She dances before man. And in the phases of the dance she unfolds successive ages. Now she is a little girl seeking toys and protection; then she is a mother giving shelter and counsel. And wavering thus between a daughter's affection and a mother's solicitude, she continues to weaken man's defenses until he becomes helpless as a child and she offers herself before him as womankind.

Parsifal, the lost youth who does not know who he is, lets himself be bound by the flower-maidens.

"Who'll play with us now?" they ask as they dance around him. Parsifal makes a move as if to flee.

"Parsifal, stay!" It is Kundry who bids him thus.

"Parsifal?"

One day, in a dream, his mother had named him so— The scene changes, the music becomes transfigured; the childish prattle of the flower-maidens becomes hushed before the grave contralto, the voice of long ago, the maternal voice that emerges from the forgotten depths to recall to the man who he is and what his name is, and to remind him of the obscure reason for his name and his existence. Now it is the unchanging voice, the enduring one, the one of long ago that is speaking, and Parsifal remembers a dream in which he had heard his mother within himself calling him by his name.

"Who art thou? Art thou, too, a flower?"

[2] Midnight Mass of the Nativity (trans.).

No. Kundry is not a flower. She is woman. She is eternal womanhood. She is youth that is six thousand years old. She saw Parsifal on his mother's breast, she heard his first crying, she knew his mother's pain. The pain of Herzeleide's heart.

Did he not hear the sorrowful outcry when the child went far astray into the night? And the laughter, the great loving laughter when the happy woman found him at last? Did not her kisses frighten him? But one day Parsifal did not return. Through days and nights she waited, until all hope was dead, until her lamentations were stilled and she was consumed by her suffering, until there came the longing for a silent death. And then the sorrow broke her heart—"Leid das—and Herzeleide died." "Und—Herzeleide—Starb."

There is Kundry. Look! The flower-maidens put to flight, the mother dead, the toys of childhood and the protective endearments of consuming mother love left lying upon the ground, there is Kundry, womankind, who came from afar. Why? To "tarry a while" in order that Parsifal might find her. She moved about, she danced, she sang, she ran, but now she is fixed in that immobility which is the profound honor, the metaphysical dignity of woman. The final step Parsifal must take.

In Machado's *Midnight Mass of the Nativity*, though without the four-dimensional apparatus of Wagnerian art, we see the same thing: the pathos of woman immobile in the final and decisive waiting. The "good Conçeição" does not lower the banner of her sex. Even if her husband's desertion and the frailty of her senses let her prowl for a time like a famished lioness around a seventeen-year-old Parsifal, they are not enough to overcome her ultimate resistance, which is something more than moral, and which comes not from virtue or prejudice but from the deep roots of her femininity.

What I have tried to say with those digressions that have consumed two hours is that by being late Eunice used to charge me the small quota she could in the game of love, as amends for and a discount on woman's enormous patrimony of patience. Woman, who herself waits so earnestly, thinks nothing of keeping others waiting. She sells us retail what she bought wholesale.

How then could I say that I waited ten years for Eunice? No, I did not wait ten years. I should not know how, I should not be able to wait ten years. Shall I be able to wait two months? No, I was not waiting for Eunice. It would be truer to say that I went about all that while, running and wandering in search of her who might call me by my childhood name, who might tell me who I am. A disoriented Parsifal, I trod again and again "the paths of error and suffering." In meditation and dreams and in long reading, I spent many days and nights traversing the ways already traversed, asking poets and philosophers—skipping long periods of time all the while and leaping over great distances—whether some one of them had by chance found the key to my life fallen upon the ground. O spirit of my mother, who will again whisper to me the name you gave me? How could I forget? How could I be faithless in all things? 'Tis only folly and darkness that dwell in me."

There in my bookcases are the motionless backs of the ten thousand witnesses whom I have heard. What have you said to me, O Greeks? And you, restless men of my own day, what have you told me? I look about: over there I see a title that brings to my mind a grave analysis, with figures, neologisms, laws, theorums, and corollaries to prove that man lives by bread; beyond, from a gilt-lettered binding, issues a voice to tell me that man lives not by bread alone. Economists, prophets, historians, philosophers who keep saying that they have seen farther because they have mounted a giant's shoulders, and philosophers who persist in saying that they have gone farther because they have unburdened themselves of ancient baggage; humorists who weep in secret, poets who secretly mock, hagiographers, exegetes, hermeneutists, psychologists, essayists; solemn voices, ardent voices, tiny voices, interrupted voices. When I cry out, which one of you will answer me, O angelic apprentices?[3]

Ten years humped over books. And now when even yet I bend "over many a quaint and curious volume of forgotten lore," I hear the crow saying "never more."

And I tell my soul that we are reaching our destination. A Parsifal without lance and without helmet, I have trod the paths of error and suffering in vain. Now I am reaching my destination. A rendezvous has been fixed. She is coming, that Kundry; in two or three months she is to embrace me. What am I to think?

What shall we do, my soul and I, when night falls in this room, in this little hiding place, which is large enough for love and death? When night falls, the "good Conceição" hovers about me, and very white and very beautiful she bends over my indecision waiting for what?—a gesture from me, an impulse, my helplessness—

November 13th

In Dr. Aquiles' Consultation Room

Several times I had felt a vague presentiment when I noticed that in a two-weeks' interval people remarked my pallor and loss of weight. I felt, too, growing fatigue; but I ascribed it to worry and to the heat and my age. No one knows until he has experienced it

[3] The first of Rilke's *Duino Elegies* begins: "If I cry out, who will hear me among the ranks of the angels?" "On the remote frontiers of consciousness, which Rilke was continually trying to extend, on the cold peaks of possible sublimity, towards which he was continually striving, stands the Angel, a being in whom the limitations and contradictions of present human nature have been transcended, a being in whom thought and action, insight and achievement, will and capability, the actual and the ideal, are one" (J. B. Leishman, *Rainer Maria Rilke: Later Poems,* p. 203)—(trans.).

himself, and that he can do only once, how fifty misspent years can weigh upon the body. Perhaps that was all it was.

However, I heard so many comments both from my University colleagues and from persons whom I met on the street that I determined to seek a doctor. It was Pedreira who recommended Dr. Aquiles. He praised his carefulness, pointed to successful cases of his in which others had failed, and did not rest until I took note of his name and consultation room.

I went there day before yesterday. I liked the man, though I found him quite different from what I had imagined. I do not know whether because of his name or because of some adjective that Pedreira used, I thought of him as tall, athletic, and nervous. I was wrong; Dr. Aquiles is a quiet mannered man of medium height, and he shows signs of an incipient corpulence that will certainly increase with the years. He is probably about my age or a little younger. In his rectangular face, whose natural symmetry is accentuated by the middle parting of his chestnut-brown hair, the large nose, the heavy eyelids, and the rimless bifocals harmonize perfectly by the law of contrasts with the small mouth, which he keeps obstinately shut as if it were only with reluctance that he uses it.

He looked at me for a while in silence, and then with a quick, difficult smile he asked me what was wrong. I spoke of Pedreira, and while I was telling the little I had to say—fatigue and loss of weight—secretly well pleased with myself for making so light of my indisposition—the doctor was amusing himself by scratching on a piece of paper. At first I supposed that he was taking notes, but by stretching my neck a little I ascertained that he was drawing a ship.

Then he filled out a filing card with my name, age, and address, and asked me about my parents; if they were living and from what they had died. When I told him that my father had died from gambling, I surprised the rapid glance of one who thinks that he has misunderstood, but his lips compressed themselves even more tightly, resisting indiscretion, and the Doctor started a second ship beside the other one, that meanwhile had acquired smoke from its stack.

"Will you take off your coat?"

He put a towel across my chest and began to use the stethoscope, lingering longer on the left side over the heart. Just as I was becoming weary of his insistence, he lost interest in that spot and began to examine me from behind. By now I wanted to reassure Dr. Aquiles, explaining to him jovially that it was Pedreira's idea, that I had come only to please Pedreira. But the doctor, whom I could not see now except for a hand placed on my chest and a leg in Irish duck trousers, persisted in probing the back of my thorax. It was at that moment that, raising my eyes, I noticed the crucifix on the wall. Was it there, I wondered, for the Doctor or for the patients? Was Dr. Aquiles a Catholic, perhaps, or might he have fastened the figure of Christ there to give the first note of consolation or the first evasion of eternity to cases that were hopeless?

"We'll go over to the scale. Have you weighed recently?"

"Three months ago I was a hundred and forty-five, which isn't much for my height. I'm nearly six feet."

"You're a hundred and thirty-six now. That isn't much. Will you lie down?"

I lay down, not knowing whether or not I should take off my shoes; I felt very humble, quite at the mercy of that vertical man. Dr. Aquiles tapped my stomach, closing his eyes occasionally in order to concentrate fully on his finger tips. Now he was slowly exploring the region of the spleen, and I was observing on the whitewashed ceiling a small gray stain that reminded me of the map of Australia. How could it have got there at so inaccessible a height, I wondered, that smudge that made pretense of being a continent in miniature? I was about to ask the Doctor. Like the criminal who tries to divert the policeman's attention, I wanted to divert the doctor from my spleen.

"Have you ever had malaria?"

"No, sir."

He was standing now, regarding me thoughtfully, and for the

first time I noticed that his mouth was entering into the play of his features, rising slightly in the left corner. Could that grimace be from displeasure or indecision? I could not discover. I lacked the previous information, conversations about politics, religion, painting, family histories, to find out the exact meaning of what the doctor would not tell me. I rose.

"Well, Doctor?"

"It's too soon for a diagnosis. I'm going to ask you for two analyses: blood and urine. If you could bring the results tomorrow. Do you have a good laboratory that you go to?"

I usually went to Dr. Rosalvo's. He declared that was excellent, and I left to get the analyses.

I spent a difficult night, heavy with apprehension. I had supposed that the doctor would advise me to give up smoking or take a vacation, and with this in view, I had already put aside a certain amount of heroism to follow the advice. It would be a bother, and it comforted me to imagine that it would really be quite an annoying one. But the request for the tests disturbed me. What would come of it all? Can it be possible, then, for a person to have a grave illness and go about with it until his casual acquaintances whom he meets on the street are kind enough to observe how thin and pale he is?

As a rule, the doctor's consultation room is a place where one acquires during the course of life a senseless optimism. One goes there ten, twenty times with somber forebodings and leaves with a benign diagnosis. The last time—it was the past year—Dr. Mendes had laughed at me and had prescribed Atroveran and vitamins. And so it is that a succession of small ailments perfidiously instills a growing optimism until the day when the doctor stands before our horizontal body, with that grimace in the corner of his mouth—

The next day, that is, day before yesterday, I again found myself in Dr. Aquiles' waiting room, with the results of the test in my pocket. There were three people ahead of me: a stout woman, middle-aged and extremely unhappy, to judge from the expression of her face, in which there was a resignation that obviously she wanted all the world to see and look upon as a mark of heroism; a thin young girl slumped down in a green upholstered armchair, who was turning the pages of a magazine; and a young man with dark glasses who had turned up his trousers with much exaggeration to show off his muscular, hairy legs.

The nurse, a plump blond girl, did not stay quietly seated behind the white lacquered table at the entrance to the consultation room. She kept getting up every minute; she would pass us with the haughty air of one who had seen many cases, and very much more interesting ones than ours, and would go over to the window to examine the street or the weather; not that the weather was threatening or that there was anything special to see down below in the street. It was just her way of killing time, the arch enemy of underlings.

"Will it be much longer, I wonder?" queried the stout woman. "Heaven knows all that I have to do at home. There's no one but me to do it." And she raised her eyes to the stuccoed ceiling as one who seeks in things on high the understanding that is not to be found at earthly level.

"The young man over there's still ahead of you."

"Not really, Dona Helena! I've been here for over an hour and I didn't think I saw anyone when I came in. Are you sure? Did you really get here before I did, young man? Would it make much difference to you if I went in ahead of you? I have so much shopping to do yet and I have to get home and prepare my husband's diet. You won't mind?"

The youth with the turned-up trousers did not answer immediately. He looked at me as if to say that it does no good to be in turn, shrugged his shoulders ill-humoredly, and not finding any way to refuse, agreed, "Of course."

"Oh, I'm very grateful. You have no idea how distressed I am!"

And again she sought on the ceiling consolation for her troubles. She was triumphant. At home, she will recount the episode to her husband in order to prove her highly developed spirit of initiative so in contrast with his timidity. She will say that you'll not be given much unless you cry for it.

The youth with the dark glasses picked up a much handled magazine whose cover was loose and that had been left on the stool. Evidently he wanted to avoid conversation, which seemed to him even more disadvantageous than the loss of time. Then the close tie that existed between the stout woman and the thin young girl was revealed.

"Mama, it's five o'clock already!"

"What do you want me to do? I've gotten the gentleman to let me have his place. I can't go and get Dr. Aquiles by force. If you'd been on time we'd already be on our way. That's always the way. Always here, there, and everywhere, but never on time for appointments. Your father's just the same."

And again she was about to raise her eyes when the door of the consultation room opened and Dr. Aquiles appeared. The two women went in, and the nurse as she passed the young man dropped the scornful comment, "That was a stupid thing to do—"

"Did you want me to refuse? People no longer offer their services. Everyone complains that there's no longer any courtesy—"

"There's no longer any time. There's courtesy only when there's leisure. I go from here to Engenho de Dentro. I get home for dinner at eight-thirty. My plate is kept for me. And no one gives me a seat on the bus—"

"But you don't ask either. That's just it. It's right not to ask—"

The nurse did not answer. She went over to the window again and re-examined the weather and the street, and when she went back it was as if she had never addressed a word to that stranger with turned-up trousers and dark glasses. And I remembered Eunice, who, likewise, after all that had happened, had passed Miguel as though she were seeing him for the first time. An extraordinary faculty, extraordinary, that of so rapidly wiping out, in this instance, a provocative familiarity, and, in that other, an adultery. Apparently they have no need for the waters of Lethe in order to forget; for them the will to do so is sufficient.

From this memory in which I was associating Eunice with Dante, my fancy leapt to the drawing that adorned Dr. Aquiles' wall a little above the young man's head. In a touching chiaroscuro, a young girl, very fair and very beautiful, was in the death agony. Beside the bed with his back almost completely turned, the venerable doctor was stooping over the lovely dying girl, struggling with the angel of death.

That was not a drawing; it was a discourse. I seemed to see the artist at the threshold of the frame declaiming with the sweeping gestures of an orator that medicine is a priesthood and that while there is life there is hope. Yes, there is hope because the Doctor is keeping vigil. Forgetful of everything else, forgetful of himself, the Doctor concentrates wholly upon that patient, upon that life. He did well, Dr. Aquiles, to hang so comforting a message on the wall, because the most distressing suspicion of every patient is that his own very special case is not being given the special consideration that is its due. His fear is that even when the doctor is not mistaken he is lost in the vague realm of generalities. The patient wants to be as an only son to the doctor, as a lover. He wants to be concrete.

I, too, am a patient, it seems. I, too, as my case continues, am going to become a child, dependent, obedient. I am going to fall in love with my case. Its first elements, the results of the tests, are in my pocket.

I pulled them out to convince myself. The blood test reads: leucocytes, 100,000; and it adds a series of odd names: myeloplasts, myelocytes, rods, segments, eosinophiles, basophiles, lymphocytes, and monocytarians. In the column on the right are the figures, 10%, 30%, 20%, 10%, etc. I wonder what those names and figures mean.

The door of the consulting room opens and the two women come out; the stout woman seems less unhappy, the girl is laughing convulsively, which is probably due to one of those professional jokes with which doctors encourage their patients. Behind them, framed in the doorway, appears what is already becoming for me a recurrent sight, the face of Dr. Aquiles, the bifocals gleaming in the blending of light and shadow.

In a few minutes it will be my turn—

"Well, did you bring the tests?"

I drew the papers from my pocket and handed him the blood test first. My heart was pounding. I must have been even more pale than usual, but an extraordinary acuteness permitted me to discern the slightest changes in the doctor's phlegmatic face. Before he took the paper that pucker reappeared at the corner of his mouth, as if to say: "Let's see if the hypothesis was correct." On his table was a paper with rough drawings. Three and a half ships. His hand reached out, took the report, unfolded it. Now the Doctor is reading—Ah! Where have I seen before that suddenly repressed play of features? Good God, where have I seen it, where have I learned to decipher the meaning of that deliberately vacant stare, that restraint of eyelids and mouth? Now I know. It was at poker—at Albino's house—Major Edwards had just been dealt four aces. And that is the very way, with an empty gaze, a quick flicker of the eyelids and a tightening of the lips, that Major Edwards masters the excitement of his cards.

"I have the other one here, the urine test."

Dr. Aquiles made an evasive gesture. I wish I could! The Major does not want any cards either. The Major looks at me with faraway eyes. Ah! How discerning I am! How clearly I see that Dr. Aquiles holds four aces in his hand!

Apparently there was a traffic jam out there in the street. The cars were bellowing dolefully.

"The traffic's worse every day," I said.

I, myself, offered the Doctor subterfuge, and he resorted to it.

"Well, if the streets stay the same and they're more cars every day—"

"What we need is collective transportation. From this point of view, our people are the most unfortunate on earth."

"The metro's the only solution. In Paris the service is excellent. Have you ever been to Paris, Professor?"

"No, I have never been able to realize that desire. Perhaps some day—if that blood test will permit me."

"That's right, the test—"

Then Dr. Aquiles finished the ship that he had left without a stack and masts. There were four of them now. I needed only one to go to Europe. One ship and the blood test.

"Are you married? Do you have children?"

"I am married. I have a son."

"Perhaps it would be better if I were to make arrangements with your wife for the diet and the details of the treatment. It's not well for a man to do things by himself, especially when it comes to treating himself. You well know that in this respect women are much more practical than we are. I have the impression you're absent-minded"—he was laughing now, almost jovially—"like all intellectuals, after all. You'd end up with the hours and doses all muddled—"

I let him talk as that day I had let Eunice talk and become more and more enmeshed in the lies that come so volubly to her lips. Dr. Aquiles was lying, too, which disclosed the lack of an upper bicuspid concealed when his mouth had been honest. I knew now. I knew for certain what the leucocytes and the myeloplasts meant. I knew for certain that my case was serious. Fatal. But I was still managing to keep that certainty at a distance. With face aflame and soul in tumult, I was managing to bear up under the fact while it was still objective. It would be worse when it pounced upon me, and of that I was afraid. I was afraid to leave the consultation room and find myself in the street, alone with myself and with the thing, the certainty that it was making ready to spring and sink its teeth into my heart.

The Doctor, beginning his fifth ship, appeared to be waiting for my answer to his suggestion.

"My wife left me ten years ago. My son, also; two years ago. I live alone."

After a pause, I added, "Fortunately." And then of a sudden, I became dimly aware that his brown eyes held a gentleness in contrast with the coldness of the rimless glasses. However, before he might say something conventional or seek some other evasion, I told him that I had understood the seriousness of my case and asked him for the complete and precise truth.

"Are you a Catholic? he asked.

"No—that is, to be frank, I don't know exactly what I am. I was educated at the Fathers' school, I was the best student in catechism and I liked to assist at Mass. The Fathers thought I had a call; but then I left school, my fervor cooled, and afterwards—afterwards life was just one hard knock after the other. I married young, I had a son, and I have come to where I am today, with my blood in the state it is, without knowing who I am or who God is. But why do you ask me this? Can it be that you wish to prescribe a miracle for me, tell me that my case is in God's hands and that He alone will be able to save me? Perhaps it's in order to broach this subject, to facilitate conversation, that you have the crucifix on the wall over there, a sort of silent commonplace that prepares the way for other commonplaces, inevitable and eloquent?"

"No," he replied in a low voice, "I have the crucifix there because I believe in God and in Jesus Christ, His only Son."

I noticed that unlike the unhappy stout woman of the waiting room, the Doctor lowered his eyes to the floor when he spoke of God. How amusing the conversation between the two of them would be were the stout woman the hopeless case! How different are men who believe in the same things and utter the very same words! Or, who knows, perhaps their God is not the same? I could see Father Agostinho telling us that the God of Moses is jealous and conceals His identity. "If you study the catechism, you will know who God is. People are apt to refer to a God-idea, which may be one thing or another. If someone tells me merely that he believes in God, I do not know what that person means. I almost prefer the man who starts out by telling me that he believes in the

Devil. That is more precise—" Then the bell would ring and the class would begin to stir, while Father Agostinho, with his nasal voice, enjoined quiet and order.

Where should I seek the true God? On the ceiling, like the stout woman, or on the floor, to which, from what Dr. Aquiles' heavy eyelids seem to insinuate, He has strayed?

"I repeat, Doctor, that I understand the seriousness of my illness. Please put aside the hypothesis of a miracle, and, above all, put aside all deception. I feel as though it were a part of me, as though I myself were the embodiment of falsity. And I hate and despise falsity."

"When I asked if you were a Catholic, I wasn't thinking of a miracle. What is more, you've made me realize that I almost never do think of miracles."

"How many years, Doctor?"

Again I saw a gleam of gentleness in his brown eyes; he was feeling sorry for me.

"How many months, then? How many days?"

Dr. Aquiles picked up the report of the blood test, and, with the voice of one speaking of an abstract problem, he began to explain that that leukemia, within that hematolytic framework, with the neutrophiles, the appearance of the myeloplasts and the diminution of the placquettes, had all the characteristics of an acute form. Of that he had no doubt. As for the length of time—he could not determine exactly. In every case there are fortuitous circumstances, many imponderables.

"Less than a year?"

"I believe so."

"Less than six months?"

Dr. Aquiles stirred restlessly in his chair. He picked up the report again. Then he folded it once, twice, and putting a glass weight on top, he clasped his hands and gave me a long, lingering look. I began to talk feverishly. I told him that at least I wanted to live those days; that I wanted to live my death since I had not been able to live my life; that I wanted to make the most of that final chance of harmony, that unique certainty, that advantage, that enormous, colossal advantage which from that day on I should have over the ordinary mortal.

"And that's why I'm asking you, Doctor, and begging you for the truth, for the love of God—"

"Three or four months."

His eyes were almost hard; his bifocals more scientific than ever. But quickly his facial expression changed, and rising with an agility of which I should not have supposed him capable, he brought me a glass of water into which he had poured some drops.

"Drink this. It will do you good."

I already knew, of course, but at that moment the certainty that I had been holding off as an objective thing in front of my eyes leapt abruptly upon my chest. Or, rather, upon my stomach. I felt as though it had devoured that. And I gazed about me at a different world. There were the scale, the bed, the crucifix, and up there that ridiculous Australia in miniature. Everything in the same place with the same properties that they had had a little while before, a half hour ago, when I still belonged to that species, that proud species of people who live on uncertainty. For me, meantime, everything had changed. The world had become faded, withered, dying, as on that day when I saw Eunice cross the street and enter the hall of the apartment house. The world was hopeless; the universe was about to die. And I had the desire to get up, to go out without a word, leaving my umbrella propped against the wall, leaving Dr. Aquiles and his useless ships—and then I should go on walking and walking—

"Do you feel better?"

"I feel better, thank you. I had told you that I knew, and I really did know. But there are many ways of knowing. Now I have the truth in my stomach. And what must I do to prolong—well, to get through those days better?"

"You can have a blood transfusion from time to time. You'll not have to take any special care otherwise. You can go out and work, so long as you don't get too tired. And come back in eight or ten days; we can arrange a transfusion."

"Is there danger of contagion?"

"None."

"And what is it called?"

"What is what called?"

"That thing that's inside of me."

"Ah! It's acute myeloid leukemia."[1]

"And where does it reside? In the heart? The stomach? The spleen?"

"No. It's not a question of a disease localized in one organ or infection. It's rather a general modification of the formative mechanism of the blood, a profound change of cancerous nature. Yes, I should say cancer of the blood."

"Cancer!" A word, a sound. "Cancer!" And I who had always imagined cancer as a substance, a monster, a parasite that was born inside of people and continued to grow with its mortal tentacles. And now, from what the Doctor says this is a fluid monster. It is a change rather than an intrusion; it is a modification of quantity, place, and order rather than a strangling body. It is almost a reasoning being, an obliquity of what should be perpendicular, a curvature of what should be rectilinear. And I shall go out from here with that half-abstract, mortal fetus within me.

"You say that there's nothing to be done—supposing, of course, that there's no possibility of error."

"Unfortunately, there is no such possibility."

"I'm not referring to the diagnosis, but to the test. Might there not be an error in those numbers? If, for example, a laboratory apprentice put a zero too many in some of those figures—"

"No. Unfortunately, there's no room for such a supposition. On the whole, the picture fits together and matches perfectly the hypertrophy of your spleen and your weight and pallor. In any case, of course, if you'd like to consult a colleague—"

[1] Rainer Rilke died of myeloid leukemia in 1926 (trans.).

"You mean that it's as plain to you as this table and that scale?"

"Exactly."

"Well. Then—I don't wish to take any more of your time. There're others outside."

"Come again. Come and have a talk. Phone me when you want a transfusion."

And Dr. Aquiles accompanied me politely to the door.

November 17th

"Iván Ilých Saw That He Was Dying and He was in Continual Despair

"Iván Ilých saw that he was dying, and he was in continual despair.

"In the depth of his heart he knew he was dying, but not only was he not accustomed to the thought, he simply did not and could not grasp it.

"The syllogism he had learnt from Kiezewetter's Logic: 'Caius is a man, men are mortal, therefore Caius is mortal,' had always seemed to him correct as applied to Caius, but certainly not as applied to himself. That Caius—man in the abstract—was mortal, was perfectly correct, but he was not Caius, not an abstract man, but a creature quite, quite separate from all others. He had been little Vanya, with a mamma and a papa, with Mitya and Volodya, with the toys, a coachman and a nurse, afterwards with Katinka and with all the joys, griefs, and delights of childhood, boyhood, and youth. What did Caius know of the smell of that striped leather ball Vanya had been so fond of? Had Caius kissed his mother's hand like that, and did the silk of her dress rustle so for Caius? Had he rioted like that at school when the pastry was bad? Had Caius been in love like that? Could Caius preside at a session as Vanya, nay, as Iván Ilých did? Caius really was mortal, and it was right for him to die; but for me, little Vanya, Iván Ilých, with all my thoughts and emotions, it's altogether a different matter. It cannot be that I ought to die. That would be too terrible.

"Such was his feeling.

"If I had to die like Caius I should have known it was so. An inner voice would have told me so, but there was nothing of the sort in me and I and all my friends felt that our case was quite different from that of Caius. 'And now here it is!' he said to himself. 'It can't be. It's impossible! But here it is. How is this? How is one to understand it?' "

I closed Tolstoi's book, straightened the red rose that had fallen over too far, and walked to the window. In the garden across the street the little boy was playing with his ball. He took a tumble on the soft grass, still hugging his ball. "It was nothing! It was nothing!" A bird dog was jumping and barking joyously around him. The child got up laughing and held the leather ball away from the dog, who was trying to get it.

That child could smell the odor of the leather ball. He was Vanya. Now Vanya is a man; hence he is mortal.

A long time ago I had read that same page of Tolstoi and had appreciated its poignant beauty, from the height of my immortality. Iván Ilých was struggling to sever himself from any identification with Caius; or with Socrates, as we who study logic in other treatises would say. And I, from the comfortable cabin of my immortality, appreciated the stages of that inglorious struggle whose outcome was so inevitable, and appreciated them so much the more, being neither Socrates nor Vanya.[1]

It has been like this for three days. I have spent a twentieth of my allotted time without making any progress in really assimilating the idea of death. I am not saying that I doubt the diagnosis. Dr. Rosalvo, of the laboratory, has confirmed it, though he doesn't

[1] In the first of the two letters *On God* written at Munich, in 1910, Rilke begs his correspondent, L. H., to read Tolstoi's story, *The Death of Iván Ilých.* Rilke's passionate awareness of life was always permeated with an equal awareness of death (trans.).

agree to calling it cancer. In regard to that, Dr. Rosalvo forgot my very special case and moved the problem into the plane of essence. What characterizes cancer in his opinion is the formation of atypic cells.

"Now, tell me please, where are they, the atypic cells? Leukemia is caused by immature cells that are injected into the circulation. But immature doesn't mean atypic. Please tell me, then, where the cancer is—"

Not being able to tell Dr. Rosalvo where the cancer was, I kept still and remembered what Juliet said to Romeo:

"What is in a name? That which we call a rose
By any other name would smell as sweet."

And what the poet said about roses I say about cancer. Let them change the name in accordance with their theories; it is still the same thing and I am just where I was.

Like Vanya, I have not yet been able to assimilate the idea of death, and it is this that distresses me, beause I do not wish to be caught unaware like a rat. I have had enough of the mockery of life I have lived. What have I done for twenty years but follow Eunice's comings and goings? She was my real death, the real and effective destruction of my freedom. Her caprice bit into the living flesh of my being; her frivolity took hold of me when least expected, in the middle of the day or the middle of the night, and my soul would collapse, like a child that has been struck down in the street.

Now, at least, an opportunity presents itself. That woman who is coming to get me has all the gravity of Kundry. Something can be attempted here in this room, in the quiet and shelter of this room. Something harmonious, something serious may be attained, when one has torn himself away from confusion and variance. The world is a jumbled depository, a monumental store where one buys stars and flowers for the secret, soundless fête that is to be held within the recesses of the soul. Is that not what sculptors do when they wrest the clay from the ground and carry it to their love tryst? Is this not what the poet does when, leaving out here and taking away there, he selects what he wants from the noisy anonymity of the common reserve? The important thing in poetry and in life is choice, and, hence, rejection. Poetry is a strike, a protest like that of the transparent crystalline minerals whose sharp edges are intolerant of the mountain's bosom and its crushing weight. No one rejects so much as the poet and the lover.

That is the way, too, that I want death: completely segregated from that confused alluvium that was my life. Let it come, but openly and desired. Let it come, but rhythmically and beautifully and not as a crafty procuress who nabs the defenseless schoolboy.

It is a curious contrast that there is nothing more certain than death, to the extent of its serving in the classic example of the syllogism and that, on the other hand, it is the idea hardest for us to admit. And the nearer it is, the harder it is. It is a certainty quite contrary to all others.

Some days ago I went to Real Grandeza, in the new district of São Jõao Batista, where the dead take leave of the living in small mortuary chambers superimposed one above the other like today's diminutive apartments. Every deceased has his cenotaph there, every family its half dozen chairs for the most overwhelming of all sorrows. The friends and distant relatives can weep standing up. Nor, indeed, is any greater comfort necessary for so rapid a leave-taking.

I was going to pay my final respects, as they say, to Ferraz, the old chemistry professor who had died suddenly of angina pectoris. However, I had not paid due attention to the door attendant's instructions, and I came to the mortuary chamber where the living persons, distorted of face, were unknown to me, and the corpse, of impassive countenance, even less known. I had come to the wrong sorrow; that was not mine; the death that was putting on its trivial little show there was death-in-general, the kind that seizes Socrates or Caius in the knots of the syllogism. Also, the suffering that was stamped upon the faces there was the kind usually designated by the generic of mourning, orphanhood, and widowhood.

When I went down and entered the room below I immediately saw Idelfonso's long face and Barata's bald pate and I saw Carolinhos with his arm around Helena, and seated in the back, the inconsolable widow, Dona Maria Aparecida. In the middle of the room, covered with flowers, which left only the face and low shoes visible, was what had been the old Ferraz. The moment I entered, I sensed an atmosphere of stupefaction.

"It seems impossible! Why just yesterday—"

"An irreparable loss, ir-rep-a-ra-ble," Idelfonso syllabified in a hollow whisper.

"It seems incredible," said the widow embracing me.

And, in amazement, I looked at the scene, wondering at the great wonder of the others. Just because it had become personalized, the most ordinary phenomenon on earth was assuming the proportions of a thing to marvel at. And all these people—a people weary of attending seventh-day Masses—were marveling at Ferraz' corpse, as if they were gazing at the Aurora Borealis.

Even for me, with those ideas of mine, it was hard to believe that that was Ferraz. It seemed that there must be some deception, some mystification, and that suddenly we would all laugh at the farce. But no; it was indeed he, Ferraz, who was lying there dead and very dead. More dead than the nails of the coffin, as Dickens would say.

The room became more and more filled with friends, students, and relatives, who were already beginning to talk of other things, since, after the first moment is past, there is little to be said about death. Even the widow was crying discreetly now, as if she were being careful not to exceed the bounds of that room that had been rented for the hasty bivouac of our individual grief. The whole building was divided thus into tightly sealed sorrows.

As I watched the flame that was flickering atop its waxen mast, I was thinking that one great fire had swept through there and left a small sample for each one of the dead. The floral wreaths, too, are kept apart and labeled with the name of the deceased in order to indicate clearly to whom those gilt-lettered sentiments, so vague and so universal, are addressed. But the bees that fly about freely throughout the building may well come from the same hive. It may be they that will blend into a single sweetness all those separate, bitter sorrows.

And I realized that sorrows remain aloof, each in its own compartment. They concentrate upon themselves and hide almost as if they were conspiracies, because men remain aloof from one another; and men remain aloof from one another because man remains aloof from himself.

Another thing that I observed at that funeral of Ferraz was that people go to the deceased as to a judge. They present themselves to be judged in that strange tribunal in which the magistrate remains motionless and silent. He does not have to accuse; the living accuse themselves. They come up against the evidence of omission. No longer ago than yesterday there could have been a word, a gesture, a smile. Today it is too late; the deceased is there to remind us what we could have done and did not do. And the living, who always count on an indefinite opportunity, are now perplexed. They would like to say something, but they encounter the dead man's stubborn silence.

I owe myself an explanation. The tone with which I am recalling Ferraz' funeral appears unfeeling, harsh, sarcastic, as though the widow's tears did not reach my heart. No. I well remember that I suffered along with Dona Maria Aparecida and that I felt the loss of Ferraz, but I suffered very much more, oh very much more, from the frightful misunderstanding that apparently pursues mankind and that in such instances leads to utter delusion.

Yes, it is this that grieves me and grieves me deeply. There are persons who almost invariably speak heatedly, with easy indignation and quick temper. At the slightest injustice they clench their fists and give vent to the exhuberant vehemence of the full-blooded. I like to see them, but in general I am not moved by the major tone of their anger. What distresses me most, what grieves me most, is the misunderstanding that I see in the world. That is my unhappy dominant, an aggrevated sense of the ridiculous. Only he who has had that experience can have any idea of the sharp pain, the penetrating glacial pain that is forever with me. They talk about a Hell of fire; sometimes I can conceive of a Hell of ice.

November 20th

Old Deaths

Not speaking of the numerous funerals and Masses that do not concern one closely, my experiences of death have been few. The first, which was my own father's death, was a frustrating experience. I did not see the body, and it was only long after that, by chance, I learned the story of the gambling and the suicide.

I was thirteen. I was at school, in geometry class, when the head Father came in with Uncle Afonso. They spoke to the professor, who interrupted his demonstration of alternate inner angles, and with a voice that was different from his usual one called me up front. Uncle Afonso placed his hand on my head, and explained that Papa had been rushed to a sanitarium to be operated on for acute appendicitis. I was to go to his house.

"And Mama?"

"She's with Edward, but he can't receive visitors—"

I did not see the body; and my father's death, robbed of its visible apparatus, left me with the impression of an artful thievery.

Mama's death was different. It found me, at the age of twenty, highly emotional and a long way from any metaphysical musings. It was a dramatic death, closely followed, intensely suffered, and deeply mourned. It did not occasion anguished questioning but for weeks on end I was shaken by an unassuming, banal grief. It was the worst when I awakened in the morning. Every morning Mama would die all over again, like a repeat showing of a theatrical hit. It distressed me that I did not dream of her. I wanted to dream, but I was not able to. Dona Edwiges, who was a widow and had experience, explained: "It's like that; one doesn't dream—"

More penetrating, more unacceptable and cruel was the death of a friend. I was reading a novel when the telephone rang. I was on page 145. "Et le beau prince, emporté maintenant au flot de la mélodie, chantait. Sa voix s'étalait, se nuait en queu de paon, se rengorgeait, et puis mourait dans des ah! ah! pâmés." The telephone rang. Robert had died, he had been run over in the street. And the world (space and time) became divided in two: before and after page 145. The handsome prince was still singing, more ridiculously than ever, in front of an abyss, and it seemed to me that life was monstrously absurd. Robert no longer existed. He had died; he had been run over and killed somewhere, on some street corner, and his last sensory impressions of this world so rich in stimuli, so rich in colors, sounds, and forms, so filled with stars and birds and flowers, had been of the sharp projection of a dirty gutter, a municipal drain, a banana skin, a fly.

I went to his family's home to fulfill my final duty, as they say. No sooner had I closed the gate than I heard hurrying footsteps and saw the brother-in-law, a fine fellow, coming down the stairs, with consternation in his face.

"He's come!"

"Come?"

I thought the verb peculiar. Most unsuitable for a corpse. Ah yes! it was the body. It was only the body that was coming from the street. First aid, or rather useless aid, had been rushed to the spot, but now the body was coming. It was being carried. It was mounting the stairs on the anxious shoulders of the living. "Up! Lift up there! To the left! Steady! Up! Up!" There is always one person who gives the orders and takes the right measures, one who knows how things should be done, and who, in misfortune, reveals the qualities of a leader.

They are arranging the drawing room. They are dragging the furniture around and bringing in wreaths. And I, who can be of no use, remain huddled in one corner of the room, absorbed within my own thoughts. I see figures bustling about, and visitors arriving for the reception of the dark ship that has brought me a dead body. Ah! The ship has come!

> Come, come see the famous brig
> with masts of wax and flags of fire!
> The ship has cast anchor. See it there in port.
> It has come back from distant lands. It has
> been on the high seas.
> It has danced about in maddened winds.
> Look!
> The cenotaph is a ship—
> Only it has too many anchors, too many life preservers,
> And its crew of one is dead!

November 28th

Between Goethe and Voltaire

Today I have come upon two statements in the same book that take me right back to the paradox that is tormenting me. The first is by Voltaire and it says: "The human species is the only one that knows that it must die, and it knows from experience." The second is by Goethe, in a letter to Eckermann regarding the death of the Grand Duchess Louisa: "Death is something so strange that it is not considered possible despite all the evidence of experience; and when it concerns a loved one it always astounds us as something incredible and paradoxical."

And at the moment I am reading, also, in Machado that very beautiful page from the *Memorias Postumas de Braz Cubas*:

"Long was her agony, long and cruel, with a minute, cold, repetitious cruelty that filled me with pain and stupefaction. It was the first time that I had seen anyone die. I knew death chiefly by hearsay; at the most, I had seen it, already petrified, in the face of a corpse on the way to the cemetery, or had thought of death all wrapped in the elaborations supplied by the professors of ancient history—the perfidious death of Caesar, the austere death of Socrates, the proud death of Cato. But this final duel between being and not being, death itself in painful, contracted, convulsive action, stripped of political and philosophical trappings, the death of a beloved person, I had never come face to face with anything like this. I did not cry; I remember well that I did not cry at all. My eyes were expressionless, stupid, my throat tight, my mind agape."

What conclusion shall I draw from such different testimonies? Can it be that mens' souls are of such diversity? Or can it be that one of them is right and the others wrong?

The conclusion that I do draw is that all are right, that the divergence is explained by a difference in perspective. Voltaire speaks from the chair, he is rational and logical, and he is right; but Goethe and Machado are at the bedside of a loved one who is dying, they are seeing from nearby, they are living the experience to which the other alludes— But then—then the paradox of the idea of death rises to the second power because we are facing a fact so much more incomprehensible the nearer and more evident it is.

"And now," I say to my soul, "what direction shall we take, what counsel shall we seek, what way shall we try in order not to be caught like a rat? If it is true that the absurdity of death increases with proximity and evidence; if it acquires a new dimension of madness when it loses its political and philosophical trappings and reaches a beloved person, if it is so unbearable when it comes so close, what is to be said, what is to be thought of that death which is on its way to us, on its way to strike and annihilate the very core of our being?"

Dawn is the hardest time. I awaken. The room is dark, with only a thin strip of light under the door.

When I had the measles as a little boy that strip of light kept me company at night. It was the hyphen that united me with the rest of the house. Shadows would pass, and I would recognize the manner of walking and the sound of the footsteps. Afterwards, for a long time the line of light would remain intact, yet I knew that the house was beyond that golden boundary.

Today the house is empty; the trace of light stays rigid and motionless until the coming of day reduces it to a secondary, mediocre tint of yellow. And I continue to lie awake, watching the crack of the door. Now and then I run my hands over my legs and chest, and, as I think of the liquid monster that is devouring me, I feel infinitely forsaken.

November 30th

Am I Discovering, I Wonder, That the Soul Is Immortal?

Today I am back to the knot that I did not succeed in untying yesterday. The chiaroscuro of death is now the main problem of my life, if that remnant, those forty days that the decomposing of my blood concedes me, can be called life. But the number of days is not important; what is supremely important is to resolve the crucial problem. For if I do not succeed in resolving it, my death will be as casual, as accidental as up until now my life has been. The cancer, in its pitilessness, keeps me in constant anguish, just as Eunice, in her pitilessness, threw me into continual distress. I shall not be the author of anything. Nothing, not even a minute of my life, nor the minute of my death will bear my signature. And it is this that I think I cannot bear.

I tell my soul that we must return to the problem. We were between Voltaire's affirmation from the chair and Machado's mind agape. The very plain, incontrovertible fact of death as it draws near and approaches the beloved person becomes an absurdity. Yet there we have a certainty that evolves inversely from the others, a fantastical certainty that shuns the light. Why is it so? What can be the distinction that instinctively we establish between the Socrates of the syllogism and ourselves?

I think that I can catch a glimmer of the solution; in Voltaire's assertion, as in the compendiums of logic, man is what he is defined to be; he is the rational animal, the featherless biped, or what you will. In Machado or Goethe, a person—and I am not saying now the beloved person—is a different kind of reality, seen from another perspective. It does not matter if he continues to belong to an innumerable species and to merit the same definition. He was man-in-general, as Iván Ilých said—now he is primarily something else; a being who exists and is aware of that ineffable fact, and who because of that singularity never tires of saying to himself that there are two worlds, the ego and the alter-ego.

What I am trying to say is that there are many ways of looking at an individual. A soldier goes by in the street. I see him, and from his uniform I say to myself instantly, "There goes a soldier." This is the superficial, circumstantial view, and it is upon this, alas! that we base our hierarchies, our calculations, and the majority of our hopes. And, above all, it is in this shell, alas! that our vanity resides.

Then I realize what I have said and I correct myself; now, with a note of respect, I say: "No, there goes a man." This is the essential view from which syllogisms, grandiloquent phrases, and cathedratic affirmations are woven. But take care, my soul. Do you not see that that view does not admit of a certain fixity? Do you not see that it has an indefinable restlessness and mysteriousness that make it waver? If not, we shall consider the question. I shall seat Dr. Aquiles over there, the good Dr. Aquiles who does not know how to lie or change the shape of his mouth. And I shall ask him if it is permissible to kill that man in order to extract his sound spleen, supposing that my disease is localized in that organ. I should have so many interesting things to do and to say, were I to be given the soldier's spleen!

Dr. Aquiles will say at once that it is not permissible to dispose of a man's life. But why? Because he is a rational animal, a featherless biped, or what have you? No. It suffices to say "a man's life" for us to be aware of a particular echo deep within us. Unless corruption is rife, everyone knows that a man's life is something sacred. But why? Let us proceed with caution, let us give heed, full heed to the resonance that the words awaken in our souls. Just now I said, "There goes a man." But that reality has two sides. The individual who is now turning the corner is not man-in-general. He is a man. *A*. It remains to be seen what meaning this *a* has. If numerical, the object of my perception enters the field of statistics and the definition shrinks. If, however, I give to the *a* the meaning of unique, concrete, complete, particular, substantial, exceptional, separate, total, then my essential view expands and I surprise myself with the question: "*Who* is that man?"

And I know and everyone knows before he is seized by the madness of collectivism that that is the fundamental question that a soul may ask—a soul that is still intact though the body may be afflicted with leukemia or tuberculosis—when it sees on the opposite sidewalk an upright being that is moving counter to all the laws of mechanical stability and that, occasionally, like the one that I see at this moment, even yields to the whim of scratching one leg with the other foot while in the air his arms are resolving an integral of the third kind which restores his compromised equilibrium, and while up there in that absurd tower of bones and flesh the watchful lookout is directing two brown objects toward the silhouette of a passing girl.

Alas, I have gone astray again! I slipped off into impressions. Let's go back and recapitulate the successive stages of our exploration. First I saw with a sidewise glance—a uniform. Then I saw more comprehensively—a man. Now I am boring down in search of a more penetrating view, in quest of the individual's identity, his singularity, his concreteness, his existentialism. Who is that being, I wonder, who is unique for whom there can be no substitute, who was misleading me by his martial appearance and suggesting evasion into the realm of general ideas wherein death is acceptable?

And I, who am I? We are at the motionless center of the cyclone. Here appearances stop, adjectives grow dim, and I look for myself in the dark as one who tries to grope his way at night among familiar objects. It is within myself that I must find the way to that understanding view of the individual. I shall be able to understand the other only if I understand myself. It may be that the inverse process will make my search easier; that is, it may be that in the face of the other I shall discover, as in a mirror, the secret of my own. Was this not what I sought in Eunice's eyes? Perhaps. But actual, definite contact is possible only within one's self. If I really find out who I am nuclearly, then I shall be ready to attribute my own identity to the other individual, which will make him my equal and set him up before me to be loved and hated.

In other words, an understanding view of the other can be attained only when I find within myself the basis, the radical principle of our profound likeness. Therefore I must dig deep down into myself; I must discover my hidden name, poor, poor cancerous Parsifal, in order to learn who I am and to learn, through an overflow of love, who that passerby is.

And death? Where was death left in all that philosophizing? What relation exists between that mystery that is the individual and the thirty or forty days that are allotted to me?

The relation does exist. We left behind the certainty of death, which is luminous in the essential view and which evolves in inverse proportion to the evidence, becoming amazement, wonder, revulsion, stupor as the reality of the individual emerges. We concluded then that within the individual, within that mystery that is the individual, there is a force that repels death, rejects it, and denounces it as a scarecrow of contradiction.

Am I discovering, I wonder, that the soul is immortal?

December 1st

The More They Demonstrate the Soul's Immortality, the Less I Believe in It

I must not hide from myself that yesterday's solution has left me in the same state of helplessness. Taking as a working hypothesis the idea of the soul's immortality, I see clearly that certain antonyms are resolved, that the aberrant impact between life and death disappears, and that a rational philosophy is substituted for a philosophy of the absurd.

All this I see clearly. Too clearly. And for that very reason it seems to me to be something imposed from outside, a marriage of convenience, a blackboard demonstration of a problem in love. I even go so far as to say with Kierkegaard that "the more they demonstrate the soul's immortality the less I believe in it."

What does this mean? Can it be that I am so skeptical that I disbelieve the operations of the intelligence and that I prefer darkness to light as appears to be the pleasure of a Heidegger and even of Kierkegaard? No. That is not indeed the difficulty. If I am truly repelled by the glare of Cartesianism, I am no more attracted by the obscurity of the Germanic philosophers. But the fact is that I cannot overcome the gap that separates me from that hypothesis, which is so suitable, so obviously meant for my leukemia. I am unmoved likewise by the demonstration that man spiritualizes what he apprehends, with its deduction that, since the apprehension is spiritual the potential and the soul itself must be spiritual, and its conclusion of incorruptibility and immortality.

The rational demonstration responds to the deepest instincts and resolves the mind's stupor before the idea of death. How can it be explained, then, that all that admirable concordance, and the residual of my Catholic faith besides, leave me indifferent?

Yes, of this point I have no doubt: all this leaves me in the same mortal anguish. Yes, this certainty, this kind of certainty does not give me the slightest help when at night I run my hands over my body and think of the earth that will fall onto my coffin.

I can imagine the man condemned to death, who, as in the cloak-and-dagger novels, receives the king's pardon when he is already on the gallows, with the rope around his neck. I can imagine the tumultuous joy in his soul. Pardoned! He will live! The world becomes cordial; houses, trees, man, the blue sky, all unite once again in harmony around that center threatened by death. I can well imagine the overflowing jubilance, that bursting vitality; but for me it has no message, it fails to touch me, it fails to move me, that document of absolution that arrives with the seal of philosophy. Do I doubt then what reason tells me? No. I do not doubt. I do not say that metaphysics is wrong; I do not reject its conclusion. But the trouble is that it fails to penetrate, it fails to become a part of me.

Therein lies the great difficulty; the intelligence is not the whole soul. The tip shines brightly, but the substance remains in darkness. Hence the contradiction. That conclusion of the philosophers lacks I know not what portion of loving kindness to make it assimilable; and that light lacks I know not what refinement of gradation, what veil to proportion it to the weakness of my eyes; it lacks, finally, any conditioning through love that would make it capable of overcoming the obdurateness that divides me from myself.

Like the person who very much wants to eat in order to recover his health, yet has not the slightest appetite and is unable to subject that aversion, though it is of a lower order, to his higher will, I, too, with vexation and no appetite push aside the bread they offer me—

And let the philosophers and apologists not persist lest their vehemence oblige me to repeat with Kierkegaard: "The more they demonstrate, the less I believe."

December 3rd

Pedreira Is Finishing His Book

I met Pedreira, who announced happily that he is finishing his book on dielectrics. Engrossed in the subject, he did not notice my thinness and he did not inquire about Dr. Aquiles. We talked about electric fields, and I agreed to go to his laboratory one of these days.

Pedreira is finishing his book. I, too, am finishing, but what am I finishing? Pedreira's book, when it is concluded, will be complete, entire, perfect. It will have a good ending. And I? What will remain of my life at its closing hour? I do not regret the book I did not write; no, I am only asking what will remain of my life, my life itself as a work, an accomplishment, at the moment when I close my eyes? What is there up until now? An evanescent memory, an echo that scatters in the air.

The day that I pounded on the table with my fist and shouted at Eunice, "I've had enough! Get out!" the air started to vibrate. In concentric waves my anger took wing, went out the window like a bewildered bird, struck against the wall, wheeled around and past the trunk of the almond tree, and soared upward. The molecules will continue their activity, which is becoming ever more tenuous and ever more fused with other movements, other accidents until the day some ten or a thousand years hence when some remnant of a tremulous whisper will stir again, and borne on an early-evening breeze, will ruffle the soft hair of a dreamy young girl, who will never, never be able to know or to guess that hidden in that wind's caress is the final lament, dynamic now and molecular, of a poor impassioned heart.

What will remain of the words that I have uttered with tenderness or fury? What will remain of the moans that I have stifled, the gestures, the footsteps, the ideas, the plans—ah! what will remain of the plans that I have made? For it must be noted that I have made more plans about my life than Pedreira has about his book. I have dreamed of a certain order for the chapters, I have been absorbed by the question of variants, I have struck out, restored, erased, amended, and now? Now I shall come to the printers with a handful of dust, or, worse, I shall tuck it under my arm, this invisible, imponderable manuscript with all the circumspection of a madman. Or, perhaps, I shall reduce it all to a three-word epitaph, which I shall hand to the stonecutter, as a crazed writer might with mysterious gestures pull from the bottom of his pocket and hand to the publisher a scrap of folded paper with the word Finis.

Music, too, flows away in time and dies. But how different! Music dies when it attains perfection. It spouts forth, but it fills a measure. Not life. It spouts forth, but it does not fill. It comes to an end, but it leaves nothing finished. What is the sense of that? I can imagine a sculptor saying to me, "I have finished my statue," and pointing to the floor white with sweepings from his marble. I can imagine an architect's announcing, "I have finished my building," and indicating with a broad, philosophical gesture, the rubble of his structure in collapse. I can imagine a painter declaring, "I'm opening my exhibit today," and, with a wink, showing me one by one his smoke-blackened canvases.

Well, I, too, am preparing my opening exhibit—my *vernissage*. Be sure to come! In a month or two I shall have smudged, by way of completion, that extravagant sketch in which one sees a clock, an eye, a viola, one of Eunice's legs, one of the balls Raul used to play with, a shower of tears, a sea of dreams with swift, white feluccas, and in one corner I shall leave a blank space where my friends may write "Regards."

The conclusion that I draw is that life and death are heterogeneous, and that life cannot be take as an object of art, as music or poetry, as is suggested by the philosopher who says that man is an existence for death. If our life were a poem, death would be the end. If it were a dance, the final step of the exhausted dancer would deserve the applause of the angels. If there is anything that strives impetuously for an end it is art. The poet is not only he who would die if he did not write, as Rilke points out;[1] he is rather he who desires an end, who desires death when he has created his poem, desires to give his all, to offer himself entirely, to go down with his phantom ship. I say of the poet what Rilke said of man in general: *"c'est quelqu'un qui s' en va,"* someone who goes away, someone who dies a little every time he produces a full achievement, an achievement that in its wholeness and perfection is a sort of magic egg. In poetry, yes, the idea of ending and death unite. Every poem is a good death. A new testament. A victorious agony.

Why cannot I apply that idea to life without immediately encountering the absurd, the heterogeneous, the ridiculous? Why is there in life that despotism of the accidental?

Heidegger himself said that in any situation man is ripe for death! I, however, dispute this: death is always accidental, and always surprises life when it has gone but halfway. It is a senseless interruption. I can understand that the philosopher would like to reduce the whole problem of man to a single absurdity, that of death. But, in truth, there are two, that of life and that of death.

Let us try other ways. Life is not a poem; it does not have the entirety of a ballet; it is not completed with music. Who knows? Perhaps it is a broken aggregate of moments with more or less protracted and more or less insipid intervals. The whole will be con-

[1] On February 17, 1903, Rilke replied to a youthful aspirant who had sent him some poems for criticism: "Would you die if you were no longer allowed to write?" Then he advised him that if such were the case "Even the most indifferent and lowly hour of your life must bear witness to this urge" (trans.).

fused, like the complete works of an author who had followed different paths; but the fragments, the volumes will be comprehensive and reasonable. Death comes and leaves a remnant behind, just as the busy writer tosses into his drawer the abortive scribblings that he had not the time to tear up.

What I must do is take stock of my moments, index my complete works, and then rest content with that discontinuity. As an epigraph I shall write: "This is what is to be got from this life." That is the way most people are apt to say in their old age: "I have got my daughter married, and put something by—I can die in peace." And it is curious to note that in that dissolution of life there is an accord between the two types of men who are most violently opposed to each other, the bourgeois and the antibourgeois, who lives as though life were a poem.

Let us examine that new proposition that already holds forth such contradictory prospects. According to it life is without continuity. And now, as I take stock of my connected instants of life, I shall be able to say whether I was happy, whether it was worth the trouble to be born. For it must be remembered that, as a dying man, I am in a privileged situation to judge life. Ovid said in his *Metamorphoses* that it is always necessary to await man's last day, because of no one can it be said, until the obituary and the funeral, that he was happy; whence Montaigne derived his essay entitled, "Qu'il ne fault juger de nostre heur qu' après la mort."

No, not even I with my cancer shall be able to boast of having been unhappy. From what the poet and the essayist say, any judgment yet is premature. Just as Priam was sorely afflicted after a long life of good fortune, the contrary may befall me. In those thirty or forty days I may discover the secret that will authorize Dr. Aquiles to write my obituary notice and my certificate of happiness on the same sheet of paper.

But, if life is without continuity, why, I wonder, am I always the same? Why the continuity of awareness and the awareness of continuity? I fail to see the necessary connection between that depressing sameness and the astounding diversity of life's moments. In other words, if life is without continuity, then it is dissimilar from my soul, and there we are in the face of a new absurdity, which divides me from myself.

"The best thing is not to think!" I can fancy a thousand faces grimacing with annoyance, a thousand grimaces expressing the superior conclusion: "The best thing is not to think." Not to think of what? Of death? Of life? Of one's self? In that case it is necessary not to think of any one of these three things, because each one leads to the others. I do not know whether this is possible. There are people who boast of not thinking. Seneca said, however, that the only way to free one's self from the obsession of death is to face it and think of it constantly. Cicero, too, taught that philosophy is the apprenticeship to death. These two, I believe, boasted inversely; but I can say that I, personally, have not yet verified the efficacy of their prescriptions. As for not thinking, perhaps there is some way of not thinking about death, one's own death, I mean. But they who do not think about death already carry it around repressed and absorbed inside of them, where, like a darkling eminence, it commands all the disconnected acts of life. A fear will be diffused in their blood, a dissolved, continual death. And those persons will have a profound, panicky, unreasoning fear of many little things: they will be afraid of becoming penniless, of losing prestige, of not being elected to office, of losing their jobs; they will be afraid of drafts, inflation, an overturned saltcellar—

But then—O monster! O chaos! O confusion!—the absurd divides you from yourself. The two selves are dissimilar, and it is hardly understood that you have a single heart. Why is it—if your destiny is to curl up and feign death as insects do—why is it that you dream of love, generosity, and heroism?

The unthinking man goes to the movies three times a week. On the screen he finds a small loan of grandeur; he is heroic with the hero, passionate with the lover, magnanimous with all the characters that display greatness of mind and courage of spirit. Afterwards he returns home arm and arm with his death. Why? Why? Why?

December 6th

Life Is but a Walking Shadow

It was two years ago. In my loneliness a hope had arisen: the idea of seeking out the young, the uncontaminated, in order to retake with them *la diretta via*, in order to flee with their help from the dark forest that was leading me, without the Florentine's immunities, to the Inferno. Who knows? Perhaps it would be possible for us to discover together the secret that was eluding me. Perhaps it would be possible with their new blood to build something free from the corruption into which my bones had crumbled. Besides, I knew in my heart that I had been born to teach, to preach, and convince, to gather them around me, to go among them as if they were so many sons, and to be sought by them each day, each hour, in a wearying and fruitful old age.

Therefore, I sought out the young. And they came, the poets, the musicians, the dreamers, the hurt.

Having gone down to the library this afternoon, I suddenly found myself surrounded by evocations. The room became filled with phantoms; the sleeping echoes awakened and a strange ballet began to unfold before me.

It is the third act. I see children sprouting from the ground and bursting into a cloud of bloom that by some magic takes on pattern and color. I see lilies being born and growing—how fast they grow!—and a moment later drooping on their fragile stems like the livid corpses of the hanged. In a stage garden Parsifal is walking among flowers, flower-children. But that Parsifal is very different from the other. He is an eager-eyed youth who makes incomprehensible motions to me from the back of the scene, dream motions, seeming to say that he is eager, very eager to go where he is being called. I want to warn him to wait, to tread with caution, but, as in a nightmare, all I can utter is a strangled moan.

Then another youth slowly enters, smiling and with the posturings of a dancer. A stout, tawney-haired woman runs on tiptoe to meet him—where had she come from?—and, unabashed, offers him a scarlet rose. They dance; they exchange twitterings of endearment whose meaning escapes me. I was about to warn them that the garden was alive, that they were treading on enchanted petals, when a strident horn sounds in the street. The door opens, and a dozen persons in loose multicolored blouses invade the scene. The one at the head of the procession is pushing a small chromium-plated cart with 200,000 records of Prokofieff, César Franck, and Scarlatti.

They all lie down on the floor. From where I am, the stout, tawny-haired women recalls the Stone Giant except that she is very fair, blond, and freckled, and with a volcano of a painted mouth where the Parrot's Beak should be. We stay as we are for two hundred years, drinking Coca Cola and listening to 200,000 of the finest English recordings. Now and again a trampled child cries, and at Record 84,253, a bent sexagenarian goes out the back door and commits suicide backstage.

Then the victrola's rotations grow faster and faster, and they all start to whirl about in a circle to the music of Villa-Lobos. But someone suggests a new game, even wilder and more desperate; a sort of old-fashioned quadrille that goes on and on indefinitely, in which the couples come together just long enough for a kiss and then separate.

Distressed, I wanted to say something, some warning or protest, when suddenly, in the midst of a silence that was like one of Beethoven's great pauses, there was heard the voice of the contralto apostrophizing me with a restrained and majestic ardor. And in an exaggerated close-up the bright face of a young girl covered the rest of the scene. Who was she? Who was that woman that was confronting me with such authority? Should I call her daughter or mother?

"Life's meaning?" said the bright apparition in a solemn voice. "Who dares to ask us for an account of what we do with life? We dance and sing. And we defy Heaven and earth to prove to us that we should not dance and sing. The one who is right is the grasshopper of that immortal fable, which is eternally new, the fable of fables both in poetry and in life. We dance and we sing with fervor because we believe in life. Life is everything. It has an infinite value; *but it has no meaning.* Life! It is everything, and it has a clear sweep on all sides, like the wind of the prairies and the sea's horizons. But meaning it does not have. Life is to be lived and to be radiated in every direction like the light; it is to be breathed every moment like the air.

"What does have meaning," interrupted the slender youth in blue, who had settled comfortably on the window ledge, "what does have meaning is the seven-forty-five streetcar, the waiting line, the time clock, the excuse, and every seven days, an idle Sunday's weekly yawn!"

"Let them not talk to me about the future," continued the bright-faced woman, let them not talk to us about highways with stones to mark the space of time. Let them not cover our light nor take away our air. Life? We want it to be luminous and breathable; we want it to be vast, free, comprehensive, penetrative. That is the way we want it—whole, and without meaning."

The eager-eyed youth, who was bidding me good-by with mysterious gestures, thought that it behooved him to speak:

"If people ask us, 'Where are you going?' we shall keep still. Do they expect me to say in a little boy's voice that I am running to look for happiness? That childish idea was buried in the last hole we dug in the backyard. The child has died and is buried inside of us. The child has died. Happiness has died. Life's soul has died; and what they have said of it, they who are not even ashamed of the abortion to which they consented, is a bare-faced lie, told in the worst petty-bourgeois style. Now they are making for it a pompous mausoleum, whose declamatory and distorted outlines, whose colonnades and capitals are to recall what?—the ephemereal heart of a little bird that saw one day in a dream the blue lightning-flash of bliss. What is that happiness that they propose to us now, that is to be attained at a snail's pace? What is that flash that has to be reproduced with pieces of glass taken from the ground? Snow White has died. She is truly dead. Neither the weeping of the dwarfs, nor the kiss of the enchanted Prince will be able to wrench from her mouth the suffocating apple of her first wrongdoing.

"And now?"

"Now we are grownups. We are standing and scanning the horizons. We are adults. We speak as adults, adults who know that Snow White is dead. Let us enter then upon life with impatient feet. Let us solve today's problem here and now. Life's to be lived and not thought about, waited for, and prepared for. We cannot await indefinitely the promotion of the living, nor can we defer the collection of what is owed us. If something exists, whatever its name may be, we want it now. So, here we are, hard, implacable creditors, ready for the collection, the auction of the Universe and the seizure of God.

They all clapped their hands when the youth finished speaking. Are they really applauding, I wonder, or are they dealing blows? Am I at a theater or in the center of an arena, being insulted and hissed? Ah! Those words that I am hearing now are genuine and belong indeed to the theater. And the character whom I see, dressed in velvet and cloth of gold, is Macbeth, who has just this moment learned that Lady Macbeth has died.

"Life is but a walking shadow—it is a tale told by an idiot full of sound and fury signifying nothing!"

December 7th

Catarina, Where Did You Put My Childhood?

One day when I was about twelve years old the thought that the world had once existed without me struck my mind with particular emphasis. That is an ordinary thought, apparently, since no one of us in his right mind claims to have been a companion in arms to Charlemagne or one of the crew of Christopher Columbus' caravel. Obviously the world was older than the little boy who suspended his play to look curiously around him; there were the older people, the big trees, the houses, the mountains—all of which bespoke an earlier time and an earlier scene. And yet the fact is that I found that very simple thought exceedingly strange.

Older people had a disconcerting privilege: they had but to exercise their will to create inside of them a world of which I was not a part and that had had no need of me. So I would ask Mama:

"Tell me a story of long ago."

She would proceed to tell me one. Grownups became children again, the dead left their graves, and children, like me, withdrew and merged into the pale death of nonexistence. Of all the transmutations that was the one that seemed to me the most incomprehensible. In the story that my mother would tell the people did not miss me; no one was expecting me. There were echoes, traces, of even the most completely dead, those that could not emerge even then at the time of the story. Yet they were there, because they were remembered. There was Barão, Aunt Elvira, who had gone to the dance at Fiscal Island, Juvencio, a Negro whose loyalty and devotion had become legendary. Their names and a nostalgic recollection of them were part of the story. They had left their mark. But not I. In that softly yellow-tinted scene that I saw taking form back of my mother's forehead, there lived again a world to which I did not belong; a world that did not even have need of me.

Mama was in her eleventh year and still playing with dolls when Aunt Dulce fell in love with the languid Tancredo against the wishes of her parents, who suspected that he had more hair on his head than money in his pocket. It was whispered that he was a poet and would not make a good husband. And indeed he did not, as became evident later, but for other reasons, of which the Muses were innocent. Tancredo proved to be what in those days was called a useless piece of furniture. Rude, lazy, always running after the maidservants, he made Aunt Dulce's life one of martyrdom. And this was still stamped on her face, when I, who had been born by that time and was incarnate and very concrete, began to be mistrustful of grownups' stupidities.

But at that time I did not exist. My mother was playing with dolls. If someone had shouted my name into her ear, "José Maria! José Maria![1] she would not have had any maternal impulse. I did not exist. Nor was there any need of my existence. The atmosphere had not the slightest whisper that might denounce me or announce my coming. There was no paper dropped on the floor of which they could say: "It was José Maria who dropped it." There was no book forgotten on a chair of which they might assert: "It's José Maria's." Nothing. Nothing. A pale transparent, innocent, painless nothing. A nonexistence of which no one could complain, at which no one could be surprised—

But I was surprised. As I looked back, I became giddy. Not they; those people of the Empire, however much they might look into the future, had no inkling of me. Mama, it is true, playing with her dolls, thought of the children she would have; but it was of her children-in-general that she thought and not of me, José Maria, unique of my kind, as Miguel Unamuno so rightly says of himself. If Tancredo really was a poet, as my grandparents suspected, inferring his genius from his foppishly curled whiskers, he could

[1] Rilke was baptized René Karl Wilhelm Josef Maria (trans.).

have said about Mama what Michelet said about the Prince de Condé's future mother, that he saw the brilliance of Rocray in the young woman's eyes. Tancredo, the poet, would not have seen the glow of battle in my mother's gentle gaze, but he could well have glimpsed the ashen pallor of my jealousy and of my acute myeloid leukemia—

For that, in addition to the supposition of poetry, there had to be a bigger supposition: that in the world there was an imperious need of my existence. Later, when I lost the metaphysics of childhood and strayed into the world of phenomena, the universe seemed to me to be a mechanism without accident. I came to think that there had already been some part of me in the first flaming nebula, and I put the thought into a sonnet. My existence was foreordained. It was part of the world's essential order that I should be born. Molecules, atoms, and electrons were pledged to combine in fixed arrangement in the body of the little boy who was to be born on the thirteenth day of March at the close of the century, during Holy Week.

But when I was twelve or thirteen that determinism of mine had not yet risen to the surface; and what is left of it today is ashes and confusion. At that time I had a feeling of helplessness; I felt that my birth had been something inaugural, unforeseen, gratuitous. I have the same feeling today, heightened by suffering, and, even more than the idea of death, it leaves my mind agape.

The death of one's elders—the Aunt Dulces, the Uncle Afonsos—does much to deaden in one the impression that one has come into being in the middle of that tumultuous intercourse which is the history of man. I remember how grieved I was when the final witness of my childhood, the old Catarina, who had brought up Mama, and who had stubbornly clung to life, died at the age of eighty-seven, a little shriveled-up old woman. I felt wrenched from the past, and never had I felt so grown-up and so alone.

> Ah! the little old lady dead in her cradle
> Her rosary in her hand!

Seeds of many an Ave Maria hanging
On a withered, weather-beaten bough
Fallen
To the ground.

Never had I felt so emancipated and at the same time so bereft of myself. Catarina was taking away with her in her coffin a portion of my past life—and it was only right that she should. For my childhood was more hers than mine. It was her treasure. What I threw away she kept—ah! what a hoarder that little old woman was! And, of course, it was not for herself that she used to pick up memories fallen to the floor. It was for everyone, for general use in the household—just in case. She used to keep my laughter just as she kept my buttons, because someone had to put aside what everyone else was throwing away.

My childhood, cast out from me, dwelt in her, intact and genuine. Behind her wrinkled forehead I still ran about on Sundays when the sun was shining. Her soul was an enormous trunk in which there was room for everything. There was room for released kites and for *barra-manteiga*[2] and *chicote-queimado*.[3] Faded memories, faintly yellow. Sickness. Troubles. You remember, Catarina? Catarina was getting old, but she did not forget. Old outwardly, older and older, but inwardly, younger and younger,

more fair, more smooth
Ah! the little old lady scorched and burned
by her own heart. Burned alive!
The furrows of her soul were rising gently
bubble by bubble
to the surface of her wrinkled skin
(lacelike and papery)
in a transfiguration.

I did not know at that time (I swear it) that inside of her was an immense, marvelous world—a world other than this world of ours

[2] A child's game similar to tag (trans.).

[3] A child's game played with a handkerchief rolled into the form of a whip (trans.).

—in which, in inextinguishable memory, I was still running about as a little child. A world outside and inside of this one of ours. Moving about the house. Sweeping. Going and Coming. Familiar. Within my reach. Catarina! I would call and a world would come. And back of that, an even bigger world! The earlier one to which I did not belong. The world in which I did not exist—

> Her body, withered and sear,
> was a cloth pulled askew
> stretched taut and flung over deep valleys.
> Her hand patched together the years.
> Her soul formed a knot between two worlds.

My childhood, as I have already said, was more hers than mine. Not that she claimed any right to keep it. She put things aside just in case and to be helpful.

And now?

When it was alive my life was suspended and gratuitous. And I did not know! In it lay my secret, the sign, the explanation, the connection, the mingling—yes, the metaphysical composition of being and not being, so that I kept on being born over and over again. The two worlds. The two worlds were united, fused; and life was for me a continuous rebirth, a continuous growth and outpouring.

And now?

"Catarina! Catarina! Ca-ta-riii-na! Don't you hear me, woman?" "Have you grown deaf?—Catarina, where did you put my childhood?"

After Catarina's death I was grown-up, irremediably grown-up, and, except for books, pictures, and statues, out of touch with the world in which I had not existed. I clung to the conviction that the universe had absolute need of me. In that way I quieted my dismay and, a solitary and melancholy god, I set myself up at the center of the universe that had been made for me.

Today, however, as the shadowy voice draws near, that same childish feeling of utter dependence comes back to me. More than ever I feel suspended; suspended between an accident of creation and one of destruction, between an incomprehensible birth and an incomprehensible death. Dangling. Helpless. Yesterday I fell by chance into an opening lap; tomorrow I shall fall under a closing stone.

And the thought that tortures me is that of my sterility.

December 9th

The Encounter in the Campo de Santana

Since I felt a little better when I awoke today, I do not know why, I decided to hop over to the War Ministry, where a paper has been awaiting my signature for over a month. By mistake I took a streetcar that put me out on Visconde do Rio Branco Street, and I found the full length of the Campo de Santana before me. As the morning was fresh, I decided to walk the distance to the Ministry. So I went into the garden. I was thinking more of the tiresome paper with all its official seals than of the trees and lawn; but soon, after I had gone a little way, removed from the confusion of the street and the danger of traffic, the peacefulness of the garden enveloped me. I slackened my pace and relaxed pleasurably. I determined to take a holiday from my cares during that brief jaunt, and I concluded that it was well to be in a garden while on my way to a bureaucratic mission. Every ministry ought to be thus surrounded by woods so that the soul might refresh itself before reaching the desert of paper. In the very halls of the office buildings— If I were given a portfolio for a month—I should have various ferns, maidenhairs and *samambaias*—placed here and there in rustic jars smelling of earth.

As I was walking along the tree-lined paths, with head and shoulders bent, the simple rolling monotony of the gravel and the sand and the grass filled my soul with a joyous sense of security and continuity. The ground is good because it always mends itself, because it continues, because it does not separate from itself; and I thought of the faithful continuity that stretches along the roadways of the earth. The proverb says that all roads lead to Rome, apart from the sea, which did not surprise me, since I saw no serious, important reason why I should stop on the smooth highway I was following until I came to the outskirts of the Eternal City.

The mineral world is compact. Even if the grains of sand do stand out from one another, they cannot destroy its good unity, its fine solidity. Now grass is another matter. Seen at a glance, it might be compared to a broad smooth brushstroke of green. But that half-drooping little blade that was sticking out from the border and advancing into the sand, plainly denoted a principle of insubordination, the timid impudence of one who wishes to be different from the rest.

Then I looked up at the trees and let my eyes run up one of the trunks. I divided my gaze among the boughs and became lost among the countless leaves. And suddenly the tree rose before me like a grotesque monster at once motionless and gesticulating. It was emerging from the earth, from the ground beside the path, to assert a new unity. It was striving to separate itself from the ground and from the rest of things, but it was a poor sort of separation, for it could not manage to conceal the knotty humility of its roots nor the capricious levity of its branches, with which the wind was sporting. It was still at the mercy of earth and sky, firmly bound, lightly yielding.

The case of the *cutia*[1] was obviously better defined. The *cutia* had jumped out of a thicket, and now there he was in front of me, applying himself to the watchful gnawing of an almond husk. With his lustrous coat and plump body, he could move about freely, without imprisoned roots or exposed branches, in a graceful and magnificent anatomy. The *cutia* was an entity that could move about and jump and gnaw an almond shell. Clearly, there was an abrupt separation drawn between those two categories: the *cutia* and the rest of the universe.

[1] A Brazilian rodent (trans.).

Had a biologist been at hand, he could have explained to me that the *cutia's* body, from hair to nails, is composed of constantly renewed cells, which the chemist, had he come along, would have pulverized into atoms, which the physicist would have broken up still further into electrons, protons, and other particles of matter or energy. The *cutia*, in the final instance, would be a sort of geometric locus, a fleeting conjunction of the grains that make up the universe, combined in the animal according to certain equations, or merely supported by certain probabilities, and maintained thus at the level of the hair and nails in a precarious and casual equilibrium. The almond shell would be another conjunction of electrons. The act of gnawing would be only a movement by which a flux of particles would give the shell's equation from the equation of the *cutia*.

Furthermore, as I thought of the testimony of certain philosophers I realized I was justified in doubting the existence of both the *cutia* and the shell. If I were to shut my eyes, those things, that would then be seen by no one, would lose color and form. What a great privilege is that of man! He has but to shut his eyes for the curtain of the lids to drop and enclose the drama of the universe.

So I shut my eyes to test whether some part of me, some corner of my mind, could hold the belief that the universe broke up into uniform particles every time I blinked. Now what I felt at that moment, the philosopher's quarrel over the existence of the universe forgotten, was something inexpressible that suggested to me the idea that I had glimpsed the substantial existence of the universe. I shall attempt an approximation by saying that in that fleeting instant I had contact with the primordial fact that imposes itself when one achieves, however slightly, the experience of self. And that primordial fact that imposes itself brutally, sharply, undeniably is that of a separation; a separation like which there is no other in the universe; a separation of a new sort, like which there is no other from the spiral nebulae lost in the depths of the heavens to the shining, scalloped shell lost in the depths of the ocean; a complete separation that is torn between everything and that mysterious center outside of everything, that essentially eccentric center that places itself, enigmatic, watchful, solitary, at the edge of all things, at the farthest boundary of nothingness.

That is the primary fact. Obviously everything has its limits, its form, and is constituted in exception within the cosmos. Yet all things, *cutia*, tree, husk are bathed in what I may call "space" or "atmosphere" and are able to communicate with one another. Not I. I can exclude myself in a strange, new way. And I carry within myself an entity, the center of an entity, that is opening up a furrow for its passage, and digging an abyss of totality and solidarity. Two things exist, two great categories: the ego and the non-ego. That is the primary intuition. Even without reaching the delirium of the idealistic philosophers, who end up by believing in a single existence, that of the self, even without destroying with my eyelids the intactness of the Campo de Santana, I was aware of that overwhelming and intoxicating separation.

That curious experience lasted only a few seconds. When I reopened my eyes I found an individual two paces away. It was a drunk. Wavering on his legs, planted in my path, he was observing with shrewd interest and sympathy that gentleman who was standing there with his eyes shut. Seeing that I was coming back to earthly reality and that he could count, therefore, upon my attention, he removed his old hat with a sweeping, patriotic gesture and exclaimed, "The oil is ours!"

At that moment, my meditations suffered an abrupt impact. Something new was in front of me. An incredible thing was standing out away from the ground and the surrounding scene in a manner that was almost as brutal as the dissection of my soul that I had a moment before experienced when my eyes were closed. And behind this new thing—the swollen, flushed face of a drunk—the entire universe was a vast décor with conventionalized trees and an animal in one corner of the frame, superfluous or anachronous, like the details that a Veronese might have painted around *The Marriage at Cana*; and behind everything else, in the very background of this would-be landscape, the War Ministry might perfectly well have been a cardboard structure without in the least diminishing the principal theme—the bloated face of the drunk.

I scarcely gave any heed to the nationalistic thesis that my man was so ardently upholding. I had observed before that drunks are almost always nationalists. I do not know why. Besides, at the moment, the oil problem seemed unimportant to me. What was occupying all my attention was the shock, the dismay, the wonder of glimpsing, suddenly, the extraordinary duplication of what I had just seen with closed eyes. It was the sight of that most separate, most detached, most withdrawn, most terribly isolated thing in the world, an ego; an alter ego, a self that was not mine, but a self, nonetheless, that, however much of a fool it might be, dragged in its wake a vassal universe.

Behind the face deformed by vice I saw, or rather guessed than saw, another ghostly face, vague and illusory, as though I had leaned over the edge of a well whose water was agitated and cloudy, and, where I had seen below, almost at the water's surface, a great mysterious water lily or the visage of a drowned man.

And then, terrified, I discovered my own image in that *ecce-homo*. He was my mirror. I was his. Our beings' single center began to dance, leaping from my world into that of the drunk. There was a brief duel between the two selves. Each one of us had at his disposal a dreadful secret weapon to make the other vanish. All I had to do, for example, was blink my eyes or loosen I know not what springs of my soul for that face quickly to lose its relief and take its place beside the animal and against the Ministry's broad facade as a mere ornamental detail in the picturesque landscape.

The garden was filled with people, to be sure; they were all around us. But at the instant when our eyes met, the whole world became a concave, expectant amphitheater with two gladiators at the center of the arena.

However, the encounter was short and futile. The man grew impatient with my immobility and continued his sinuous way, carrying his thesis on oil to more appreciative ears. I, too, went on my way. A few minutes later I was on the fourth floor of the Ministry, the sealed paper before me. And no one there could have had the slightest suspicion that I had just come from the depths of an abyss.

December 11th

There Is a Luciana

Pedreira introduced the girl who was seated on a stool, noting the readings of a milliamperemeter, "Luciana, my assistant."

And when she got up to greet me, he added, "She's my right arm. Without her my work wouldn't be where it is."

Luciana smiled. And then I saw—

Yes, I saw in a flash, standing before me—real, alive—in her gleaming white apron with its little blue flower-bud buttons and its small pockets like just so many recently opened envelopes of good news, the girl with the soft brown hair whom I should have met twenty or thirty years ago, the girl whom I could have loved with a quiet, tender affection. With its sweet brightness, her smile lighted up a vast expanse of possibilities. There was a Luciana. In that tenth of a second that encompassed all of life, I was filled with wonder by the discovery that what I had always desired existed. There was a Luciana. Is she more beautiful than the other women I have met? Is she more beautiful than the blond and radiant Eunice? I really do not know. I do know that she is gentler, paler, more expansive— I began to dream— I was far away, in distant lands and remote seas, taking possession of the earth and life, with that linen-clad figure beside me. I did not even have to turn around to speak to her or to make sure that she was there. The important thing was that she was there. The important thing was that she was beside me— No, not even that. Not even that mattered. I set out, leaving her behind, far behind, and, through the years that her smile endured, I ventured, alone and courageous, through dark tunnels and dense forests. The important thing was that she was still back at the place of my departure, quietly, dependably waiting for me— No. Not even that. Not even that mattered. The important, the truly important thing was that she existed: and wherever I might be, in the East or in the West, at the poles or in the deserts, her existence would be elucidating the realities, explaining the seas, interpreting the Infusoria and the constellations. I should live alone, gentle Luciana, motionless Luciana, in a solitude of profound whiteness. I should live alone, like a solitary monk, surrounded by transparent love, which expands and dims to allow the soul to breathe. I should live—and I did live, for that tenth of a second, within the four white walls of a cell that had all the freshness of the convalescent's linen sheets, and the intense sweetness of friendly silences. I felt my mother's hand upon my head; I heard the whispering voices of the sisters whom I had always wanted; and the world expanded, Luciana expanded, as the dawn expands, and all the world, yes, life itself became fused into harmony upon that modest bosom into which plunged a little silver chain. O longed-for solitude! O gentle whiteness!

Pedreira was explaining in great detail his most recent research on dielectrics. I had gone to see him at his insistence, because he needed to exchange ideas, or rather, talk about his investigations in order that they might take on more body, actually or by agreement, in someone else's ears. He had inquired most perfunctorily about my health. I told him that I had consulted Dr. Aquiles and that it was anemia, and then he began to talk about his equipment.

Luciana went back to her stool. The tenth of a second had expired. From the threshold of that momentary intuitive vision that I had had of life, I said good-by to Luciana. She had passed by—I was kissing a breath of air from a swallow's wing—and all was over. The twenty-eight–year–old girl sitting with her back toward me on the stool, doubled over the frequency count, was only the charming assistant who had been introduced to me.

And I left the laboratory accompanied by my tattered fifty years and my cancer.

December 12th

On a Dream Adriatic

I am going to ask Dr. Aquiles to give me a transfusion and then let me have one of his facile ships. I shall set out. With a loan of blood and one of the ships of the Doctor's fleet, I shall set out; thus I shall die a little in Paris, and a little more in Vienna, until the final day, which I can fancy drawing to its close amid the rocky promontories of a dream Adriatic.

Since the medical profession cannot prolong my life, I shall expand it. The Doctor gave me three months, I shall transform them into three years, into three centuries, filling them with variety, activity, and emotion. What is time? A kind of space, a kind of vacuum. What is a month? A compartment to be furnished in the fourth dimension. What do I care about the astronomical, physical, or biological smallness of those walls that science has drawn for me? Did I find the room on Ipiranga Street too small?

I do not have love now, that wonderful interior decorator of secluded moments, or that great explosive that makes an ocean rise out of a kiss. No matter. Poetry will guide me in death as it guided the Florentine upon the pathways of the Inferno and upon the escarpments of Heaven. So I say to my soul, "Let us go. Let us reinforce our blood, let us prepare the good sacks of flour and the good skins of dark wine that gave new life to Telemaque, and let us set out, let us set out upon the final journey."

Where am I? What place is this to which I have come? What

quiet, unique afternoon is this, with golden sky and green sea? We are drawing near. Step by step, with extreme fatigue, I am approaching the edge of the abyss. I am alone. The world has stayed behind. The wind has brought fragments from it still—torn, scattered bits of news that dance in the air. I hear only murmurings from the transient world of the living that stayed behind. The torn pieces that are borne on the wind stick to the rocks of wet basalt; and there I can read, in truncated form, the latest news. They say there is a war, that there are conflagrations, that young men are falling like leaves, that ministries are uniting and armies retreating. There are pharmaceutical products that advertise happiness and smiles for hire stamped upon the billboards of the world.

But I am alone. In a lonely spot, in a stone cave of a poet's Adriatic, I am going forward, ever forward, fascinated by the abyss. I lean over the edge of the precipice. "The wind and the sea murmur prayers." The wind, a great soaring eagle, draws the world with leather traces that creak upon its mighty wings— The sea, a slab of porphyry and emerald— And I, leaning over the abyss. Night is falling—

Shall I cry out? Who will hear me? "If I cry out, who will hear me among the ranks of the angels?"[1]

[1] From the opening lines of the first of Rilke's *Duino Elegies* (trans.).

part 2 BURMESE RUBIES

December 14th

My Roses

Today[1] I bade my faded roses farewell. Of the radiant youth of three days ago and of yesterday's splendid maturity this is all that was left: four old things, four crazy old maids who were still putting on paint and arraying themselves in petals unbecoming to their age.

Have I already said that my roses have names? To free them from the indefiniteness of genus and species I give them proper names—women's names. They keep me company better that way. Their personality reinforces my personality, and their rhythm expands mine.

Today's dead ones had a glorious life. The first one was named Fedra; it was scarlet, tragic, and headstrong. I called the second Brunhilda, because it was fair and vigorous as a Germanic heroine. Isolda was the ephemeral name of the third, a velvety, mysterious creature of the night, with the perfume of love and death. But the most beautiful of all—no one would say so now, seeing her in her decrepitude—was Esther, an erect, golden rose, that took precedence over all of them to demand the freedom of her people from Ahasuerus, who was captive to her charms.

[1] Rilke was deeply fond of roses. His garden at Muzot was filled with them, and throughout his life he was haunted by their symbolism. "It is highly significant to note the evolution this symbol underwent in the poet's mind. During those early years of what one might call his belated adolescence, the living red rose, universally accepted symbol of love, immediately evokes a death fantasy, for at that period of Rilke's life everything erotic inevitably becomes macabre. At the end of his life, the sleep-image of the countless closed eyelids suggested by the petals of the rose calls up in him the transcendental idea of wakefulness and immortality" (*Rilke: Man and Poet* by Nora Wydenbruck)—(trans.).

Le roi est mort, vive le roi: applicable to opaline vases as well as to thrones. Since I have settled in this cramped, hermetic little planet, roses have come and gone just as do dynasties, pontificates, and regimes in that other larger vase, more crude and confused, that stands in a corner of the universe apparently forsaken by the gods.

I can see their phantoms. I remember Susana, for instance, the most limpid, the most chaste rose that I have ever seen, with its broad petals in the form of a shell, few and single, light at first and afterwards deeper in color, with a crimson blush of innocence, clinging closely together to conceal the bud, which never opened fully and never revealed its inmost secret. The blossom died without losing its petals. It clad itself modestly in its own nudity, a successive and concentric nudity that hid the closed petals with the open ones—

There were, too, Eunice, saucy and of a pale copper hue, Catarina, blood-red, free, generous, and in their midst, in the same water, Dona Antonia, a huge common pink rose, profuse and motherly, whose talk was of forgotten anniversaries and recipes for sweets.

Then, during the worst days of last week, between two most ordinary little gossiping red roses, the white Beatrice opened like a gleam of moonlight. "Funereal Beatrice with icy hand, unique, consoling Beatrice." When she hung pallid and dead, it seemed to me that the others, whose names were Sandra and Suely, were talking about my Beatrice, her pallor and her quiet funeral, with the inconsequential volubility of those who frequent Masses and death chambers, yet consider themselves immortal.

Later there was a crisis in my vase. Lacking the courage to run around the market and resist the hardy Portuguese who confont one with great mounds of dahlias and long lengths of gladioli, my vase was empty for two days and nights.

I sorely missed my flower-women, who had left me alone with the ghost of Kundry. On the third day I went out for a stroll in the neighborhood, and in a dimly lit shop where pottery, and little birds, and faded flowers are for sale, I bought three pitiful buds. They were three Marys, little orphans, all with the same ugly little dresses.

Today I have changed the water and the roses. I have three choice buds. One of them is red, of a noble, royal hue. The florist told me that it is a Saturnia. I have kept the name, personalizing it. The other bud is pink, with creamy tones, and is a Ninon Vallin. But the rose-child for which I felt the deepest affection was that golden, wheat-colored one with rosy cheeks that worries me now because of the listless way that it is leaning against the robust Saturnia. The florist told me that it is an Otto Kraus, but it is obvious, most obvious, indeed, that that name which suggests a shaven-pated Teuton in no way suits my wheat-colored rose. Quick, what name shall I give it to conjure away that ponderous specter that smacks of the brewery? If its origin is truly Germanic, if its seeds came from the Valley of the Rhine, we shall not hide its glorious blood as Esther kept hers hidden—it shall be called Gertrude.

The three buds are in place. The tallest is Saturnia; Ninon and Gertrude are lightly balanced to the right and to the left, held by frail supports of maidenhair fern and Japanese bamboo.

And now the blossoms begin their infinitely slow posturings. They awaken, they stretch, they dance in a rhythm that is foreign to my own, concealing in its slowness, a slowness that promises centuries of life, the immeasurably sweet wonder of their gestures.

Ah! The loveliest of sleeping beauties does not so gracefully bend her arm into a curving amphora handle, or—suspended in happy breathless surprise, and overtaken by sleep—so gently droop and sway her neck in unvarying rhythm. Nor does she have the delicate flickering of the wondering eyelids that disclose the blue corollas' secret, or the daring, modesty, and harmony of these my silent dancing maidens.

Can one imagine a loved face that would take twelve hours to unfold a single smile only to die a moment after? And what confuses me about that dance of the roses, about that rhythm that is foreign to our rhythm—as if it were directed from on high by a gigantic heart, a metronome for stars and roses—what amazes me, leaving me lost in endless meditation, is the obscurity, the independence, the gratuitousness of that spectacle that no one ever sees.

When I awake tomorrow my rose-children will be young girls. Yet they will appear motionless. If the wind stirs them lightly, and they sway and bow, their very mobility will be only the more hidden from my eyes; for my eyes, slaves of a frenzied heart that must still beat some fifty thousand times, cannot adapt themselves to the broad rhythm that beats only once and then dies. At most, I can see only the stages of the roses. Buds today. Half-open tomorrow. Then glorious full blooms. And, finally, withered remains. I notice their transitions like the distant relative who from year to year observes that his little girl has grown, developed, and become a woman. How Saturnia has grown!

I may see pictures of their development; let us say that I see a dozen, two dozen, that every five minutes I come to examine the work of the petals. Even so, the continuity, the complete meaning of the movement escapes me. A dance is not a succession of statues. If one were to take two hundred photographs of one of Nijinski's ballets one would still not know how a Russian's soul dances. If one were to go into a concert hall from time to time to find out what passage the musicians were playing, one could never learn the dimensions of Mozart's soul.

The flowers' rhythm is foreign to our own. Even were I to sit up all night, staring fixedly, I should not see the dance. The more closely I watched, the less I should see. The greater my effort, the more would the secret be hidden. There is, to be sure, the recourse of the accelerated camera to show us a flower's marvelous awakening. Whoever has looked through that tiny aperture which the technique provides can form an approximate idea of that great spectacle that is constantly being wasted on the world and of that immeasurably sweet wonder with which all things are suffused.

How many are the spectacles that are unbeheld! Imagine that vast theater without a parquet, that dark stage, that infinite hidden beauty. Imagine the lovely mountainsides at dawn, the concerts of the birds that the flowers do not hear, and the concert of the flowers that the birds do not see; imagine the jewelry of dew that the night strings into necklaces without number and that the sun undoes. But there is no one in the valley to say to the night, to the birds, to the flowers: "How beautiful! Thank you." And there is the growth of the vegetation from the tiniest blade of grass, a tender sword in miniature, to the mighty trees that grow and move in two directions, dancing, in the air a sprightly nymphs' dance, and with their writhing roots in the damp, black earth, a darksome sabbat. But no one says to the grass and to the cedar; "How beautiful! Thank you, grass. Thank you, cedar." The celestial roses, the stars are born and grow and die, they too. They too are diverse; each from the pale ones to the red ones has its own very special personality. They glow upon the confines of the universe, yet though their brilliance which falls upon us like a blade of light may be visible, no one sees the totality of their extreme incandescence and no one cries out to them while they burn: "How beautiful! Thank you, Betelguese! Thank you, Rigel! Thank you, Bellatrix!"

How many the spectacles that are unbeheld! And I say to myself: "Imagine the soul's infinity, and think of the elegies confined to the silence of that infinity. Think of the odes that dissolve in tears and that no one will ever hear, for which no one will ever give thanks. And the dreams, imagine the dreams, and the desires, ah! think of the desires that life has never brought to light!"

How many the spectacles that are unbeheld! And again I say to myself: "Imagine all the lives that no one ever sees, except in stages of development and still pictures, and that unfold and wither without anyone's ever perceiving their continuity, their rhythm, their entire movement, their complete secret—yes, their secret—"

December 16th

The General's Roses

It is a gala day at the General's house. Jandira, the cook, explained that his Excellence is having a birthday, and I conclude that the gifts and flowers that keep arriving at the Minister General's door must come from contractors who are having a difficult time of it and from hopeful purveyors.

The first messenger came early in the morning with a showy *corbeille* of roses. There were more than fifty roses in the basket. Later throughout the day came dahlias, bird-of-paradise flowers, Transvaal daisies, gladioli, and Agapanthus. At dusk came still another truckload of roses. I could see them distinctly. They were choice roses, similar to my frail Gertrude, but strong and hardy. They passed by me like the haughty countesses that the Revolutionary tumbril bore to the Conciergerie.

When they arrive the General will be well pleased and he will say: "A pretty *corbeille.*" But he will not see the roses; he will not know that they have names, that their sister Gertrude is suffering from some mysterious malady, and much less will he know that in the night they dance slowly, slowly. Though his Excellency sees the basket, the mass, the agglomeration, he does not see the roses, just as on the days when excited mobs have gathered, he sees from the height of the presidential platform the square jammed with people, but does not see their faces, or guess their names, or suspect the troubles and secrets of each. The square filled with people is also a *corbeille,* a gift for his ministerial eyes.

Now, in private, the General is a demagogue of roses. He receives enormous quantities of them, in commissions and collective manifestations. And the flowers' shamelessness seems to me even more shocking than that of the poor fools who crowd around his platform. Just see how those bird-of-paradise flowers, complex and pedantic, strain upward and contort themselves to please the man of state. Look at the Agapanthus; it seems that they have pushed forward one of their number, a sorry-looking individual, pale and thin, but with the gift of gab, to address the eminent man. "We, the Agapanthus of this wonderful city—" And the dahlias? They puff out and flaunt themselves provocatively in their baskets so that the Minister's fat hand may seek among them the card of the gallant contractor. And even the roses, perfidious creatures, fill the air with fragrance. What relation can there be between a purveyor's flattery and the fragrance of roses?

Did I say that though the General does not see the roses, he does see the *corbeille*? I was mistaken. He does not see the *corbeille* any more than he sees the roses. The whole thing has no existence of its own. It is a token. It belongs to the category of telegrams, honors, decorations. It is no more than a token. The courtiers could send the receipt stamped with the price of the flowers and the effect would be the same. Because it is not the flowers or their number or arrangement, not the combination of colors or the unusual form of the petals that the General notices when the gift is brought to him. What he sees, through the token's transparency, is subservience. Behind the rose are bent spines and subaltern smiles; in the blossoms' fragrance, the incense of abject and self-interested flattery. And that is what the Minister sees in all that wealth of petals and hues; the shrewdness, the hypocrisy, the elemental astuteness of the servile flatterer.

But if that is so, how can one explain the statesman's pleasure over so ugly a spectacle? He knows, surely, even from personal experience that adulation is an ugly, despicable thing. Better than anyone else the statesman knows the true worth of obsequiousness. How, then, can one understand his unctuous smile of satisfaction at the repulsive sight of the roses' hidden meaning?

I believe that with one more reflection I shall be able to explain the phenomenon. I said just now that behind the flowers the Minister sees the smiles of subservience. But no. The pleased eyes of the powerful man who is today celebrating his birthday do not linger on the faces of the contractors and purveyors. Obsequiousness too, is indirectly a token, and it is not upon it that the General's gaze rests. No. What he sees in that trick of mirrors, with roses here and purveyors there, is his own importance, his own face, the one big reality, for which the whole world is an enormous frame.

December 18th

The World Reduced to Atoms

Thinking again of the General's many roses, I discovered today that the world is dying of collectivism. Ah! How I detest that cancer that is strangling humanity! With a crusader's zeal I should begin the fight right away, were it not for my own cancer. Yesterday Eunice, today Dr. Aquiles; I have never had the serenity, the quiet, the whiteness of a spacious and fruitful life. Why does that feeling come to me now? Why does it torment me precisely at this moment, the thought of the work that I have not done, the battle that I have not fought?

The collectivism from which the world is dying and on which modern adventurers live is the theory of conjunction without unity; it is the attempt to find meaning in numbers, since the meaning of the individual could not be found; it is a conspiracy of those who are ignorant of themselves; the union of those who isolate themselves; sociability based on misunderstanding; the locus of error.

Mankind, who has lost the secret of the soul, isolates itself at times and congregates into masses at others. Human history is a dance of twofold measure with error for a pendulum, and thus the world follows its swaying madness. So long as there is a certain complacent egoism men manage to live in a sportive competition, the law of supply and demand (each man for himself and God for every man) dividing society into airtight compartments (social relations and business relations) and are able to formulate and live a doctrine of individualism tempered only by that association which is inevitable, by a social contract of extrinsic accord. However, when the euphoria of that state, which might be called social atomization, is exhausted, and when solitude weighs heavily on men's souls, they rush to pile up together and jam the public square, raising now the right arm now the left as a sign of conciliation. And in the warm contact of shoulders, chests, and buttocks, in the tepid shelter of the corral, the men who have come together smile, comforted, a plebeian smile, happy to have escaped from the horrible nightmare of possessing a soul. Then they talk of human solidarity, by which they mean the sensation of sticking together shoulder to shoulder, chest to chest, buttocks to buttocks.

Which of the two is the worse, I wonder, the egoism that seeks isolation or the egoism that congregates? It is difficult to decide. The one of which the world has grown weary is probably the worse, whereas the better is the one whose disadvantages the world has forgotten. And so, like the cabinless traveler who spends the night on the sharp edge of a bench tossing about, shifting his position, finding a moment's alleviation in the very posture from which he has suffered cramps, we, too, go from one contortion to the next, from one alleviation to the next, and, what is still worse, from one enthusiasm to the next.

Had I the time, I should like to prove that true sociability is possible only when its roots go down into the depths of subjectivity; for it is from those depths alone that true generosity can well. In other words, what I should like to prove is that man's genuine sincerity lies deep within him, in the secret cloistral garden of his heart.

That would be my banner if I could still assemble the strength that I have dissipated during a ridiculous life. But I have come too late. Today, the mere thought of the undertaking overwhelms me with an intense feeling of sickness and my mind is assailed by the infinite wearisomeness of the controversies that I should have to maintain, the individuals who, with that profound manner peculiar to the mediocrity who has discovered a doctrine to his just measure (la poule qui a trouvé un sou), would seek me out to prove that two and two are four and that four times four is sixteen, and that sixteen minus nine, is seven. I should have to explain a thousand times sincerely and convincingly that I am not unaware of the fact that it takes four Portuguese to carry a piano and that the subtlety of the rule whereby ten men can put up a wall in less time than five is not beyond me.

Indeed, the majority of socialistic arguments begin with the supposition of bringing to the world the sensational discovery that two and two are four. Even if I were not ill I do not know whether I have the courage for the Herculean project of saying the same things every day, of resuming the same reasoning a hundred times, merely to find myself at the end of ten, twenty, or a hundred at the point from which I started, explaining that man can solve the outward problems reasonably only when he has discovered, at least in its vague lineaments, the secret of his inner being.

Because of my illness, I shall bring my eager apostleship to a close with these notes. The little strength that is left me is barely enough to observe in three or four rosebuds what I should like to see in the lives of man: the rhythm and harmony of perfect unfolding.

December 19th

Comical Errors

My window is a box; the Minister's reception room in the mansion across the street, a theater. That is the impression I have from the ladies and gentlemen whom I am watching from here. They are acting. Each one is obeying the sequence of a play of his own invention; each one is evolving, moving about, laughing, gesticulating, and speaking according to the secret directions of an inner prompter. Each one has created a personality for himself; so no wonder the play is so insipid and its pretense of harmony so ridiculous.

Man is ridiculous. Yes, ridiculous. Before the spectacle of adulation, injustice, and the abuse of power I might still become angry as I used to when the blood seethed in my veins; I might passionately clench my fists at the thought of the countless numbers out in the world who are defrauded and deceived so that a half-dozen characters may assemble that disconnected comedy; but now, in the isolation of my observatory and with the ghastly illumination that I project on all things, I see only the ridiculousness, the glacial, melancholy ridiculousness of man.

I believe that I have discovered its cause: it is the mistakenness—the practical, the colossal deception—that oppresses human destiny. Perhaps that is why there is something comical in the figure of a man. In his subtle treatise on laughter Bergson has said that comedy lies in the mechanical appearance of human attitudes. Would it not be better to say that it is not in the mechanical but rather in the nonhuman appearance that the cause of comedy lies? To me it seems that it is this persistence in error that constitutes the essence of vanity and comedy.

At the circus people laugh because it is the business of certain individuals to err intentionally, deliberately, professionally, but with an apparent spontaneity that momentarily hides the intention. And that laughter is actually a hissing *sui generis.* The circus comedian is the clever professional of stylized banter who goes out to meet the crowd's hissed disapproval halfway and transforms it into applause of his art. The clown diverts our constant, tyrannical desire to censure, correct, denounce—and hiss.

Outside of the circus, the intention and the art that sublimates hissing into applause disappear but the same explanation of the ridiculous subsists: it is error, practical error, the mistake that man makes in his own identity. Everything is a comedy of errors. Is life, I wonder, a divine comedy?

What we see most often in life is the other fellow's mistake. Every individual is a play and every group, a parquet. Sometimes the mistake is so obvious that it sets the involuntary artist apart as in the middle of an improvised ring. Such is the case, for instance, of the poor devil who drinks the water with its circular slice of lemon that the waiter brings for the ritual of finger dipping. The act is not in itself absurd, since water is for drinking as well as for washing and especially since the slice of lemon suggests more quickly the idea of a beverage than that of ablution. The ridiculousness of it lies in the fact that the individual has not conformed to conventional behavior; he has muffed the part that was his to play in that scene.

Comedy, as Bergson has so well pointed out, assumes the social structure, that is, it assumes the possibility of imagining a ring for the person who is to be singled out and rows of seats for his judges, who are to pronounce their curious verdict in laughter.

Who, then, will laugh at that generalized spectacle that involves three billion clowns? Occasionally we achieve the illusion of being in a box from which we can laugh at the others. But whence comes that resonance, that echo of a laugh that is much louder than my own? Who is there? Who is there in those empty chairs laughing at me?

The world is a circus in which the arena and the rows of seats are relative. Three billion poorly rehearsed actors spend their lives seeking amusement by pointing out the other fellow's weakness, or, if you will, the mote in his eye.

One error, a deep-seated one, has the peculiar property of being visible to others but invisible to the one to whom it belongs. That is the error that I am watching from my observatory. Those people in the General's reception room are amusing, most amusing. Like the individual who did not know how to use the water with the slice of lemon, they do not know what to do with their own souls.

They are not familiar with the great conventional pattern; they do not know the scheme of the play, the right time to laugh, the precise gesture, the adequate word. What is my hand for? What is my spleen for? What is my soul for?

Here we are examining our own hearts, like a native of Polynesia who has found a sextant half buried in his island's sand. He will probably use it as an ornament, or, perhaps, as a lance, and no one of the tribe will laugh, just as no one laughs in the General's reception room.

I am reminded of bovarysm, "that faculty that men have of conceiving of themselves as being different from what they are." But Jules Gaultier's analysis based on the mistake of Mme. Bovary, who considered herself a *grande dame,* seems too superficial to me. If, for example, I were to consider myself a great singer or an exceptional dancer, I should be hissed. If I were to fancy myself Napoleon or Charlemagne, I should be locked up. But I do not know what nor who I am; and thus I am living this fag-end of life between comedy and madness. I was certainly wrong many times where Eunice and Raul were concerned. Like Mme. Bovary, judging myself to be different from what I am, I have probably committed many an adjunctive blunder. Now, however, I am thinking of a more inherent error, one that divides me from myself. That is the important one, the one that begets all the others. The feeling that I lack inner unity impels me irresistibly to seek a borrowed personality, a part to play, a mask to put on, as it impelled Eunice to be repeatedly unfaithful.

The case of Mme. Bovary, to my mind, was oversimplified by its author. A borrowed personality never has the coherence, the harmony that one sees in Flaubert's character. It may have stability to be sure, but a disconnected, dissimilar stability that approaches automatism. This recalls a few pages that I wrote long ago in an imaginary letter to Miguel about Eunice's inconstancy when good old Alice was trying to defend her by saying that she was only a little flighty—

Alice broached the subject of Eunice. Apparently our misunderstandings were becoming too obvious. It was a most painful conversation, in which I strove to conceal the secrets of our intimate life. Very delicately, Alice pursued me and cornered me, trying to convince me that mine was the greater fault because I made no effort to adapt myself. She concluded by saying that Eunice "was only a little flighty."

Yes, Miguel, Alice thinks that is only a trifling thing. And you? Do you know what it really is, that thing that she has so monstrously distorted that one can only smile with condescension or quickly forgive? I didn't know either, but today I know. And I can assure you that I've paid dearly for that knowledge.

I'm not unaware that the consensus of society is almost unanimously against me. When a pretty girl assumes an air of gaiety and scatters her smiles and idle chatter at random, she seems the loveliest and most exciting of creatures, a true source of joy. Yet, actually, capriciousness is a sad thing. I don't know whether you've ever seen those frightful sores that eat away the nose and open a cavity in the face. They have a wealth of color, so that if one were to look only at them, without taking into consideration the nose and mouth, those features that give expression to the human countenance, he could not deny that they have a certain exotic beauty. On man they are horrible. Well, capriciousness is like that.

Capriciousness is characterized by sickness rather than health, rigidity rather than mobility, death rather than life. I have used the word "rigidity," which I shall explain more fully. During the course of life we all suffer certain psychological shocks—fright, amazement, sudden sorrow—all of which leave some residual. Now everything in our lives depends upon our ability to assimilate those residuals. If we succeed in dissolving them into the substance of our being, then those marks of our experiences will be fruitful, and the result will be a truly human, profitable experience. If I convert the stones along my path into blood and soul, I shall have thereafter sensitive antennae that I did not have before, I shall be capable of intuitions which were impossible to me before. I shall compose verses, I shall discover new planets, or I shall simply have a harmonious balance that will allow to live a broader life.

The capricious person, on the contrary, is one in whom the residual of his experiences has tumefied. It has sensitive areas, buttons, and keyboards and is controlled from outside, like a machine. One presses a button and he says "good-day," wrinkling up the muscles of his face. One presses another button, and if it controls a minister he makes a speech; if it controls a twenty-five–year–old girl she tosses back her hair.

I knew a poor woman who spent her whole life, and many bad moments, upheld by a *leitmotiv* that probably originated in her early girlhood. On a certain day, at a certain favorable conjunction of stars, someone had said: "What a good disposition Fabricia has!"; and from that day on, with all the constancy of a Vestal Virgin, Fabricia had kept that motto alight. She made a point of being faithful to that chance obligation, even achieving, in certain more difficult situations, a veritable heroism in defense of that good humor that she had received as a loan and of which she was taking such systematic care. I remember that I went to see her the day that her son was run over and killed. She was weeping as any good mother would, but I believe that I'm not very wrong if I say that back of those honest tears I saw a brightness that seemed to flash the message: "Such is life; I shall be equal to it, you'll see what a good disposition Fabricia has."

That case is one of the best, since it involves, as it were, a demon of pleasing manner. But the trouble is that generally that demon is not alone. There are others that, having taken advantage of the open door, augment and complicate the inner choir. I could prove, if I were to write the unhappy Fabricia's whole story here, that there's nothing more sad, more desolating than for a person to have reached the age of fifty, methodically striving all the while to live up to a good disposition.

In Eunice the switchboard is formed almost entirely by the inhibited desires of a girlhood spent in poverty. One of her main ideas is to be a determined person; another is to possess a natural distinction, which closely relates her case to that from which the term bovarysm is derived. And in addition to these ideas, there are innumerable lesser ones, formed by words and objects that have remained within her just as they entered and continue to operate in such a way that they can give back the reactions that originated them. As I have felt and observed them I have discovered one by one the buttons that make my puppet[1] laugh or cry. Alice is right in one thing: I could please her in most instances. I know what I ought to do. Viewed objectively, the things are easy. But I cannot do them. I cannot. Do you understand me, Miguel? I cannot do those things—

Our life has become impossible. Or rather, my life has become impossible. Something has broken inside of me, severing me from people and the world. A profound lack of interest and affection gives me the impression of being on the verge of madness. My disillusionment is no longer in Eunice alone; born of her, it has grown and now encompasses everything. The flavor of fruit and the color of the sky have changed. Everything around me is dying. I see clearly now that it was the presence of others, chiefly Eunice's, that gave meaning, color, scent, and savor to everything. It was because of Eunice, Raul, and you that I relished the taste of coffee in the morning. Because of Eunice, Raul, Alice, Pedreira, and you the sky was blue and Mozart's music beautiful. The fold of the fresh sheet was good, the rain running down the window pane was good, and the cigarette that I used to smoke in my armchair after dinner while I heard Raul telling his mother what had happened at school. Eunice killed the universe for me. I see now that she was the

[1] "As we now realize, the doll or puppet occupies an important place in Rilke's symbolism, and all unconsciously it becomes the prototype of everything that is soulless, inert, the dead weight of matter eternally at variance with the upward and outward urge of the spirit" (*Rilke: Man and Poet* by Nora Wydenbruck)—(trans.).

ground I walked upon, the water I drank, the flower I smelled. Intermediary for all things, light of my eyes, through her nearness she brought me near to all things and was my salvation.

When we had misunderstandings, when I found out how terribly fickle a person can be, there was still a close union between the world and me; a painful one, indeed, but it was contact. I still had the sense of taste, although the taste was bitter; I still had an interest, though it was a sorrowful one. Today I am dead. It is putting it mildly to say that nothing interests me. It would be better to say that the life of things around me has diminished.

I used to be a living man whose happiness started in the soles of his feet. All things were good. Now the universe has grown prodigiously old, and if I do not laugh at the absurdity of the stars and the clouds and the trees it is because even that laughter I cannot find in me.

They usually say that woman is the frail sex. All anthropometric measurements prove that Eunice is smaller than I. But those measurements are dreadfully misleading. Eunice is enormous. What I hear going clickety-click-click-click around the house, what moves about and talks, expressing its thoughts aloud, making remarks that bore me to death, is only the nucleus, the very tiny and visible concentration of a substance that is dispersed in every direction from the depths of the seas to the depths of the skies. We men are only the restless little drones flying around in that vast feminine world. Yes, Eunice is enormous. And the part that I am playing is that of the neglected little boy who sees his mother hurry off to a game of tennis, taking along the clouds and mountains in noisy confusion around her legs and breasts and golden hair.

Can you imagine such a thing? The whole cosmos affected by capriciousness?

I see now that it is through love that one apprehends things, separating them, distinguishing them but keeping them all together and immersed in the same atmosphere. And if there is no love? Then the entire universe becomes a fantastic heap of ruins. Raul! Raul! yesterday my son, today a shadow. I hear Eunice's footsteps upstairs; yet I am alone in my study. Again I spoke my son's name in a loud voice. Raul! And once again I called, stressing the R, RRRaul! I listened intently, hearing the echo of my own voice. And I found that Raul, too, no longer interests me—

I remembered our conversation about Heaven and Hell, and somehow I suddenly found myself a ten-year-old boy playing on the lawn of our house at Petropolis. I was playing alone, drawing from out my imagination the brothers that had not been born and plotting with those little spirits a game of fighting and adventure. Finally, tired of running around with phantoms and doing the talking for four or five, I lay down on the wet grass, with my face in the leaves close to the earth, smelling its fragrance. Then stretching out full length and flinging my arms wide, I lay gazing up at a very blue sky in which a few filmy white clouds were sailing. I watched one of them. It looked like a foreshortened cat. But it lengthened out, scattered at the place where the head was, and in a little while I had to exert an effort to make it still look like a cat. Then I gave up the creature and accepted a new starting point. Now the cloud formed the head and wings of a chromo angel. Again, as when one holds on to a rubber band that is stretched to bursting, I clung to the shape from which the cloud was fleeing. The angel burst—

Tired out, I closed my eyes. When I opened them, the cloud had gone and there was an enormous blue hole in front of me that was terrifying. I had the impression that it was beneath me and that I was going to fall into that immense blue cavity. I turned over then, and buried my face in the fresh grass. Ah! I preferred the earth, the grass, the smell of the earth, the freshness of the grass, because the sky was empty. The cloud had fled the sky, seeking the mountain peaks where it, too, might rest. And I said to myself: "I don't want to go to Heaven because the sky is empty. In Heaven I couldn't smell that fragrance, pull the grass out by the roots, watch that little insect go by in the dark, that little creature that looks like a lost jewel in search of its owner—

And now, Miguel, I ask you where, how, and why man first conceived the idea of seeing that bluish fluid as a symbol of eternal felicity. Today when I think of the Heaven of the saints I feel the same giddiness that I felt long ago. Felicity needs a ground; it needs things to which it can be anchored. I should like a Heaven with this table, that chair, Mama's picture. A Heaven with Eunice. With Eunice's new dress.

What can I do now, if it is the very ground and the things that are fast upon it that make me giddy and give me a hopeless sense of emptiness? The whole world is in crisis. Everything is a shifting, speeding cloud. The only thing that seems fixed and palpable is the grief that I bear within me.

Miguel, I shall have the courage to say: "If that Heaven of the saints existed, I shouldn't want it. I should be profoundly unhappy, unhappy as one damned, in that translucence where there would be no room for my passionate grief."

And that is what the inconstancy that Alice thinks a trifling matter has done to me. That is what Eunice has succeeded in doing. She has killed my very desire for happiness. I don't know whether there is a Heaven, but there is a Hell. I'm already there.

December 20th

Dead Jealousies

It was curiosity, and mainly extreme sensitivity to gesture and attitude in which the spoken word is implicit that aroused my first distrust. A chance meeting on the street was the spark that kindled those two ingredients into a flame of jealousy. I wasn't jealous before. When we were married in Uruguay, and even after the first years of disillusionment and suffering, I didn't know that searching and corrosive passion of the completely jealous man, who doesn't even need suspicions—the woman may be an angel of purity—to taste wormwood.

Pure, innate jealousy doesn't consist of mistrust; rather, it's an avarice that cannot tolerate that any part of a woman, her appearance, her warmth, her fragrance be accessible to anyone else. A casual contact in an orchestra seat is enough to fill him with unbearable anguish, even though he may be convinced of its fortuitousness and inconsequence. Pure jealousy doesn't feed on drama; it has no story; it doesn't depend on plot. It's a stark tragedy, whose action, all of which takes place in the present, is based upon the miser's idea of absolute possession. He who is afflicted with this pure jealousy would like to hide the woman whom he loves, as the miser buries his treasure. I knew a man like that who locked up his wife and even went to the incredible length of having a dentist's chair installed in the house. He wanted, in every way, to keep his wife from scattering and evaporating on the street. He corked her up as if she were something volatile. Everyone felt sorry for the woman, but I was able to learn that she wasn't so unhappy as was generally supposed. I believe that she even enjoyed playing the uncomfortable role of a cherished treasure.

Besides, one of woman's greatest tyrannies is to provoke that of man and set herself up as its triumphant victim. Anyone who knew the Cerqueira couple will probably say that Samuel tortured his poor wife not by jealousy (that was not their case) but by the constant commotion in which he kept her. He couldn't take two steps without calling her: "Fidelia! where's my brief-case? Fidelia, get me an envelope! Fidelia, phone the drugstore—Fidelia! Fidelia! Fidelia! And she in her quiet, serene way, would do this and that, and go here and there to wait upon the petty tyrant, the poor petty tyrant, who as he grew older retrogressed to the point of no longer being able to cut his nails or knot his tie. When Fidelia died, Samuel was like a sixty-year-old orphan. He killed himself.

Innate, pure jealousy is a metaphysical rather than a moral attitude. If distrust is part of it, it is a distrust of everyone and everything rather than of one woman! Rather it is a generalized suspiciousness of the universe and of existence. It senses fraud in the air, a sort of universal betrayal, and it locks itself up with its treasure.

But that wasn't my kind of jealousy. Nor was mine the flaming and explosive jealousy of Othello. Furthermore, now that I've remembered the Moor of Venice I should note that I don't even consider him a jealous man. No. Othello wasn't greedy or suspicious of Desdemona. Othello was a great and noble man, credulous and trusting, who in the drama of jealousy enacted only the scenes of anger and violence. His rage was commensurate with the betrayal of his trust. That was the dramatic thing about him. What jealous man needs the astuteness and perfidy of an Iago, or could say, as did Othello, that he would prefer *not to know* and that all would be well even if his army were to file through Desdemona's bedroom, so long as he did not know it? No. Othello was not miserly, nor was he a curious and suspicious intriguer; he was the trusting man who cries out his need of confidence, confidence incarnate, and the impossibility of living without it:

> Farewell the plumed troop and the big wars,
> Farewell the neighing steed, and the shrill trump,
> Pride, pomp, and circumstance of glorious war!
> Farewell! Othello's occupation's gone.

The curious and mistrustful man has a jealousy (like mine) that is dramatic, inventive, restless, and conspiring, and he forgives every plot and snare because no one contrives them better than he. He's in a fever to investigate and learn the truth, even experiencing a ghastly satisfaction when he sees his suspicions confirmed. Rarely does he punish. Confronted by the evidence of betrayal, he enjoys that strange intellectual pleasure that prompts the most compassionate people to say "I knew it" when they see the confirmation of their forebodings.

That afternoon when I happened to see Eunice going along on the opposite side of the Avenida, I conceived the idea of following her at a distance, out of curiosity, to see in part an aspect of her that, as yet, I didn't know. In the beginning it was almost a game; then it became a piece of fiction, a story half-invented and half-true, in which I was playing a role. The part that was true grew and encroached upon the other; and then, by dint of this performance, feelings that had been repressed rose to the surface of my consciousness. Her words, "That's what they tell me," crossed my mind. It had been months before. I was speaking of the color of her hair, which changed with the time of day. She had smiled and spoken those words: "That's what they tell me." *They* tell. An indefinite subject. Or hidden. They tell. How is it that I didn't realize the peculiarity of those words at the time? The fact that on that afternoon when I was following Eunice from a distance the scattered fragments began to acquire the outline of a spirit. A masculine spirit. And so it was, with a germ of suspicion, half-invented and half-real, that all one afternoon I walked behind Eunice through the city streets—

There goes Eunice. I see her green dress disappearing and then coming into view again in the midst of the crowd. She stops. She stands a moment in front of a window display of lingerie, and then she goes on. She has a different way of walking in the street, very positive and self-assured. She doesn't turn her head or notice the furtive glances attracted by her thick, golden hair and the proud bearing that befits Diana the Huntress. She turns the corner of Ouvidor and goes up Uruguaiana. Then, all of a sudden, I lose sight of her. Can she have turned the corner of Uruguaiana? Deeply distressed, I start to hurry feverishly and almost bump into her. She is coming out of a china and glassware shop. I hide in a doorway and let her go by. At the corner of Sete de Setembro she hestitates a moment. Then she turns and starts again for the Avenida.

Occasionally she lingers in front of a window, and then resumes her serene, self-assured walking. It is not the hurried walk of the shopper nor the bored walk of the stroller. It is self-assured, serene. What is its meaning, I wonder?

How becoming that dress is to her! From a distance, she looks more slender, almost thin— Now, she's going down the Avenida again with that same resoluteness, without noticing the furtive glances, apparently.

Did I say "apparently"? I did. I did, because that is what I thought. And the seed of the thought grew apace, put forth branches, and bore fruit. Yes, apparently she doesn't notice. Actually she's aware of that mute approval of the passer-by. She goes on her way without turning her head or issuing a receipt, but she's aware of it. And she walks the way she does precisely so that she may be conscious of that anonymous tribute and so that she may garner it and store it away for her pleasure.

She doesn't have to give anything in return; she has only to receive. It could be said that her sexual etiquette and mine, and, indeed, that of all us men, are different. We need to look, she needs to be looked at. When our interest is aroused, it is projected as a dart or as a lasso that is flung forward to envelop the coveted object. Not so with her; her interest remains within the sphere of her own body. A masculine form, an arm or a leg, means little to her. What does interest her is our attention, the gestures, however slight, with which we acknowledge that we are within her range of gravitation. She is the end of our desire as well as of her own. She stands still, waiting, and we hasten forward. Man's desire is to go forward; woman's is to receive him. This game doesn't involve two bodies of equal weight that exert mutual attraction and come together halfway. To the contrary, just as between the Earth and that fertilizing dust that according to panspermy explains the origin of life there's a great want of proportion. The halfway point of that collision between the sexes is woman herself.

That is why the "good Conceição," after she has made all the rotary motions compatible with the dignity of her sex, waits in vain for the student to take the masculine step that will restore her to her true self, as an ultimate goal, motionless and powerful.

All this is plainly relative, since sex is rather a matter of predominance than one of absolute difference. Hidden somewhere in everyone's nature is a companion of the opposite sex. There are anomalies of course too; the under-sexed and the over-sexed. But I'll warrant that in general woman's typical motion is rotation, whereas man's is translation. For the game of love is not symmetrical: on the one side there is a rectilinear activity that is projected in search of the desired object; on the other, a potential activity, as of a star or a flower calling to the restless and volatile hearts of men.

To offer an example illustrating the theory, I suggest that if, like the alarmed moralists, we wished to neutralize the interest aroused by that reciprocal attraction, we should have only to cover women's bodies or else men's eyes.

And women's eyes, those celebrated eyes that have by now exhausted every adjective and worn out every metaphor? Capitú's eyes that were like the surf? The pre-eminence of the feminine eye in love affairs is well known. I shall take a backstitch in my theory with the observation that the eye of a woman is a thing of light rather than of vision, a lantern shining into the night rather than the lookout's spy-glass. Or I might say that women do not use their eyes for seeing but for encouraging and responding to the eyes of men.

And as Eunice walked along, she was showered with admiration from masculine eyes. It lingered around and over her, making her seem to expand. One can actually see—I did see—that aura that thus clothes a woman as she walks along and thus fabulously increases her size. As Eunice goes along the streets it is not she that moves; it is the street; everything. So I shall abandon the Copernican theory for the Ptolmaic and place the center of the universe in Eunice, who is standing still.

My anxiety, implanted and carefully tended, has grown. Ah! Miguel, you can't imagine how distressed I have been! I'm afraid of her frailty. Not that she is provocative and would throw herself away like a wanton. Not that she is simple and would get into trouble unknowingly. But I'm afraid of her automatism, which is her weakness. I am afraid that they will touch one of her secret keys. She prides herself on being what she is not, and there is no greater weakness than that of the person who is mistaken about himself, especially when that misconception has been methodically planned. It is easy to have one's way with a person who is enacting a part that he's created for himself. One has only to enter into the game; for the lone actor immediately comes to life when another picks up his cue.

You can have no idea, Miguel, of what my life has been like with that thought working inside of me. Just yesterday we were talking about the situation in Spain. You were prophesying wars and calamity, and then from General Franco's deception we drifted into a philosophical discussion of the mysterious ways of history and of life. And then I put my hand into my pocket. Do you remember? No. Of course you don't remember; you don't pay attention to insignificant gestures; you don't know the language of gestures— Well, it is true. Just as you were speaking of the worldwide yearning for brotherhood, I put my hand into my pocket. And do you know what I had in my left coat pocket, wrapped in pink paper? A duplicate key of Eunice's desk which I had had made a half hour before at a locksmith's on Assembleia Street.

All this is fearful, I know. I could argue with myself and prove mathematically that it is her happiness that I am protecting thus. But it wouldn't be true. Of this I'm sure, because I can't even bear the thought of anyone's having seen me ransacking the drawers of Eunice's desk in search of some clue. I dare not tell even you. No. There are certain moments when one needs to forget even old friends, so that he may feel completely alone and free to do anything he wishes.

This is what I have come to. And she? Is she to blame for her inconstancy? I don't know. All human relations pose a moral problem, for which there is never any answer. What I do know is that I suffer while she goes about gaily, tosses back her hair, and lights her cigarette with a nonchalant elegance that exasperates me.

I have said, I believe, that Eunice is dead and that her movements are purely galvanic reflexes. No. I haven't yet lost all hope. Just yesterday an unexpectedly profound peace flowed over me. She was asleep. And so was Raul. I was pacing back and forth in my study, mortally unhappy. I sat down on the sofa and tried to read a book. As it was warm, I opened the window, and a whiff of jasmine came into the room. A dog barked in the distance, up on the hill. The house was asleep. I closed my eyes and then—then as in an open sky, I saw our life fall into harmony. It was probably a fantastic vision of mine, the result of my analytical obsession, a nightmare. Life was before me for the taking. And life was Eunice. The fragrance of jasmine was Eunice. The open sky was Eunice. And we were walking along hand in hand on a quiet afternoon through old quarters of the city where little girls with their hair in braids were singing.

Entrai na roda, o linda morena,
Entrai na roda —[1]

And we, hand in hand, wordlessly enjoying a deep understanding—

There I was, once again, going along the Avenida, ten feet behind Eunice. Already I felt dizzy because of the close attention with which my eyes were fixed on her scarlet dress. At times she would be lost to sight in a more compact group, and I would hold my breath until I saw that bright spot of color again. She went up Ouvidor, turned the corner at Gonçlaves Dias, stood for a while looking at a florist's window, and went in. I remained at a distance,

[1] Come join the circle, O pretty brunette,
Come join the circle—(trans.).

with my eyes on the door. Then she came out and started in the direction of Carioca Square. There, consulting her wrist watch, she stopped as one who is uncertain. It was half past four. I noted that detail, as though it had great importance. Who knows the value of a detail?

After a short hesitation she called a taxi. I was about to take note of its number (again a detail) and make a dash for another, when some one grasped my arm and jovially called me by name. I had run into Rodolfo.

"What a long time its been!"

The taxi had disappeared up Senador Dantas Street while Rodolfo was giving me a detailed account (details again) of his operation for acute appendicitis. I hated him. What did I care about his appendix or the rest of his viscera which, it seems, were healthy enough? I could feel that my face was cold and paralyzed. He kept on talking in a voice that seemed very faint and far away and the good humor in his face, which was close to mine (because he has a mania for talking in a confidential tone like that), was as shocking to me as though it were something obscene. I tried to talk and smile, but my muscles would not conform to conventional behavior. Finally I broke away. Tomorrow or next day, Rodolfo will tell everyone that he finds me changed, that I have grown arrogant.

I went into a coffee bar. At a side table a middle-aged individual, whose face was puckered in an effort to make up in expressiveness for the inadequacy of his words, was explaining to two other patrons the process of acquiring a permit for something his firm had put out. Apparently his listeners found the whole matter with its details about applications and rulings more fascinating than one of Marco Polo's tales. How can anyone be interested in a story that revolves around stamps and protocols? It appears that one can be. It must be their passion, as mine is the number of a taxi and the color of a dress. After all, every passion feeds upon just such trifling details.

On the other side of the room an old man was sitting alone at a table, motionless and absorbed. His ravaged face was a sixty-year-old planisphere of failure and misunderstanding. Probably he was no longer suffering, but out of habit the creases and tendons had maintained positions corresponding to the friction, the anger, the humiliation, the nights of sickness at home, and all the rest that makes life an absurdity and a sexagenarian's face a museum.

Fifteen minutes past five. I telephoned the house; Eunice had not yet returned. Plainly it wasn't the house address that she'd given the driver.

Something is going on. Nebulous doubts are being dispelled by the light of certainty. Definitely there is something. Eunice came home late for dinner. She came in gaily, tossed me a "hello," and stooped to kiss Raul. She was flushed, her eyes were brighter than usual, she talked vivaciously about the manicurist, the dressmaker, some good buys she'd made. I was watching her. She had expanded, grown, and an atmosphere hung around her. Some time before, we had gone to the Mendoncas' when Lidia's engagement was announced. Lidia had been like that, and Lidia had a suitor. Could Eunice have a suitor? Who was he? How had they met?

"Are you all right? You look queer!"

Raul laughed. Papa looked queer. I forced myself to laugh as best I could. Eunice went upstairs to change her dress, and halfway up the stairs she announced that she didn't care to go out, she was tired. Dinner was eaten in silence despite Eunice's efforts to start a conversation. Raul observed us, first one, then the other. He appeared to be suspicious. Or was that just a notion of mine?

After dinner, while Eunice was talking with Raul, I went upstairs, saying that I was going to change. I had an idea. I locked myself in our bedroom, and, cautiously as a thief, I opened the connecting door, closing the door of her room that opened onto the hall. There was the scarlet dress, crumpled and limp. What had become of all the admiration showered upon it during the four times she had walked up and down the Avenida and Ouvidor Street? I picked up the dress. It was extremely light. How frail their armor is! I lifted it into the air with arms widespread, like an amorous scarecrow. I examined it. It might have retained some sign. I smelled it. There was Eunice's perfume, and that was all. Nothing else.

Suddenly I had an intuition: her handbag! It was on top of the dressing stool. I marked its exact position so that I could put it back in the same place, and with shaking fingers I opened the clasp—

At that moment, the nature of my jealousy had changed abruptly. No longer was it timorous and preventive. On the contrary, I now wanted Eunice to have deceived me and I wanted the proof to be there in the handbag. A feverish joy overwhelmed me with the certainty that I was to have proof.

In the bag were some five hundred milreis, a little handkerchief with a small crimson stain in one corner, a lipstick, three cigarettes, a picture of Raul, a pencil stub, a bit of ribbon as a sample, and a tiny pad the pages of which were blank. Nothing else.

I was about to close the bag when the pad caught my attention. I examined it close to the lamp. A sheet had been torn off, but what had been written on it still showed faintly on the blank one. With some difficulty I managed to read the address: street— number— . Below was our telephone number and her name: Eunice. Evidently the address was for her and the telephone number for him. They must have torn the sheet in two, which indicated a certain haste, a meeting on the street perhaps. And the taxi? The taxi gave proof of a meeting deliberately planned. — Ah! It is very simple; the address preceded the taxi by a few days, yesterday perhaps. Who is it, I wonder? Someone whom I know or a stranger? I run over in my mind the most likely names; Walter, Fernando, Luis—

"Papa! Papa!"

Raul was calling me. I kept the memo-sheet, replaced the bag, hurriedly changed my clothes, and went down. I was remarkably calm. Raul and Eunice were laughing. When I entered the room, they turned toward me, like two children, a little boy and his elder sister, who are awaiting the solution of a difficulty that only a grown-up can solve.

"Papa, see if this is the way to work this problem— Mama insists, but it doesn't come out right. It's like this: a man made a will leaving three thousand cantos to four sons—"

I bent down over the paper. Eunice's face was close to mine. Raul, on the other side of the table, almost lying on it, was repeating the part of the problem that was given. "The first son was left a third, the second, two fifths—"

"That isn't the way you told me," Eunice broke in.

"Yes it was, Mama. You got it wrong."

"Wait," I said, "we'll name the four sons. Names will help to make it clearer. Eunice, you name the young men."

Eunice hesitated, as if it were difficult to find four names, and at last, slowly as one who is treading warily, she began to say our names while I watched the movements of her lips and eyes.

"José—Raul—"

"No, our names won't do. Give some others."

"Mario— Rodolfo— Paulo— Antonio," Eunice said slowly, and finally, she added, "The father's name is André."

"No," I said crossly, "the father doesn't need a name. Now let's see; Mario got a third—"

I don't know how I stood those two hours. If anyone went by and saw through the window the warm lamplight and the three forms bent over the table he probably said to himself, and with envy, perhaps, "There's a happy family." I am calm now. Eunice and Raul have gone upstairs and are asleep. And I am remarkably calm, walking back and forth in my study, gathering my thoughts together. They think that I'm the one who's deceived. They don't know, poor things, that they are my puppets, they're not aware that my eyes are coldly watching their movements through a skylight. Besides, whatever pathetic effort they may make to think of something new, there can't be much variation in those things.

All of a sudden I thought of checking on the address in the telephone directory in order to find out who the person was. Why had that simple expedient not occurred to me right away? Feverishly I turned the pages. There they were, the street and the number. It was an eight-story apartment house with three or four apartments on each floor. I should have to telephone each one in order to identify the permanent residents and the dubious transients.

The first voice that answered was a woman's; I hung up. I tried the second number; no one answered, so I jotted it down. At the third call, I heard a man's voice. I jotted that number down, too, with the notation that it was not likely to be the right one. At the fourth, as I insisted upon finding out the number and then apologized for having called the wrong one, I had to listen to a lecture. One shouldn't make a mistake at that hour of the night— I could go to so-and-so— I smiled superciliously, pitying that stranger, who was annoyed by such a little thing. I didn't jot that number down, for surely it must belong to a family. Only in a family can there be that picayunish annoyance that bristles at the ringing of a bell or the barking of a neighbor's dog.

I went through the whole building that way from top to bottom. I felt as though I were in a control room bombing an enemy fort at long range. A great thing, the telephone! I had only to twirl the disk to penetrate those vulnerable homes and make contact with those happy families— or with those vacant apartments that are used only for casual rendezvous. Probably, one of those symbols would set a bell to ringing in the very room which some hours before had echoed with Eunice's voice and that of her companion. Already I had, as it were, a surreptitious part in their secret. That was all it was that day; the next day we should see—

I made out a neat list. In all there were eight possible apartments without counting the recently occupied ones that I had not yet put down. Could it be that Alves or that Sousa? I did not know anyone with the names of the suspected occupants. Tomorrow we should see.

I went upstairs. Eunice must have the other half of the memo-sheet. Where? I tiptoed into her room. She was asleep. I examined her slip, hoping to find a bit of paper pinned to it. There is invariably a pin somewhere in such intrigues— I found nothing. I examined her shoe. Nothing. Then I leaned over Eunice, spying upon her slumber, watching every move of her face and breast.

"Eunice! Eunice—"

She half opened her eyes and then closed them again, turning over to the other side.

"No— I'm sleepy—"

At lunch time, I still wanted to make sure. I asked Eunice to go to a movie with me in the afternoon. She had the afternoon free; we could even have dinner together in town.

"No, I must go to the dressmaker's; she's already behind time and I don't want to provide her with any more excuses."

"You can go to the dressmaker's first."

"I've already made an appointment with her. Can't we go tomorrow?"

I agreed that we should go next day, and we finished our lunch in silence, each busy with his own thoughts.

Yes, the apartment house did have eight stories. Its entrance—monumental and pretentious—in its unhappy combination of marbles was reminiscent of a tomb. The elevator was at the back, to the right. I was undecided as to what I should do. Why had she not written the complete address? I tried to imagine the scene, putting myself into the place of each. The handwriting was hers; so he must have been the one to dictate. But how explain the absence of the floor and of the apartment number? Was there something peculiar about the number, or was their tryst to be downstairs in the reception room? No. That could not be. A due period of waiting and preparations to receive the other into his intimate surroundings have been a part of such affairs ever since there have been men, and women, and adulteries.

I had been in the street since three o'clock, examining the location and studying my plan of action. I had put on the new suit that the tailor had delivered recently and that I had not yet worn. I was taking precautions in that way against the possibility of being recognized from a distance in case I should do anything rash.

Opposite the building was a small barber shop, and next to the barber shop a coffee bar. I sat down in the coffee bar, opened a paper; but I didn't read. Over the paper I kept my eyes fixed on the entrance to the building. Four o'clock. Five after. Ten after. Impatient, I went out to take a turn, always keeping in sight of the house. Every car that passed made my heart leap. I went back to the bar. Half past four.

I didn't see her come. When I looked, she was already hurrying into the hall of the building. I got up without thinking. I felt an intense hatred. Had I had a rifle in my hand, I should have struck down that bluebird right there and then. I could see her in front of the elevator in the dimly lit hall. As I ran across the street, I heard shouting and the sound of brakes. The driver was cursing me in a fit of rage.

I got there in time; the elevator indicator was moving slowly and was now stopping at Number Four. A great invention! A notable convenience in this age of electricity and electronics. The elevator tenderly carries young women from the street to their lovers' arms, but behind their backs it tells their husbands the number of the floor. A great age!

I consulted my chart. On the fourth floor I had crossed out 403; 404 was suspect; the rest didn't appear on the list. I realized that I could have tried to find out something more, but now it was too late. I had to act quickly.

I pushed the button for the elevator and went up. When I got there I was able to make out the four entrances in the dark hall: 401, 402, 403, 404. At that moment the door of 403 opened, and a stout woman came out carrying a valise and calling back instructions. They were not to forget Iolanda's medicine. One could hear a child's voice. My chart was confirmed: the presence of a child obviated any possibilities of an assignation. But there were still the others, and I had to act. Yes, I had to act. How? Without thinking, I knocked at 401. I heard footsteps, the door opened, and a freckled young woman in blue pajamas asked me what I wanted. From inside came a coarse and impatient voice. "Who is it?" I inquired if Dr. Lourival were in.

"He doesn't live here." And the door shut with a brutal slam.

It was then that I had an idea. I should remain unseen, and I should bring my quarry out of its lair. I went down in the elevator, and when I got down, I tore two pages from my notebook and wrote in a disguised hand: "Raul in accident, come quickly." On each sheet I put one of the two remaining numbers: 402 and 404. A boy delivering a box of shoes happened to be going by.

"Hey, boy! I want you to do something for me. I'll give you ten milreis."

He looked at me suspiciously. No doubt my face was terrifying. I explained that I wanted to play a joke. I would give him twenty milreis. I would have given much more, but I didn't tell him lest he should be even more alarmed.

"Take the elevator, get out at the fourth floor and deliver one of these notes to 402 and the other to 404. Now remember, if anyone should ask who sent it, you're to say that it was a stout woman. And keep an eye out to see in which one of the two apartments there's a tall, blond young woman in blue.

I made the boy repeat his lesson and went with him as far as the elevator.

Ah! She'll call the house! I ran to the barber shop across the street and rushed to the phone. I dialed. With immense relief, I heard Maria's voice. She said: "Hello! Hello! Hello!" and seeing that no one answered, she hung up. But I held the line. Another great invention of the age, the automatic telephone! Then I began to talk very volubly so that the assistant who was sitting and waiting for a customer would not be suspicious. I was talking with Eunice, an imaginary Eunice. "Woman, why did you do that to me? Why?" The assistant thought I was in love. He looked at me pityingly as if to say: "He's mixed up with a skirt, poor fellow!"

On the opposite sidewalk the boy with the shoebox, who had completed his errand, was looking for me in perplexity. I slipped the barber ten milreis and asked him to call the boy over. Without letting go of the phone, I gave the boy twenty.

"Well?"

"I didn't see any young woman, but there was one in 402 who screamed when the man gave her the note."

"Now get going!"

The boy fled in fright. And I went back to the phone, resuming the fantastic conversation while the proprietor, a solemn Portuguese, interrupted his shaving from time to time and peered at me over his spectacles. It's quite likely that my loquacity had a note of madness, because the puzzled assistant, who was near me, was smiling now with the melancholy malice of one who has seen worse cases. I believe that I recited poetry. Sweat was pouring down my face, and my throat was constricted as if to keep my heart from leaping out. Then she screamed! My shot had hit the mark. The quarry was wounded. It was going to come out of its lair.

From my post I could see the entrance to the building, and I kept by eyes fastened upon it. But noticing that the proprietor was observing me more closely, I composed my features in an attitude of listening. I smiled. I nodded. I said: "That's right, that's right." Meanwhile the proprietor came toward me, razor in hand.

"Are you going to be at the phone much longer?"

"Just a minute, just a minute. I'm taking a message. It's a case of illness."

"Oh, come now. You were reciting poetry just now. Not that that matters, but a business phone's not a plaything."

"My friend, I've already explained, it's very important—I'll give you whatever you ask."

"It's not a question of money," the proprietor said loftily, making a sweeping gesture with his razor; "it's a question of business, but since you're nearly through—"

Not for anything would I have let go of the phone. I could visualize the scene in 402. She, at the telephone, hearing the busy signal: buzz, buzz, buzz. He, at the window, irked by that intrusion of mother love, was trying to quiet her: "Let's be reasonable, woman—" And the telephone: buzz, buzz, buzz—

"Many thanks!"

I dashed out. Eunice had appeared. She was signaling a passing taxi. I ran, shouting, "Eunice! Eunice!" I wanted to tell her that it was a lie, that Raul was all right. How could I have done that to a doll, a poor doll that was manipulated by strings? But the car was rounding the corner. Then I suddenly felt a mortal hatred for the one who had stayed behind up there. I crossed the street like a somnabulist. I brought down the elevator. I got in and pressed the button for the fourth floor. I went up, and my hatred went up with me. I reached the fourth floor, and the elevator door opened automatically, as much as to say: "Please—" But at that moment I had no thought of gratifying the little automatic courtesies of the modern age. I stopped a moment in front of 402. I felt hardened, congealed. I pushed the button and heard the buzzer sound inside with a muffled tone. When the door opened slightly, I stuck my foot inside so that the person couldn't close it again. I shoved; the other person resisted; I shoved harder.

Then in the partly open space a serious, scared countenance appeared. And without a word we stood facing each other in the now wide-open doorway. It was André, Eunice's husband. Her first husband.

At that moment, despite its intensity, my jealousy fell apart like a pack of cards. It was André. And since it was André—I can't explain. A dozen lesser feelings came upon the stage of my imagination, like the circus hands that, during the show's intermissions came in to roll up the carpet and remove the trapeze on which the gymnast has just performed feats of prodigious skill and daring. The pantomine had ended, and now we were living an illogical interlude.

He was turned away from me, facing the window. Finally he said:

"I don't know which of us can complain to the other."

"Is this your apartment?"

"No, it's been loaned. I'm just passing through."

"Are you staying here in Rio long?"

"A week maybe."

I made no reply. The apartment was tastefully furnished. A roomy divan, pictures, a carpet, a low, glass-topped table on which a tea service for two had been set out. The tea was still steaming. I noticed then that she had left her bag on the divan.

"She left her bag."

"That's so. Take it with you. Look, wrap a newspaper around it—"

In the door André came closer to me. He was deathly pale and trembling, but he managed to say:

"Look after Eunice. So long as we're the only two, it doesn't matter much."

I had the impression of standing in front of a mirror, seeing my own misery. Then the door of 402 slowly closed.

Miguel, however, was at that time my best friend.

I got up and went over to the window. Those pages written so long ago had wearied me dreadfully. The General's car went by. It looked as though it were going to rain.

December 22nd

The Coffee-Bar Waitress Who Stands All Day, de marré deci

I entered the coffee bar and took my place as contestant behind a big, sweaty individual who was already tentatively sipping the cup that had cost him so arduous a struggle. On his thick wrist he displayed a heavy gold watch, and he was bending his athletic torso a little in order not to drip coffee on to his light duck suit. How things have changed! It used to be that a coffeehouse was a place of leisure. A literary group would get together there for half an hour and for a tostão anyone could hire a box seat for the passing show.

Now that the habit of drinking coffee standing up has become so general, the infusion has lost its former nobility, which consisted precisely of serving as a pretext for higher things. The beverage was secondary, subordinate, but there are certain subordinations that confer greater dignity than independence. Today coffee is independent. One takes it for itself with the same rational and functional dispassionateness with which one partakes of a laxative or an analgesic. One drinks a cup of coffee in egotistical and erect loneliness. And as there are more people everywhere now, one must await one's turn behind the lucky fellow who has already been served, watching his ease and enjoyment with a certain amount of resentment. Therefore, with ticket in hand, I was waiting for my corpulent predecessor to drink his fill and yield his breach beside the marble counter. Imprisoned behind its narrow confines a boy and three girls were performing the same rapid gestures over and over, dispensing crockery, serving coffee, taking in the tickets, and putting the used cups into an enormous caldron of boiling water. Then I saw my frustrated wheat-colored rose. She was the one in the middle. The dishwasher had just told her something amusing, and she still had the trace of a smile on her face when she held out my cup. It would have been a pretty smile, perhaps, were it not for the fact that everything about her was frustrated. She herself, with her irregular features, prominent cheek bones, and slightly hollow cheeks could be a lovely Russian princess whom the adversities of a revolution had reduced to that humiliating employment.

What employment? What can be the name of that business, standing for eight hours and handing out cups with the motions of an automaton? I believe—I fear that it has no name. It used to be that every business had a name. The young woman who had to earn her living would be a seamstress or a florist, and on summer evenings the little girls of Santa Alexandrina Street used to join hands, dance in a circle and sing:

I am poor, poor, poor,
De marré, marré, marré
I am poor, poor, poor,
De marré, deci –

I want one of your daughters,
De marré, marré, marré,
I want one of your daughters,
De marré, deci –

What employment shall you give her?
De marré, marré, marré,

I'll employ her as a steamstress,
De marré, deci –

How could we put the long specification of that nameless employment into a song for little girls to sing as they dance around in a circle? A young woman who stands in the cafe and hands out cups all day, *de marré, de marré, de marré*? But if the profession itself does not have a name, its classification has one that is distinct and rigid. If the girl's employment is nameless, the institution to which she belongs has a name. She is a working girl, *de marré, deci.* Tomorrow or the day after she will no longer be here with her coffee-stained apron and the crescent of folded organdy that they have put on her chestnut brown hair as a crown of servitude; she will not be here to smile at the last part of the story that the blond boy has just told. Tomorrow or the day after she will be in the corridors, in the elevators, and in the waiting lines of her enormous institution. And later she will find herself surrounded by other aprons whiter than hers, and with a grizzling head pressed against her breast that will be panting like that of an exhausted swallow.

"Cough! Breathe—"

For it is evident that she will not live long. There is still some alertness and animation in her face, revealing what she would have been had she been given a chance to live. But the hollow chest, the frail waist, the emaciated arms indicate a disharmony with her true self, a cruel discord that only the proximity of death can explain. And I see, or, rather, I saw there in the bar, while I was waiting to be served, that my wheat-colored rose will not live much longer than those sisters of hers in my vase. Who will be able to support her fragile stem? When a flower has a tendency to droop, the florist on Gonçalves Dias Street puts a wire around it to compensate for the hardiness it lacks. Who will be able to support the little body of that child condemned to serve as a croupier in that fantastic game played with tickets and crockery?

She must have a strange outlook on the world and everything in it. There at her counter—her rosebed—she serves—let us see, how many cups. Let us calculate: three or four per minute, sixty times, for seven or more hours; let us say seven. That makes 1,180; let us say 1,000. She serves 1,000 customers a day! At first glance it seems that that is a suitable employment for a woman. In our childhood memories do we not see a woman's form perpetually bent over a set of dishes, cutting bread and passing around coffee with milk? The romantic Werther is as enraptured as before the most beautiful sight in the world when he sees Carlota passing bread to the children.

But there were probably three children. Four. Let us say ten, which is still very different. When a number exceeds certain limits it produces a cruel and complete change. It is one thing to serve ten cups of coffee and another, essentially different, to serve a thousand. It is one thing to walk around a table with a teapot, and quite another to stand behind a counter and see waves of strangers surging forward. Scarcely is one onrushing group served before another piles up. Scarcely are a dozen adversaries beaten down at the edge of the trench than another dozen rise from the ground. Or it might be likened to the assault of a ship, an attack renewed again and again, with which so small and weary a crew is unable to cope. To be sure, those pirates who appear eight and ten together at the gunwales of the assailed vessel are benign. They demand coffee rather than blood. But they demand it in such quantities, and their demand is so frequent, so monotonous and inexorable, that the crew can no longer sustain it. In the end it really is blood that they give. It is their lives that they are dispensing.

And once again the waves of people are advancing. I am being pushed along now. A youth behind me is saying to my frail rose: "Merry Christmas! Merry Christmas!" He is a genial fellow. And suddenly I see the assault on the marble counter transformed into a cotillion. There bubbles to the surface of my memory the figure of a jovial uncle of mine leading that round dance in Caxambú. He had enormous whiskers and sparkling black eyes. He would call out in the ball room of the hotel, "En avant tous! changez! and there would be a whirl of enormous whiskers and enormous skirts, while in a semicircle at the back of the room the elderly women would fan themselves with enormous fans. And I, who was just a very little fellow at that time, would watch that world in caricature, which was to imbue my soul with a lasting dislike for jocose people and conventional merriment. Can there be anything worse than the jocular relative who pays a surprise visit on Sunday when you are reading a novel of Sir Walter Scott and pokes his head through the dining room window, shouting with convivial familiarity: "I've come for a drop of coffee. How about it?"

"This cup's dirty! See here!"

It is an irate, fastidious customer who has found a trace of lipstick on his crockery. Gertrude takes the cup, tosses it into the caldron and puts another in front of the customer. She did not look at the cup or the customer. Because, if she did look, she would go mad. That is her defense, her only defense. She cannot pay any attention to what she does. It is impossible to exercise equal care a thousand times a day; it is impossible to take any interest in that game. And so she acts as though she were waiting on phantoms. Spirits. She looks through them; she fixes her eyes on the infinite, leaving the business of dispensing crockery, taking tickets, and removing used cups to her somnambulistic hands.

The irate gentleman is the center of the universe. His cup is his cup. His case is unique. His person is sacred. And, in all that, I am compelled to acknowledge that he is half right. The idea of receiving food, bread, wine, or coffee from somnambulistic hands really is senseless. The gentleman is right; it is only fair and reasonable to demand clean crockery. Yet, my dear sir, once in your life, before you die—for, after all, I am not the only one upon this planet who is mortal, nor shall I be the last to corroborate the compendiums of logic—just once—perform this absurd feat of gymnastics: in spirit jump over that marble counter, reduce your age by half, change your sex, swallow the tubercle bacillus, put on your hair that derisive crown by which waitresses are identified, and then tell me if anyone in the world has the right to make any demands of anyone in that frightful job. Have you not noticed that she is coughing every minute? Why, just now, she coughed over my coffee and into my cup. She served me a little of her death, which makes me laugh, of course, since my own is so much more potent. She will die soon after I do. Ten days? A month? I do not know exactly; but I do know very exactly, that it will be soon after.

I am sure of this. And why not? Is it not true that one sees the most tenuous emotions in the faces of others? When a friend is annoyed, even ever so slightly, does not the mark of his annoyance appear immediately in his face? When he disagrees is not his disagreement evidence even before any words are spoken? And likewise one sees joy, sorrow, fear, hope. Of every emotion one sees the species, subspecies, variants, and combinations. When Dr. Aquiles raised the corner of his mouth a little, disclosing the lack of a bicuspid, I saw that he was lying, and when Eunice, that night, told me that she had gone to the dressmaker's, I saw that she was lying. Ah! the perspicacity of the jealous man! The keenness of his eye, the rapidity and precision with which it interprets the fleeting shadow, the contrasting muscle, the quivering lashes, the frantic hands that seek a natural pose in the hair— A face has more ideograms than written Chinese. The point is to learn them: whoever, like myself, is a past master in facial geography will have no difficulty. Besides, not his face alone but also the rest of his body makes man an eloquent semaphore. When I was living with Eunice I was able to guess whole sentences perfectly. She would stir in her chair, and I would know what she was going to say. Sometimes I could even place the words in their proper sequence. And then, at such times, when I could guess and was indeed right, I would reap the bitter reward of mortal ennui; for it would seem to me that I was the only living being among puppets.

Now will not he who discerns discreet emotions be able to discern also that profound disharmony which is the essence of sickness? And will he not see the shadow of death who sees the shadow of resentment? I suspect that with a little practice I should be able to pick out the fatal cases. I should offer my services to the gross doctors who must see myeloplasts and eosinophiles under microscopes. I should be held in their hands like the rod that divines subterranean waters. I should divine death.

I have divined that of my poor Gertrude. Whether her sickness is tuberculosis or cancer I cannot say, as I lack both statistics and repeated observation. But I do know that it is fatal. I see her withering and drooping in the opaline vase, poor, poor Otto Kraus from the corner shop. She has not yet lived, and already she is dying. She does not know, as I do, that she is going to die. She will not be able to arrange her death. She will die an ordinary death, a working girl's, *de marré, deci.* I can see a hospital. An ordinary bed, Number So and So, vacated to make way for her. She is in the agony of death—and the coffee, and the cups, and the tickets, and the irate customers, and the genial ones, and the general run of customers, from whom she defended herself by fixing her unseeing eye upon the infinite, will all return to swirl about within her in waves swollen a thousandfold and to fill with the vulgar clatter of crockery and loud talk her final moments—

the final moments of a little girl, who never had a chance to live. She will die with a vision of cups, cups, and more cups.[1] Aprons and caps will flit by. Grotesque customers will lean over her body, as if she, herself, had become a cup and they had come for the last coffee from her entrails—

"Well are you going to get a lot of Christmas presents? Are you going to put your shoe behind the door?"

A tall, blond, self-assured fellow was addressing my Gertrude.

"Poor me!"

She laughed. The idea was amusing. The fellow laughed, too. The idea was decidedly amusing. I had the feeling that the whole bar might burst out laughing, that the customers might intone operatic guffaws in three voices as in the second act of *La Bohème*, at the mere mention of the possibility that the girl behind the counter might, on the mysterious night of December twenty-fourth, tiptoe barefoot to the door and put her shoes behind it.

Gertrude's companion whispered something into her ear. I think it had to do with the fellow's means. Gertrude shrugged her shoulders with a smile. Now the girl was talking aloud about an adorable bracelet that a customer had promised her. Studded with brilliants that no one would ever guess were imitation. An adorable thing.

"What about you? Don't you like jewelry?" the tall, blond fellow asked.

Gertrude handed out cups in silence. After a while, in the low tone of one who is revealing a grave secret, she said that she liked earrings.

"I like earrings—"

But the fellow, I think, did not hear her. He was talking with

[1] One is reminded of Rilke's poem that begins:

"Da steht der Tod, ein bläuchicher Absud
in einer Tasse ohne Untersatz."

"There stands our death, a glaucous decoction
Poured out into a cup without a saucer" (trans.).

someone else, a short, skinny individual in an extraordinary blue jacket. And the two of them disappeared into the street.

December 23rd

Merry Christmas!

It is Christmas Eve. The activity in the streets has doubled, trebled. The cars, immobilized in the jam at the corners, keep honking; the shops are regurgitating; the clerks do not have enough hands for all the measuring to be done; the customers are going in and out, bargaining, making themselves small, elbowing their way through, but they are smiling all the while; yes, they are smiling; apparently everyone is very happy.

Everyone except old Scrooge. The bitter, unhappy usurer is thinking only of himself, and does not have ears for the cheery voices that crisscross the air with greetings. Merry Christmas! Merry Christmas!

Civil-service employees of Groups O[1] and N and M form part of the throng and their wives, likewise, their superlatively virtuous wives, each with her happiness wrapped in fancy paper portraying bells and candles. Merry Christmas! Merry Christmas! Everyone is joyful. Apparently everyone's soul is alight, and filled with the music of hymns.

Everyone except old Scrooge, who looks askance at that irksome profusion of useless spending.

In the crowd mothers meet mothers, aunts bump into aunts, and the air is vibrant with calculations involving dolls, rifles, and tricycles. To be sure, the calculation mitigates the joy somewhat. The

[1] In Brazil government salaries are bracketed by letter, beginning with *A* as the lowest (trans.).

mothers, whose husband's boss heads Group M, linger pensively at the entrance to toy shops; and there in the doorway they make more difficult computations with actual figures—additions and subtractions—as a result of which the rifle shrinks to a cork pistol, or diminishes still more and is reduced to a clever plastic toy which works well, as time will prove, only in the clerk's skilled hands. From their dreams, when treated by the reagent of figures, comes a precipitate of ashen hue. The clerks wrap fancy paper around the rifle that has become a plastic thing. It is disillusion that they are wrapping. "Cash! Cash! Cash!" The tricycle is left for next year when there will be an increase in pay. Besides, Toninho is too small yet for the tricycle. And the clerk wraps up whatever the tricycle has turned into. "Cash! Cash!" "Mama, look at that adorable doll over there!" And the mother pushes along the little girl whose father's boss heads Group M and who wants the doll that belongs to the little girl whose father's boss heads Group O. "Cash!"

The toy resulting from the judicious combination of a dream and a salary is hidden now in the parcel, and Mother M, away from the other toys in the shop, which make her unhappy when she compares them with what she has, ties together the threads of her dream and rationalizes in order to recover its integrity. Toninho is going to like what she has for him; Toninho's going to be delighted.

Parcels, too, form part of the crowd, parcels leading people by the finger. Look! That accumulation of immature cells has made its appearance in the city's blood. Where is the rifle? Where is the tricycle? They have become myeloplasts, the detritus of dreams, young cells, rods, segments. Let them test the city's blood, and then let me see Dr. Aquiles' face when he opens the report!

"Merry Christmas, Dr. Aquiles! Merry, merry Christmas!" Everybody is happy. Toninho's mother and the mothers of all the Toninhos, who live in Copacabana, Itapiru, Jacarepagua, are dividing, branching out, disintegrating into a dense multitude of feminine backs. The streetcars are packed with legs, Legs M and Legs N, and the festive myeloplasts wrapped in bells and candles are beginning to circulate throughout the city. Everybody is happy except old Scrooge.

But do you suppose it is really true, my good Mr. Dickens, that everybody is happy? What about the rifle that turned into celluloid? And the tricycle that is being left for next year? Disagreeable as he is, it is old Scrooge who is right. Mean as he is, he at least understands one very important thing: that it is extremely hard to give. It is the last thing we learn and the first that is requisite for an inhabitable world. And that is why I view with sadness that procession of packaged blunders. Who will have a heart so hard that he will give a stone to the son who has asked for a fish? Yet the problem is solved as soon as the stone is wrapped in gay paper; and Mothers L, M and N manage to convince themselves that the stone is a new kind of fish. That is what is painful, so intensely painful! Spurious happiness, happiness that has turned into plastic. I do not say that true happiness, a child's happiness with a poor lopped-off toy is impossible. No. It is clear that a broken piece of celluloid may give a child pleasure, superlatively clear that, however much people may try, they have not succeeded in drying up the fresh springs of childhood, the wealth of a young heart that is content with little. No. Let them continue thus, for centuries to come, deceiving children and the poor. The poor will always be with us and so will children. It is not that kind of deceit, however, that distresses me most. It is evident, too, that the day of Jesus' birth has deliberately been chosen to inflict a festive humiliation on the poor. One has but to remember the Christmas of the Poor. The streets are filled with wretches standing in the gateways of the rich mens' mansions. If only it were raining, the sight would be perfect. But it is not that, Mr. Dickens, that pains me most.

What does pain me is the fraudulence, the spirit of its being the thing to do that presides over man's sorry merrymaking. It is a day for giving. The calendar sheet has marked it as a day for buying presents. The neighbor to the right has bought, the neighbor to the left has bought. So one must buy. It is the thing to do, it is done, it is what everybody does. And everybody is glad to be equated by custom. Everybody except the disagreeable Scrooge.

What sort of a Christmas is that which accentuates injustice, intensifies passions, amplifies error? Let us allow the city, and the country, and all mankind its festival. Let us allow the celebration of an event that is of interest to us all. Let us allow the world to commemorate day after tomorrow, the nativity of the Savior who was born of a Virgin in a cave in Bethlehem since there was no room for them at the inns. But with this hypothesis, my dear Mr. Dickens, I demand, in the name of that logic that is bringing me to my death, that the happiness be of a different order and that it not depend primarily, as it does now, on calculations and salaries. There are many kinds of happiness; there are degrees of happiness from the tickling of a child's foot to the peace that is born of perfect harmony; from the noisy explosion of a giant firecracker to the unfolding of grateful stillness in the sequestered places of the soul.

Yes, I demand another kind of happiness, resting doubtless on visible things, on celluloid if people wish, since man lives by visible symbols. But resting lightly, as befits things of pure love. Is it not so with lovers when they treasure little keepsakes? Would it not be better to give gifts of rose petals, fragile petals, the diaphanous wafers that are the body of perfect friendship?

My attention was attracted by a dialogue in the doorway of a toy shop. The lady in blue, majestic and authoritative, was arguing with the obsequious clerk, who was already beginning to show signs of impatience. Passing back and forth from one to the other, now in the clerk's professional hand and now in the soft, beringed ones of the wealthy customer, a little black doll with wide-open eyes and a small basket of bananas on her head, appeared to be aloof from the argument.

"It's too expensive."

"It was marked down, madam. You'll not find a doll like this for less than a hundred cruzeiros— But, if you wish, we have others that are less expensive. How high can you go?"

The lady in blue frowned slightly.

"It's for a little poor girl. My maid's child."

Obviously she could not set a hundred cruzeiros as the limit of "how high she could go," as the tactless clerk wanted her to; so by saying that it was for a little poor girl, she was able to explain more clearly. It wasn't for her; not for her daughter or niece or any child of her kind, class, or station in life; it was for the maid's child.

The clerk understood at once that the problem had shifted to a system of measurements. No one, of course, measures the diameter of a globule of blood in kilometers or the distance from Sirius in millimeters. For the globule there is the micron, and there are the light years for the stars. All things in this harmonious universe have their own dimensions on a scale adequate to them.

While the new system of measurements was being established between the clerk and the majestic lady, I was looking at an astrakhan bear in the window. With his fixed, blue-bead eyes, he was trying to outstare me without laughing.

"Bear, my friend, will you tell me, please, where they have hidden the child Jesus?"

The child Jesus was at the intersection of Assembleia and Quitanda Streets, in the lap of a beggar woman. The people who were going by ("Merry Christmas! Merry Christmas!") did not see the child Jesus in his niche of misery. Nor could they have been expected to. The child Jesus was hidden in the poor little fellow that the beggar woman held in her lap. Sallow, grimy, filthy, he looked as though he had been taken from a trash can.

When I passed he was trying to pick up a rubber nipple that had fallen into his mother's dirty rags. He raised it to his mouth, putting has little fingers on his lips, from which a clear, innocent saliva was dribbling. The mother, with outstretched arm, was soliciting alms, for the love of God. Was she really the mother, I wondered. They say that children are hired out for begging. Then it is all a show, the beggar, the child, the mother— And it is of that falsity that everyone is suspicious.

The pacifier was falling again and becoming lost in the wretched breast. At that moment, when I was nearly by, the child looked at me. His eyes rested on mine. Yes, his eyes rose from out of the depths of his innocence. And the child smiled. At me!

December 26th

My Volumes of Jules Verne

I prefer birthdays. On those days, at least, only one person celebrates. The injustice is not so shocking, the person can enjoy his gifts any way he wants to; and the child Jesus, there in his niche of misery, can smile without piercing the heart. I do not care for holidays. I have always found them more tiring and depressing than gay, and I have always suspected that if on such days there are more widespread manifestations of jubilance there is also increased suffering of the soul. Therefore, I prefer birthdays. Only one little boy has his on the thirteenth of March, or if others, too, celebrate the same date, they are few, remote and unknown; and those widely scattered, hidden jollities make no change in the city's traffic.

I used to get a pile of playthings. Papa with his melancholy and Mama with her nervousness really got together for that day, the former to obtain a brief respite from himself, compensating with balls, games, and weapons for his inability to show affection, and the latter to give free play to her excitability. And there were also relatives, and friends (we were well off at that time), and some of Papa's colleagues, to augment the pile.

But the present that I still remember today is good old Dodo's. She was a kind of poor relation, though actually she was not related at all. She always showed up on festive days. Some poor relations specialize in coming for a visit on doleful occasions. The relative who belongs to that dismal species comes when the household's hierarchy is disrupted, when each individual's pride is temporarily softened. That day is hers; its atmosphere of gloom is the air she breathes. Everyone has a vague presentiment that she is associated with sickness, misfortune, and death. She comes and takes over. She installs an emergency regime that lasts as long as there are telephone calls to the drugstore, injections, sleepless nights, and dire forebodings.

But my Dodo belonged to the festive species, which shows up for birthdays, baptisms, and weddings. I believe she was the widow of a professor for whom my father had done some favor in time of trouble. She had attached herself to the family, but joined us only on special occasions. And she never forgot to bring a present. Probably someone had told her that I was very fond of reading. "That child's crazy about books!" It was my father, who, when she asked him what book she should give, suggested the works of Jules Verne.

The first volume to appear in my life came on my ninth birthday. It was *The Southern Star.* I did not read it, because it had come too soon. But I was delighted with its red cover, on which a boa constrictor was coiled in a banana tree, symbolical of the tropics, and a lion was galloping toward a ship aground on the ice, while, overhead, against the blackness of night, loomed the bulging body of a balloon. The print was uninvitingly small, and there were only two illustrations. The first, described as "Marvelous Diamond" showed a black stone glittering on a small pedestal, in front of which two photographers had set up their apparatus; the second, between pages 112 and 113, and described as "Hanging by the Hands," showed a man wearing boots, entangled in a net that was being borne aloft by eagles, while, down below, a Chinese and a European, mounted on giraffes, were observing the unusual spectacle.

It was not until two years later, when Dodo brought me *Michael Strogoff*, that I discovered in wonder all the riches that can be hidden in a finely printed text. I read it several times in succession. I learned some passages by heart. And, though I already knew the happy outcome, I held my breath in suspense when the savage Tartar said to the courier of the Tzar:

"Then open your eyes, open them wide!"

The saber that was to blind him was flaming in the brutal torturer's hands, and the face of the old Marfa Strogoff, who had been flung into a corner, revealed the bloody marks of the knout.

Dodo had hit the mark that year.

Mama said to her afterwards, "You've no idea how much he liked it."

And Dodo smiled. She had found the key to my happiness. Later came other volumes: *Journey to the Center of the Earth, Around the World in Eighty Days, The Five Hundred Millions of the Begum.* There were enough for Dodo to continue giving me until I was sixty, if she and I lived that long. But as others, too, had found the secret way to my happiness and brought me a single volume occasionally, she had acquired the habit of verifying. On the eve of my birthday she would telephone Mama.

"He already has that one— and that one— no, not that one, he doesn't have that one."

Next afternoon they would call me, "José Maria! See, here comes Dodo!"

From a distance I would see the shape of the package.

"Guess what it is!"

"Jules Verne."

"What a clever boy!"

And Dodo would wait for me to open the package, eager for the vicarious pleasure she got from my shining face. I would turn straightway to the illustrations. There were aways two, one on the first page and one on page 112.

"Don't forget to thank her, Son."

Then I would kiss Dodo's old face, which had the smell of something that had been put away.

I grew up, but not Dodo. I galloped through the years, making new discoveries. Dodo was marking time with the good collection she had made by then. For her Jules Verne was still the same. But not for me. Nothing had remained the same. On my sixteenth birthday, when I had already composed a poem that began:

> In my breast my heart beats the measure
> Of this fevered dance of madness –

and when already I had wept and bitten my pillow with thoughts of love and death, Dodo, good old Dodo, the same old Dodo, brought me a Jules Verne in two volumes: *Keraban, the Inflexible.*

December 29th

In the Blood

When the nurse had me go into the consultation room Dr. Aquiles was already there, with his back to the door, conversing with another doctor, who was listening intently, gravely nodding his large head with its silvery shock of hair. In a chair at the side of the room, paying no attention to the doctors' conversation, absorbed in his own thoughts, was a dark, strapping youth with a dazzling white Palm Beach suit,[1] two-toned shoes, and a gold wristband. He was the donor.

" 'Thirty contos for gloves! No,' I said to him."

[1] In Brazil such a suit is called a Panama suit (trans.).

" 'Forget it, nothing doing. Thirty contos!' "

"And he said: 'They're boxing gloves'."

The silvery-haired doctor laughed at his good story. Dr. Aquiles agreed that it was funny and was probably about to adduce some pronouncement on the difficulties of the housing situation when he saw me in the doorway.

"Come in! Well, how are you? This is Dr. Noronha of the Blood Service—and Esteves."

I greeted ceremoniously the man who was to give me a pint of his blood. Dr. Aquiles had received my message the day before; he was all ready; if I wished, we could begin the transfusion at once.

"I'm a little late, Doctor. My bus was in an accident."

"It's hard to set an hour, these days when everything's topsy-turvy."

"Unfortunately there're still certain appointments that don't wait on traffic—"

Dr. Aquiles' eyes met mine in a rapid glance, but quickly shied away. And I was not able to tell whether he thought me late or early for the appointment I had implied.

In the room off to the side were two beds three feet apart. I lay down on one, the donor on the other, and Dr. Noronha, standing between the two, whispering to the nurse and preparing an odd-looking metallic apparatus, gave me the impression of being an intermediary in some kind of accord or conciliation that was like nothing I could remember. Had there been only one bed, the situation, though painful, would obviously have fitted into my memory; but the two beds, the two bodies three feet apart, placed me in a painful psychological position.

There beside me was that youth, that stranger, whose dazzlingly white suit I should scarcely have noticed had I passed him on the street a half hour earlier. And now it was from him, that nameless man, that any-man, that I was going to receive a good pint of youthful and universal blood.

What shall I do with that blood? What action will the blood of a fellow who wears such extraordinary shoes produce in my musings, my questionings, my anguish? What kind of tie, what kind of fusion can be made between him and me, sealed in this way with blood?

Now there is silence. Contact has been established. A needle here, another there, and Dr. Noronha between us with his massive graying head and his rhythmic bulb. I feel nothing physically. It's my mind that flutters in trepidation and inspires a dozen unrelated feelings, the chief of which is an intense nausea. If that young fellow's body were pressed against mine, if I felt his sweat on my skin, his breath on my face, the contact, even so, would be lighter than that which is being diffused all through me.

After today, as though it had not been enough to have that cancer, which is a foreign thing and divides me in two, I shall have that foreign blood that will divide me in three. I shall carry around in my body a part of someone else's body, which is something more than if I merely had a piece of skin that had been grafted on to mine, or hair and teeth that had replaced my own.

And besides that, the operation is of no use. Dr. Aquiles himself said so. That pint of blood put forth is a useless gift, a useless sacrifice. I wonder if Esteves realizes that he is putting forth his blood? That the ceremony is as inexpressive as a Christmas telegram? Imagine! Imagine the fool who would empty a dozen inkwells writing conventional thanks and congratulations in blood! It is all right if people want to use up tons of paper, mobilize whole armies of deliverers, and set a roomful of telegraphic apparatus into motion; that I can understand. But to go so far as to write conventional greetings in blood is to my mind colossally abstruse. Dr. Aquiles is well aware that this bloodshed is futile. Dr. Noronha, too. And yet, what the dictators of Europe are doing on a large scale they are doing here in a small way with the metallic bulb.

Of course, the fellow is just doing what he is paid to do. Some sell the strength of their muscles; others sell sleep and tranquility; others, in public exhibitions, display their secret emotions transformed into dramatic scenes or ecstatic eloquence or conveyed by a phrase drawn by the violin bow from the nerves—externalized and stretched taut—of that small singing box. There are the professional mourners, too, who hire out their eyes and sell their tears. Well, this fellow sells his blood. He ought to be called a blood vendor, but no—he is called donor.

It appears that when it comes to blood men still have scruples about confessing their business. They dare not employ for such an article the ordinary vocabulary of mercantile transactions. So they have created the title of donor, which separates the two sides of the equation: blood on one side, emoluments on the other. Two parallel acts, two straight lines in two distinct planes: the man gives his blood; I give the money.

There are the Blood Banks to be sure. There one does not see the donor. Nor are there two beds, two horizontal bodies. And then, scruple overcome, the vocabulary takes a prodigious leap from personal generosity to the cold, numerical, impersonal organization of the bank. What is a donation here is a commercial transaction there, and the commodity lacks the transitional stage, that is, the small, modest, personal business, the bootblack's doorway, the prostitute's bed, business on a scale as small as a cigarette tip. Here we have a very personal donation, body to body; there, where the various bloods are stored namelessly in scientific phials, there is a bill of exchange, a discount, an almost abstract operation.

Esteves is giving his blood. Lying beside me in that vital half-hour meeting, this stranger is becoming an intimate; he is becoming part of me. Afterwards I shall get up, put on my coat, and awkwardly place an envelope on the table—

"No! I don't want your money. I don't accept alms!"

And I, standing in the middle of the room shaded with blue curtains, was looking at the dressing table covered with *bibelots*—powder jars, atomizers, tiny rats of Copenhagen porcelain, translucent birds and fishes, French perfume flasks of various colors and shapes, bringing to mind a most feminine and most whimsical game, chess or mah-jongo, perhaps, with a topaz pawn boldly advancing against the frivolous army that from the other side of the mirror was deploying on to the duplicate crystal top. The thousand-cruzeiro note had its futile counterpart, too, there in the looking-glass world; and farther back, away toward the back of the wide mirror, I saw another dimly lit room, a spacious bed, a crumpled dress, and in the midst of that *décor* of voluptuous pleasure a common little twenty-year face that at the moment showed vexation.

I put the money away without the courage to turn around. I did not know what I had done, and scarcely remembered how I had come, led like a somnambulist by the slender form of a girl of the streets. It was the first time, and I was forty years old. Since Eunice had left me I had lived in a state of bewilderment and had walked through the streets trying to decipher the impersonal, generic Eunice in those women without a name. I felt a dreadful loss as if I had been emptied, as if everything, absolutely everything in the universe, were stricken with a fundamental loss. There was no solution for me outside of woman, because woman is the foundation, the support, the ground, the Earth from which we recover the strength that we men expend on our expeditions. We men set out. We go through the complicated epicycles of our masculine orbits; we fight in the air and on the sea; we are strong. Yes, we are strong so long as the unseen, flexible umbilical cord that holds us to the rear guard does not break. And the rear guard is woman.

In our adventures, like the fugitive Parsifal, we forget what we are, what name we bear, the definition that is our guarantee. Then we speak of the human condition and human nature, as one might speak vaguely of a lost address. What am I? What is man?

Now man is woman. When she is stripped of the accidental titles with which mankind obscures its essence, we men see that she is nuclearly more human than we. Her loss, therefore, hurts us unbearably, and her dishonor is universal dishonor.

"Farewell the neighing steed and the shrill trump. Farewell! Othello's occupation's gone." With Eunice lost to me, I had no place to turn; no house, no essence of humanity.

I walked the streets, like an exile seeking the road his parents had taken. The earth had shattered, and the highways had become a jumble. The world had become a labyrinth, and my eyes traveled among the women scattered there, as if Eunice had broken into countless fragments strewn upon the ground. In that sea into which womankind had dissolved there were different ways of walking, hair of different colors and legs of different shapes—differences that made quite plain the reconciliatory nature of fashion. Fashion has been created for our confusion. That multiplication of the identical shoe, the identically styled dress makes women all alike. Where does Filipa begin and Sandra end? Like so many adjustable circles on a planisphere, they continually bring before our eyes a disturbing view of universal womanhood. And I saw Eunice everywhere.

I accompanied the slender, bright-clad form that had picked me up on the street. And now there I was in front of the mirror in whose depths I could see that disconcerting image. What had happened? Almost nothing. She had already slipped out of her dress, when, suddenly noticing the time, she exclaimed, "The serial! It's time for the serial I'm following. It's a good one! Just wait a little while."

She turned on the radio, and the sobbing voice of a woman whose love had been outraged came abruptly into the room.

"No, Alberto. It's all over between us. I don't want your pity or your explanations. It's all over!"

The invisible Alberto, whom I visualized as having a small, neatly trimmed mustache, was saying in a conciliatory tone:

"But, woman, you understand—"

And he launched into a detailed explanation that referred to previous episodes and persons whom I did not know, Helena, Fernando, Rita. My lady of joy was enthralled, and she kept turning to me with mute signs of sympathy, revolt, fear, and commiseration. Then began a dialogue between father and daughter. In a sententious voice appropriate to persons trained in the radio theater, the old man proffered lengthy admonitions of prudence and understanding, which struck and shattered against the panting, sobbing despair of the young woman whose love had been wounded. She repeated the fatal scene to her father. She had gone out to shop; she had already reached the street when she saw that she had forgotten her list, which was probably on her dressing table. She had gone back. And when she opened the bedroom door, she stopped at the threshold, petrified wtih fright—

"What does petrified mean?"

The radio theater had brought its episode to a close with a deep, paternal sigh accompanied by pathetic invocations to destiny. Then I explained to the girl what "petrified" meant, and suddenly, at that very moment, I felt shocked to have her sitting there on the bed beside me in her slip. Whatever might have happened after that would have seemed to me to partake of incest. An absurd radio theater, one without sound and without previous episodes, had been set up in the room. I was the father who lays his hand on his daughter's curls and explains what "petrified" means. I got up with an effort. I stammered a few incoherent words. And mechanically, as I stood in front of the mirror, I opened my billfold and put a thousand-cruzeiro note on the dressing table beside a powder jar of Bohemian glass.

The transfusion was over. The donor, sitting on the bed, was drinking the orange juice that the nurse had brought him. I had thought it was for me and was already holding out my hand when the girl laughed and said:

"It's for the donor. You've had the blood."

I laughed too, in order to hide the shame I felt at having made such a blunder. I was a vampire, wanting everything—human blood and orange juice—for myself.

January 3rd

Gertrude's Earrings

I was passing by absentmindedly when I smelled the aroma of coffee and heard the clatter of the cups. I remembered the girl I had seen the other day, and I went in. I saw at once that she had not got the earrings she wanted and that in a week her illness had progressed. She has had no one to give her any blood, and she is losing her own to the thousand customers who, like so many leeches, come every day to imbibe it in the form of coffee. She is not laughing today. She is hustling at her work, repeating the same simplified motions over and over.

Why do they not invent a smiling, pink-cheeked doll with the four articulations necessary for those four motions repeated a thousand times a day? There are people who look upon the machine as one of the principal causes of the evils of our time. Everything can be mechanized as far as I am concerned so long as the mania does not touch the twenty-year–old girl who has never had a chance to live. Yes, either let there be invented an automaton to dispense the cups or let everyone have his coffee at home, because there is absolutely no sense in restricting a living, brown-haired girl to those leverlike motions. It is an obvious waste. What is the hair for? What is the narrow chest for? And the heart within the chest? And the blood, the vessels, the organs, and the nerves, what are they for? And the whole body, the waist, the hips, and the legs hidden under the counter? What are the sad eyes for? And the soul, what is the soul for?

I leave the coffee bar, and I realize how easy it is to pity other people. One comes, one gives free rein to noble sentiments, and then one goes away. That is the way one visits the sick. One does one's duty, one is sorry, and one leaves. The sick person remains. He sees the world in a different perspective from that of the visitor. He sees a world that comes, leans over him for ten minutes with facile commiseration and then takes its leave. The sick person remains. By definition, he is someone who remains behind. From his bed he sees the visitor turn once more in the door and say he hopes he will get better; then he sees him turn quickly and hurry away; he hears his footsteps on the stairs, his last cheery word of comfort to the member of the family, who is thanking him for having come; finally the gate creaks, the car door slams, the motor starts—and pity has left.

"José Maria!"

"Augusto! After all these years!"

It was Augusto. How changed he was! We had not seen each other for thirty years. Augusto had married. He had four daughters, one married, and he was about to have a second grandchild, about to be a great-grandfather, as he said.[1]

"And how have you been? You've gotten thin—"

Augusto laughed and took hold of me by the elbows, the shoulders, the buttons of my coat, while I stood looking in astonishment at this caricature of the person I had once known.

When we used to fly kites together on Barão de Ubá Street he had been a lively, plucky little fellow always ready for anything. Out of a dart and some tissue paper he could make better kites than anyone else—great marauders that were the terror of the neighborhood. He graduated the lead string and the weight of the tail so that the body could curvet about in the air in pursuit of any kite that dared to come near.

"Let out your line! Let out your line, stupid!"

And the plundering kite would go bounding after the other one, which might, indeed, be larger but had to depend more upon the

[1] The Portuguese word for great-grandfather is *bisavô*, literally, "one who is twice a grandfather" (trans.).

strength of its stout string than upon the agility of the arm that controlled it.

"Let out your line, stupid!"

Augusto would run across his yard taking in the string in order to straighten the kite, and then, with feigned alarm, he would pay it out until he secured a position under the enemy's string— I can see him still, balanced on top of the wall, with the sun beating down on him and encircling his head,which was the head of a young hero, with a bright coppery halo; and I can hear him shouting to the Negro boys in the vacant lot, "Let out your line! Let out your line!"

Suddenly, like a ferocious spider, the body of the kite would pounce upon its prey. Unmindful of getting hurt, his body arched and distended, Augusto would fall to the ground and then, with torn shirt and bleeding shoulder, would run across the yard, lean against the house, and, first with one hand then with the other as if they were the cylinders of a perfectly functioning machine, he would draw in the line behind the defeated enemy. With his penknife gleaming in his hand, he would deal the final blow and then turn toward me with the flushed, radiant face and noisy laughter typical of fearless marauders and barbaric heroes such as he.

That was the vivid, colorful picture hanging in my memory. And now? What I was to do with that caricature that was pulling me by the sleeve and by the buttons of my coat and offering me hospitality on such and such a street at such and such a number? I had the impression that that emaciated face of an old man was playing a joke on me. Changed as it was, consumed and macerated, it seemed to mock me with somnolent malice. But no, it was not malice with which it was furrowed. It was affability rather.

"Come to see me, come to see me—

And for the first time in sixty days I felt a certain pride in my cancer. To be sure, it is devouring me, strangling me, but, at least, it is not making me so ridiculously wrinkled. Yes, I was proud of my cancer. I imagined it coiling through me with powdery tentacles—and in comparison with Augusto I felt like a kind of Laocoön.

The waitress at the bar has become a caricature too. I never knew the little girl, who, ten years ago, used to join hands with her companions and dance around in a circle. I never saw the innocent eyes that looked dreamily out upon the world with infinite confidence in life. I know nothing of her little pink dresses and her rag dolls. But I do know that she has become a caricature, a deformed puppet. And she will never become a grandmother.

The world would appear to be an enormous shop for man's impairment. Decomposition begins long before the grave. No sooner is man put together, than they begin to take him apart in the workshop as though he were a puzzle-game set up as a pastime and of which they had soon grown weary. Where is the turning point in our lives? On what day did I begin to be dismantled by careless hands? Not, as one might think, at the approach of old age. No. Already at twenty, I was swiftly moving away from the promise of my birth. And it is not Augusto's stomach ulcer or his fifty years that are making a marionette of him either. Long before, surely, when his body was still following the upward curve, he had begun to leave behind the barbaric hero of radiant face.

Actually I should say that the puzzle was never completed in either Augusto or me. At a certain point in the game, when there was only the barest trace of what I might become, the outline was destroyed as if the gods, on holiday, had been exchanging ideas and proposing temporary models, roughly sketched and immediately erased, for the fashioning of a new creature to be inserted, if it came out right, between the brute beasts and the angels.

Sickness and old age are merely the wasting away of the body which is worn out by the wasting away of the soul. The old man exists already in the youth, and the corpse exists in the old man. Augusto does not know it, but he is carrying his corpse around along with enough remnants of galvanic energy to pull people's sleeves and buttons and to contract the muscles of his face. Gertrude does not know either; she has no thought of the light-weight coffin that will hold a little girl.

I was returning home earlier than I had planned. At least, I should have the pleasure of finding a seat in the bus. I should have a little respite from Augusto and myself—and everything.

I did indeed find a seat, and I sat down. I settled in my corner, through this brief occupancy experiencing a little the pleasure of possession. I stayed in my corner and kept perfectly still. Let others scurry to their shopping and social engagements; let the bus roll along; let the earth and the planetary system and the Galaxy spin about: I was seated in my intimate forum, a disgruntled spectator, yawning, or hissing the incongruous pantomine.

The presence of the other passengers, however, quickly spoiled my comfort. There were shoulders, bundles, trousers, blouses, and souls in the way. There were enigmas, challenges, provocations. What could that reserved young girl, apparently absorbed in thought, be thinking about? What could be the dilemma that was besetting her soul? And what about that old man who had resolved to adopt a facial expression that publicly proclaimed his poor opinion of life and humanity but withheld the reasons?

The bus was parked at the terminal, awaiting the scheduled time for departure. The driver, a grizzling Portuguese, was telling a workman about an abscessed tooth that he had had pulled—three roots it had, like a cobbler's bench. The girl consulted her wrist watch. The old man opened his paper with the air of one who promises not to be startled by the disasters in the headlines.

It was at that moment that we heard the unusual noise; dishes being broken, tables dragged around, loud words, cries of anger and pain. I looked out. The disturbance was at the restaurant opposite. Perhaps because of a mistake in change or a steak that was overdone or underdone, or some other incident that I shall never know, a dark-skinned, burly individual was struggling in the middle of four waiters, who were endeavoring unsuccessfully to quell him. His gray coat, which the violent agitation had turned into a dynamo, was assuming monstrous proportions; his thick arms were describing in the air rapid, extraordinary gestures of unleashed fury: tables were overturning; from the cigarette counter, suddenly smashed, was streaming a cascade of white, green, red, and yellow packets, while an unexpected welling up of coffee was spurting into the midst of the tumult a black spout the like of which I could never have imagined.

How wonderful! What a wealth of new forms and situations, what strange realities appear in the world, this weary, repetitious world, when a man dares to exceed his limits!

I observed my passengers. They were fascinated. The old man had a look of dismay on his face, but I swear that behind the dismay I caught a flash of a little boy's glee. He was regarding the man-who-dared with envy and admiration. The girl who had been fighting a spiritual battle of her own, was also following the struggle. I saw its glow reflected in her serious face; I noticed her ill-concealed excitement, I detected the slight quivering of the nostrils, the almost imperceptible parting of the lips as of one who restrains a desire to speak. Beside the girl, a middle-aged woman, laden with bundles and with anxieties, obligations and prejudices as well, was also amazedly watching that swarthy athlete improvise coffee spouts and cigarette falls.

Now it was at that moment, just at that very moment, that I decided to present the coffee-cup-girl with the most beautiful earrings in the world.

I gave a start. The girl in the embroidered blouse did not start nor did the old man. Yet their souls, too, I know, had been kindled by a spark from the struggle they had witnessed. When the girl gets home, she will lock herself in her room, while in the living room a despotic family gathers for dinner. "Marta! Marta! dinner's on the table!" The girl will shrug her shoulders. Dinner—hard faces, mumbled words pregnant with implications. She will open her closet, and, like one seeking himself among the lifeless pieces of cloth, she will slowly run her hands among the garments. Here is the plaid suit, there the voile, the silk crepe, the white chiffon she had worn to the graduation dance— Suddenly she will fling herself on the bed, weeping convulsively. The fuse has gone off; the powder is burning. Where will she go tomorrow? To the apartment that a suitor has hastily adorned for the falsehoods of love? Or, who knows? who knows? Perhaps she will take another direction— She will climb a steep slope. I see a steep slope, a churchyard, an old wooden bench. I hear a bell—a porter in religious habit appears at a partly open gate—a small bell rings—and then, then I see, in a confusion of superimposed images, a conflagration of contorted faces and writhing arms, and I see profiles of dejected old people in front of a useless closet, and, forgotten in one corner of the room, a young girl's pair of small shoes—and, there, a long way off, at the very tip of that decision, that decision that draws a flaming furrow, at the culmination of that impulse, a silent nun walking in a cloister—

I entered the jewelry shop and said that I wished to look at earrings, the most beautiful earrings in the world. The young man who had come up to wait on me was startled, apparently, for he went to call the manager with whom he exchanged a few words in an undertone. But my appearance is reassuring. The manager looked at the young man with scorn and at me with every mark of consideration. For one curious moment his face held two hemispheres, one of contempt for this underling and another of reverence for the well-dressed, apparently rich customer who wished to look at costly jewels.

He took me up to the third floor and put me in contact with another stranger, stout, red-faced, and obsequious, who all during the time of our dealings maintained a one-hundred-and-sixty-degree angle between his thorax and his legs.

"We have magnificent earrings, magnificent, sir, you will see. Please—"

I went into another small room, where under a chandelier of profuse and intricate ornamentation was a glass-topped table and a stool covered with crimson velvet. I sat down. My man, who had disappeared behind a curtain, returned in a little while with a tray of jewelry.

At first I was confused by the profusion of pearls and diamonds. It was a bad combination. They had been put together at random and were completely out of harmony. I hesitated, not knowing how to isolate them.

"Look at these beauties. Notice the luster of these pearls."

They were two pink pearls in a platinum setting surrounded by smaller pearls. They were pretty, perhaps, but I thought the rosette pattern ostentatious. I did not like it. Besides, it is hard to distinguish the real pearl from the false. One is always suspicious about them. No. I did not want pearls. The diamonds did not please me either. Their white, diaphanous beauty would not suit the sad, wheat-colored Gertrude. Much less would the cheerful, beatific sapphire. No, blue had no part in the girl's story, either.

Discouraged, I went back to the pearls, reconsidered the diamonds, even examined the amethysts. I no longer felt the impulse that had brought me to that third floor. No. No one of those jewels corresponded to the impetus that had wrenched me from the bus. Had it been a question of unemotional engagement, or a brief adventure, it would not have been hard to choose one of those elegant jeweled ornaments that the jeweler was showing me, with his eyes fastened on me in an effort to guess what his queer, hesitant customer had in mind.

We reached an impasse. All I wanted now was to get away somehow. I gathered my strength to tear myself from the crimson stool. Though by now the Jew was apoplectic from his efforts to please, I was determined to leave, no matter what he might think of me.

"Wait a moment. I'll bring you something worthy of a princess. Excuse me."

He removed the tray of spurned jewelry and again disappeared behind the blue curtain. In a few minutes he came back, holding a small box in his hand and smiling triumphantly.

"Look!"

And I saw against a background of cream-colored velvet two huge drops of blood.

"They're rubies from the Orient, from Burma!" said the jeweler, almost in a whisper as though he were speaking of something holy.

"From Burma?" I, too, spoke in a low tone.

We seemed to be plotting a conspiracy or sharing some ancient, romantic secret that had originated within the confines of Hindustan, there amid the Brahmans' temples and the canebrakes that crackle at night under the tiger's paw.

"These stones are priceless. Yet, they're unassuming. Jewels for the connoisseur. Notice the simplicity of the setting, the contrast with the lines of onyx and malachite. The large stone stands out. Very delicate work."

I gazed at the earrings that the jeweler was holding now in his hands. Two drops of blood. Look! It is my turn now; now I am the donor. And I shall give what I myself do not have: blood and happiness.

"How much are they?"

"One hundred and fifty thousand," replied the Jew with extreme gravity, increasing somewhat the angle between his chest and his legs.

"A hundred and fifty thousand?" I repeated indifferently. I was not thinking of the figure. I was preoccupied with the thought that I was the one who would now be the donor.

"A hundred and fifty thousand," the merchant repeated, wondering, doubtless, at the total absence of shocked surprise to which he had become accustomed. Then I came to my senses. One hundred and fifty thousand. The price of a good car. The price of spending my final days in various places scattered over the world and ending them on a dream Adriatic. The price of 150 transfusions. I swung partly around on the stool and consulted my checkbook. I had forgotten to write on the last stubs, but, after a mental calculation, I concluded that I had a little over 120,000.

"I'll give you 120,000."

The man opened his arms in a gesture of consternation, and invoking the crystal chandelier, which was witness to his grievous perplexity, he declared that the reduction I asked was impossible, absolutely impossible. Two rubies of that size! From the Orient, from Burma! The most valuable stone in the world!

"A hundred and forty," I proposed finally.

We were leaning over the table, one in front of the other, like two fighters studying each other. A big bluish vein was swelling on the Jew's forehead; I, myself, must have been less pale than usual, because I felt my heart pounding in a ridiculous effort to diffuse through my body a few remnants of adulterated blood.

We stayed thus for a long, tense minute, while the stones, disdainful of our petty dispute, like two barbaric princesses whom the fortunes of war had brought to a slave mart, continued to glitter and radiate the deep, red splendor that had accumulated for centuries in the rocks of Hindustan. Not for anything would I give them up. I do not know whether my adversary could perceive that. But not for anything would I give them up.

"The fact is that I don't have 120 at my disposal; I have just verified."

"If that's it," the man exclaimed in relief, "we can arrange a mode of payment."

"No, I wish to pay cash, now or never."

"But it's impossible! impossible! Alexander, O Alexander!"

The man who had received me on the first floor appeared, and they went over to the embrasure of the window to confer. They whispered. They gesticulated. And I saw my two Burmese rubies, lying on the table outside of their box. Finally they came over, and my man's fat, oily face was shining with an idea. Alexander remained standing somewhat behind to await developments in our game.

"I'm going to suggest a solution. Don't misunderstand me, but it's impossible for us to go below 140,000. Is it not, Alexander?"

"What is the solution that you propose, then?"

"You'll forgive my being so bold, but, after all, it's a solution; you have a diamond there that would cover the difference—"

It was my scarf pin he was speaking of. It had been my father's, even my grandfather's, I believe. I unfastened the safety catch and tossed the diamond onto the table.

"Here's the check, 120,000. And here's my address and identification folder."

"It's not necessary; we'll accept the check."

"The point is that I wish to take the jewelry with me; and you can't cash the check, because the banks are closed."

The man straightened and shot me a rapid and quite different look; immediately, however, he resumed his bent posture of humility.

"Give me your address, then. Is it an apartment?"

"No, it's a house."

"Your own?"

"My own."

"Well, then, leave your identification folder with us. You understand—we'll have it sent to your address tomorrow. You may take the jewelry with you."

I was not tired now as I walked along the street. I felt an inexpressible rejuvenation and affluence. Sometimes, at certain moments of the day, our childhood, brought by an imponderable—a fragrance, a voice—comes back to us with all the sudden violence of a rush of wind, and scenes of long ago and people long-forgotten rise up within us. Then we feel that through memory and the imagination we have recovered, in a certain measure, our lost selves. But the experience that opened my heart today was of a different, more subtle nature. The remembrance that came to me today was without sensory perception; it was of my very soul, a piercing remembrance that brought back the self I had once been, and sewed together the fibers of my life and being into a deep continuity, making me inwardly a child once again, even without Jules Verne and Augusto's kites.

It was not until afterwards that the images and conscious recollections came, and then I had the impression of having bestrode thirty years of failure to resume the aspirations of the young man whose expectations of life were boundless.

At that time I did expect everything from life. Everything. I wanted to be a poet and extract from poetry inward enrichment and the outward fame that would make people point me out on the street as they did the young Alighieri, of whom it was said: "There goes the man who can descend to Hell and come back at will." But had they brought me a golden salver with the original manuscript of the *Divine Comedy* to sign on condition that I give up the other quadrants of glory, I should have dismissed the offer with contempt.

I wanted, too, the inward exultation and the outward prestige of scientific research. I wanted to know the matchless thrill of seeing a secret unfold for the first time. I wanted to be the daring traveler who wanders over the face of the earth, in various climes and among exotic costumes. I wanted to be in Hong Kong, Singapore, Moscow, and New York; I wanted to freeze at the poles, burn in the deserts, experience the weariness and the hunger and thirst of the man who has had a long day's journey, the fear of stupendous perils, the joy of the discoverer who sees the continent of his dreams loom on a horizon at dawn.

I wanted everything from life. Of what use the treasure contained in a small square of the immense planisphere of possibilities, if the rest remained beyond reach to torment me? Of what use the *Divine Comedy,* the discoveries of Plank and Einstein, if music were forbidden to me? I was not willing to be a prisoner even in so grandiose a palace as the souls of Dante and Camões. Were I to be excluded from anything that man can attempt or possess I should have felt excluded from everything.

But from day to day the inclosure was narrowing around me. I should be obliged to choose and, consequently, I should be obliged to renounce the infinite. I should have to decide upon a career; in other words, from among all the possible dungeons, I should have to prepare with ardor and perserverance one of my very own. Engineering, for example.

At that time Cousin Anísio was already preparing to take his examinations at the Naval Academy. He had discovered a propensity for the sea. Ah! how well I remembered that story!

One day—let us suppose a fine May morning—the little Anísio went for an excursion with his dear parents to Governador Island. After a hurried awakening and a drive that seemed like the continuation of a dream, the little fellow came to Quinze Square, and saw from the swaying gangplank the boat, the slowly brightening sky, and the sea. Ah! the sea that the boy was seeing for the first time close by like that, very close by, that he feels beneath his feet, alive, gently surging, that he divines to be vast and mysterious though they tell him that it is only water, the same kind that is at home in small, controlled quantities, the same kind that trickles between the fingers of one's cupped hand (child, don't play with water) or that falls in brilliant drops down one's shivering body that Mama has lathered with soap; ah! this water that has neither pipes nor limits! This water had become a world in itself, and the house was rocking on top of it.

Then came two sailors, who had stepped right out of a storybook picture, and released the enormous cables that held the boat. The wheels began to make foam, like a mill wheel, and, as soon as the boat was untied from the dock, it became suspended like a bubble between sea and sky.

And just let us suppose that the happiest sea gull in the world hovered over it for an instant and that as he hung there, poised motionless in the air, he bestowed his blessing on the boat and on the five-year-old Anísio, who was at that moment the happiest boy between sea and sky.

Uncle Belisario, seeing the boy's pleasure just then, stooped down, and tweaking his ear, affectionately said:

"Do you like it, sailor? When you grow up, you'll be an officer in the Navy."

That was how Anísio's calling had originated. From that minute on they had begun to talk about the Navy, and even the child felt an inclination toward it in his heart, since the word was mysteriously associated with the boat, the sky, and the gull suspended between sea and sky. His good uncle's joke had taken hold.

I felt that I could write a twelve-volume treatise on the influence of uncles' jokes on young men's vocations. Somewhere back of a young man's despair there is invariably a grownup's jokes. Why? Why do adults laugh at children? And, above all, why do they tell them falsehoods? I should like to have someone explain that dark mystery to me. But it is too late now, and I shall die without knowing why it is that we cannot see a child without a falsehood's coming to our lips.

The joke, then, had taken hold, and, acquiring substance, it became one of those inexorable, familiar axioms from which the victim can never escape. Anísio had a propensity for the sea. Whenever callers came to the house inevitably some kindly middle-aged gentleman would question the little fellow.

"And what do you want to be?"

"An officer in the Navy."

And the kindly, middle-aged gentleman would place his large hand on the child's curly head and prophesy:

"He'll get to be an admiral."

And this is how man's itinerary is outlined. Let us go back: as point of departure we have a five-year-old boy, two color-print sailors, the sea, the boat, the sky, and, in the sky that day, at that moment, the gull with outspread wings that paused to cast its benediction on the world. This is the starting point, the germ. Then the uncle appears on the scene, places his hand on the boy's head, and from that instant's contentment, from that gleam of happiness in the boy's eyes, deduces what his training and his career shall be, as if he held a piece of chalk in his hand with which to demonstrate at the blackboard the theorum on right-angled triangles. Then comes the caller, who, in his turn, places his hand on the boy's head and foretells the glories of the admiralty. There is missing only the one who might have come next in line and, with the same gesture of the hand, have said to the boy, "Mr. Bigwig, I know that you want to have a fine monument in São João Batista—"

No one, so far as I know, formulated that final wish, but it was implicit in the way they kept pushing the little Anísio. Apparently no one can see a child happy without drawing inferences about his career. Life is never worth anything at the point at which it is. One cannot stop even to enjoy happiness. Life is a race; it is like a rabbit race with its mechanical carrot that moves along the track always at the same distance, impelling the line of simple, unsuspecting competitors. The reward is always just ahead. The final reward will be a first-rate funeral, that melancholy carrot to which no one ever makes any allusion. The more farsighted refrain from predicting the promotion to the rank of admiral, which is the next to the last, and say nothing at all about the last, which is to the rank of the deceased.

I became lost in the digression. Where was I? Ah! yes, I was in that state of mind that brought back my youth, the time when I expected everything from life. I wanted everything, the plenitude of life and the unconditional surrender of the universe.

And then it was that I discovered Eunice and love. I found that I had discovered the key to life, the sum, the entirety, the unity, the synthesis that I had vainly dreamed of acquiring in adventures and fame. Eunice was completeness. Love was the synthesis, the great synthesis of life. Eunice could give me everything. For me she was the *Divine Comedy* without a signature. She was the solution of the mysteries hidden in the atoms. She was the sea, the land. Did I wish to travel, roam distant countries with exotic customs? Each new smile from Eunice brought me the surprise and novelty of the streets of Hong Kong; I found Singapore in her hair; Moscow, Paris, and New York in her arms. And when later we became lovers in Ipiranga Street, I found in Eunice the dream continent that the bold discoverer sees looming from out of the mists on the horizon.

I was walking along the street, conscious of the box of rubies in my pocket. I felt that I had succeeded in striding over a heap of decayed rubble and that I was regaining my absurd faith through an absurd love, a love without any demands, almost without any foundation, and yet, a love that despite everything convinced me that love, the synthesis of life, really existed. I had lost Eunice, I had lost Raul, I had lost the child Jesus that had smiled at me the other day from his seat of misery. I had lost Luciana's whiteness and Augusto's picture. I had lost my blood, everything. But now here was a light shining, here was a voice telling me that it was through a breach like this, through a miracle, that the mysterious world of love is abruptly assailed and that everything is saved. What did that mean? How was I to interpret what was seething inside of me?

I stopped in front of a display window where the reflection of my slender form was superimposed on a profusion of electrical appliances. A chromium-plated toaster gleamed where my heart would have been. I was startled. I must resist that demon inside of me that prompts me to investigate and analyze everything. I clutched my absurd rubies tightly.

Truly absurd. Would it not have been more sensible to leave the 120,000 contos to the girl for streptomiacin and a decent room at the sanitarium? Would it not have been better to distribute the money among the poor? Of course it would have been more sensible. Of course. I could imagine what Eunice would have said and the woman in blue who was passing, if I had told them that I was taking to a waitress jewels that were meant for a princess. And then, too—the thought had just occurred to me—not knowing the value of the earrings, the girl might lose them or be robbed. Might it not be well to put a note in the box stating their value?

No! No! Such an attempt to interfere in someone else's life and take measures for someone else's happiness would be even more absurd. I had tried to make Eunice happy. Raul, too. And this was the result. Besides, most of the tragedies in this world are not caused by cruelty, that is, not by pure, unmitigated malevolence. No. Tragedies, the big ones, are caused, rather, by benevolence, by the blundering, and the tyranny of benevolence. Yet the merest trace of pride left in that generous wine is all that is needed to corrupt the great impetus of love with the corrosive force of egoism. Had I really wanted to save Eunice? Had I really wanted Raul's happiness?

No longer do I presume to bring about anyone's happiness through my offices. It is not within my power to save that poor girl or give her true happiness—calm, enduring happiness. What I am still able to do, and what I should still like to do—because, in spite of everything, without deep analysis or closer consideration, it seems strangely possible—is to carry out that childish idea that sprang from my heart and that I wish to conduct now with all the care with which one holds a bird or a flower in his hand. What I shall be able to do, I think—due honor and glory to pure love!—is to make a reality of that childish notion that occurred to me. I shall be able to hang a pair of blood-red stars upon a poor girl's dying delirium.

The sad little waif with whom I have come to play, the poor little drudge, will be able to die without that inferno of cups in her agony.

"Do you want to exchange deaths with me, Gertrude? Come, in the little while that's left between now and eternity, let's swap! You take my death, and I'll take yours. Here, here's some poetry for you. You give me your apron and your agony."

As I neared the coffee bar, a sudden timidity came over me. What should I do? A boy in shirt sleeves happened to be passing. He had an alert face.

"Do you want to earn ten cruzeiros?"

"Sure."

I explained what it was about and what he should do. I gave him the little box and pointed out the girl inside who was hustling to serve her leeches, and I stayed in the doorway from where I could watch without being seen. The boy went up to the counter, said something to the girl that I did not hear, and handed her the parcel. She looked surprised. She took the box, tested its weight, untied the string, and opened it. Then I hurried away, so that I might not see her happiness.

part 3 JOURNEY TO THE CENTER OF THE EARTH

January 12th

Professor Leidenbrock's Training

As I was running my eyes over my books, looking for one to dispel the long hours' tedium, my attention was drawn to the volumes of Jules Verne, the very ones with which good old Dodo, who was belated at times and anticipatory at others, tried to keep up with my troubled adolescence. The one that attracted me most, perhaps because of the analogy between the situation involved in it and my own, was *Journey to the Center of the Earth.*

Of all Jules Verne's tales of adventure that was the one that had most stirred my imagination. Doubtless, *Michael Strogaff* was more exciting and dramatic, but its clear, horizontal unfolding at the earth's surface lacked the secret force of that other story, whose mystery was one of space rather than of time. It was not a question of experiencing progressive events but of discovering a secret already in existence, hidden in the here and now. It was a vertical adventure.

The story begins in a tranquil house in Hamburg, where an old cook is preparing to announce an excellent Sunday dinner that would be served with punctuality and eaten with good appetite had Professor Lidenbrock not found among the pages of a half-forgotten old book that mysterious cryptogram in runic characters.

As soon as the document is deciphered adventure starts with a rush, what with the tribulations of the cook, who sees the soup getting cold, and the sight of the young Axel, the scholar's nephew, who bids farewell to Gräuben, the pretty seventeen-year-old Estonian girl, very blond and very beautiful. A few days later, following the document's instructions, the exultant professor and his disconsolate nephew embark for Iceland, where they are to descend into the crater of an extinct volcano on their way to the earth's center.

But, foreseeing the perils of the journey and knowing his nephew's delicate nerves, the scholar conceived the idea of taking advantage of their two- or three-days' stop at a Danish port of call. At the top of a steep cliff in this city was an old church spire served by a narrow outer stairway, and it was there that the professor imposed upon his unfortunate nephew a rigorous training against dizziness. Before their descent into the depths he taught him to scale the heights, and he called those salutary exercises "training for the abyss."

Who will give me such training? I, too, am going to take a journey to the earth's center, though a less interesting one than that of the scholar from Hamburg. My penetration of this planet's crust will stop at a depth of six feet, in that most superficial layer that is without either geological or paleontological interest. My crater will have the dimensions of the gravedigger's shovel, and my monsters the diminutiveness of the earthworm. Then a new phase in my story will begin: that convocation of the worms, that fattening of the maggots to which the melancholy Hamlet refers with the comment that not even kingly flesh escapes that underground carrousel.

I can take no heart, however, from such survival; I find no consolation in the pantheistic idea of entering into the great life-cycle whereby I shall be diluted into animals and flowers. In that respect, I agree with Job, who insisted that he would keep his identity: "And though after my skin worms destroy this body, yet in the flesh shall I see God: Whom I shall see for myself, and mine eyes shall behold, and not another."

I glance over at my bed. That is where it will be. I shall have the three spatial coordinates and little need for the fourth. With a bit of imagination I shall overcome its fluidity, I shall seize it in the state *of becoming*, and shall install my corpse there upon the bed.

I shall clothe it in black, I shall put new shoes on it and then stand back to see if my adventurer who is going down six feet into the earth is properly and decently arrayed.

Then anyone of my neighbors or acquaintances who may chance to come to see me will be able to see the pointed toes of my new shoes from the head of the stairs, and through the partly open door, just as navigators catch their first glimpse of mountain peaks on the horizon. After that, they will cover me with flowers, nameless flowers like those of the General, who is receiving his wreaths while he is still living.

January 15th

On the Inside of Things

I remember very clearly; I was probably five or six years old. I was sitting on my heels, watching the gardener transplant. I followed his every move closely. I saw his shovel extract a damp, black clod of earth; I saw his calloused, grimy hands plumb the stalks and then replace the overturned earth, pressing it down with affectionate little pats.

Then, suddenly, I saw a live, translucent earthworm squirming in one of the holes. I bent over that miniature landscape, and it seemed to grow and grow and become filled with tiny inlaid stones, hairlike roots, microscopic insects, and transparent monsters. The ground then, was not so definitive and terminal a thing as I had thought and as children brought up on city streets conceive it to be. The world of living things continued indefinitely beneath it.

There are two kinds of curiosity. The first, which I shall call moral curiosity, or that I might perhaps, call feminine curiosity, is that which is interested in the dramatic or merely episodic aspects of a situation. It glues the eye to the keyhole, alerts the ear to malicious tittle-tattle, and stands young girls at a wedding on tip-toe to see the bridegroom's face and the bride's gown.

In more morbid instances, it is that curiosity that prompts the landlady to rummage through her new boarder's desk drawers in search of his genealogy and his fortune, good and bad.

The other curiosity is what I should call metaphysical. More penetrating, demanding, and relentless, it makes straight for the heart of things. If it peers through the keyhole, it is not just to see what is inside, but to examine that thing thoroughly, whatever it may be. When it is directed to a person it is concerned only secondarily with the episodic: what it seeks is the person's core, wherein lies his innermost secret.

Now, for me, one part of Jules Verne's *Journey to the Center of the Earth* is highly symbolical. Unlike Marfa and Nadia, who in the tale of the Tzar's courier, accompany the hero in his adventures, the cook and the young Gräuben remain behind; they are abandoned, so to speak, the more distinctly to emphasize the masculine nature of curiosity that is piercing and vertical. I doubt, however, that the good Jules Verne, himself, had any such subtlety in mind. The symbolism of a work of fiction may be as unconscious as that of one's dreams.

One day I was given a little music box. One wound it up, and it sang. It was always the same faint little tune over and over, as if the box were eager to disclose some prodigious secret that no one had as yet deciphered. I had a wild desire to see what the box had inside. Not that that desire came from a precocious propensity for engineering. No. It was not the logical operation of its various parts, not the functional aspect that interested me: it was purely the metaphysics of its inner workings. What I wanted was to arrive through a direct and piercing apprehension at the vital part of the thing, its essence. When finally I managed to ravish that little coffer of cedarwood, and when I saw a coiled spring inside and a device with strips of metal that emitted a plaintive tinkle, I was as rapturously triumphant as the discoverer of buried treasure. But boredom followed quickly, and the poor broken hand organ lay in a corner, forgotten.

Not until much later did I discover that I was an ego, that is, a hidden and isolated thing, segregated from the rest of the universe. Then came the confused and inexpressible idea of there having been an extraordinary coincidence in the fact of my being myself. Not that I judged myself to be better or worse than the rest. Evaluation came afterwards, and when it did come it devastated my life. But what I discovered in myself at that time was something that because of its essential nature I could attribute to no one else. It was a category that excluded itself from everything and denied any comparison.

If I tried to project that self, shift its center to wherever another self might be, then immediately that other self would disappear—crushed, pulverized, annihilated by the invasion of the impenetrable self that drives every other entity from its place of occupancy.

At that time I did not state the problem in so many words, of course, nor had I read Rilke's lines ". . . and even though one of them [the angels] suddenly took me to heart, I should die of his stronger existence."

Unconsciously, I, myself, was a sort of apprentice angel, clasping things to my breast only to see them die from the youthfulness and domination of my being.

The universe was divided thereafter into categories, the self and the non-self; and between those two orders there began a conflict without truce. The non-self, of course, exerted a potent force as if, in counterattack, it were endeavoring to neutralize the incendiary power of the angel's wings. And the little boy who had discovered the immense treasure continued to be a poor, dependent creature. When it rained, for example, he could not run and play in the yard; with nose flattened against the window pane, he had to watch humbly from inside the great washing of houses and trees. Yet, in compensation, the vast non-self, with its thunder, and its mountains, and its clouds in the sky, was in one respect at the mercy of its young master. Whenever he was a lone spectator, then everything round about obeyed him. He had only to move for everything else to move, only to stand still for everything else to stand still; and when he spun around, heaven and earth, all in a tangle, spun too.

If anyone saw the little boy playing alone in his yard that afternoon, running and standing still, and gesticulating, he probably found it amusing, not realizing that the child was exercising his sovereignty over all the universe.

When I was fifteen, in the full flush of adolescence, I tried to emerge from myself, as one who puts on airs. I composed poetry. It was an attempt at communication. Its rhythmic hammering could, perhaps, be the telegraphy of imprisoned souls. But the verses that I composed did not come from within, from my incommunicable self, and, hence, were not communicable. They came from others, and I, like an automaton, merely repeated them.

Then I applied myself to observing others to see whether I could find myself reflected in them. How often the friend who was talking with me was all unsuspecting of the sustained tense, feverish attention with which I was following every fleeting movement of his face, noting it and keeping it, so that later I might organize in secret the enormous dictionary of unspoken words!

I discovered the remarkable way in which the imitation of someone's outward features may enable one to identify himself with that person. The important thing was to put myself in the other person's place without destroying him; then, with every precaution, I would begin from the outside and by imitating his gestures, his voice, his carriage, I would proceed to the penetration of his soul. Gradually, by following that method, I succeeded in understanding many things that I had thought inaccessible. For instance, I had only to thrust out my chest, clear my throat, give my voice a nasal twang, to understand a whole series of inner associations that constituted my Uncle Heitor's rather disagreeable personality.

Even today, in spite of all that has happened to me, including the cancer, if I were to go to the beach with shirt unbuttoned at the neck and with a bearing more positive and confident than my usual one, I should feel the cheerful well-being of Copacabana's successful, sherbet-licking citizens take possession of me. What is the meaning of this? Am I so little a thing that I depend on a shirt? Am I an empty thing?

The truth is that many a personality is explained by the thickness of the neck, the voice, the hat brim. Actors on the stage are much more real than one thinks, or else the real world is much more of a stage than one imagines.

The problem of which I caught but a glimpse in childhood has come back to me today. I am returning to metaphysics after a long and painful pilgrimage through moral problems. I shall abandon all the exciting questions concerning other people, since I, myself, am for myself a closed drawer, a compact rock, a bottomless gulf. For myself I am a little hand organ whose coiled spring and plaintively tinkling device the anatomy charts have shown me. And what else am I? For myself, I am a hidden presence, a rattling nut, a sealed bag, a pocket sewn together.

Now, everything that is said and done, everything with any degree of sense or nonsense, depends on the solution of that enigma. Who am I? For life to have meaning and for death itself to have some decency, I must know who I am, why I am living, why I am dying, why I am weeping. Of what use to learn the million relationships of the outer world if I cannot apprehend the substantial reality that they convey? Of what good is it to measure the sun's distance and analyze the configuration of the uranium atom if I do not know the length, breadth, and depth of my own being? What will it avail me to gain the whole universe if I lose my soul?

January 20th

The Broken Clock

Would it be correct to say that a religious thought entered my mind today for the first time since my school days of long ago? No. I do not believe that I can say that. That thought which came today with a certain clarity has never been far away. Silent and discreet, it has been here, there, and everywhere. Like those things to which our eyes have grown accustomed—this wardrobe, that bookcase, the clock, the vase—the thought of God, a familiar, forgotten thought, was part of my surroundings. And so were its details. Yes, in an old setting to which I no longer paid any attention God's details surrounded me: The Cross, the bells, the candles, the painted images, the angels, the saints, and the veiled and elaborately clad figure of the Virgin. I never used those things, I never paid any attention to them, but now while communing with myself I proposed the following experiment: to conceive of a world without crosses and candles and images of Our Lady. And at once I registered my soul's first impulse: such a world would be horrible.

What am I to think of that reaction? Do I still, I wonder, have the same faith more deeply rooted than I thought? Or in those reminiscences am I seeking a remedy for my fear of the death that is devouring me?

Again I make the experiment and I ask my soul, "Should you wish to live (or die) in a world without the signs of Christ's passage?"

Now the answer is slow in coming. Forewarned and wary, my soul no longer knows whether that reaction of a few minutes ago was really its own. And it is precisely this that torments me: to be able to distinguish between what is my own and what others try to inculcate in me or rather what everyone tries to inculcate in everyone else. I do not say that I can accept only those truths that are of my own fabrication. There was a time when I almost went so far as to consider myself a solitary god in exile, and I can guarantee that that is quite an uncomfortable experience. No; what I demand of truth, whether it come from outside, from heaven or earth, is the possibility of a profound assimilation, a transforming fusion that will make it truly my own. I want a truth that can be transformed into my flesh and blood and not one that is mechanical and orthopedic. I have a horror of the rubber-stamped soul's unperturbed objectivity.

How can some souls, Dr. Aquiles' for example, echo and re-echo with faith? I know, of course, that theological faith, a gratuitous gift from God, is an infused virtue that hides in the soul's depths, like the oyster hidden in the depths of the sea. I know, too, as though it were a lesson learned by heart, that the *luz tenebrosa* of which the mystic speaks illuminates but dimly the surface of our sensibility. Yet, even so, hidden and wavering, some presence must manifest itself, some echo must be heard. How? How does so extraordinary a presence—the presence of a God—manifest itself in the acts and gestures, and in the thoughts and dreams of Dr. Aquiles?

I remember that when I was a pious little boy at the Fathers' school religion was one of the things that I used without being fully conscious of them. Later, when I discarded my uniform, though I was unaware of it, I discarded my piety as well. Then came the crisis of growing up. And then Eunice. After that, I cannot recall any consciousness of religion. When I tortured Eunice, or, like a thief, followed her closely in the street, it did not enter my mind that I might be sinning. I was horrible and repellent to myself, but it did not occur to me that I might be doing something that was ugly in the sight of God. Nor did I think of Eunice's faults as wronging the Creator. The only one wronged was I.

The problem therefore, did not exist; or if it did, it was forgotten in the background, like the pictures on the wall, chairs, and aunts, when one is agitated by the flame of passion.

There are many things like that around us of which we take no notice. There are many things that remain hidden because of our inattention. I well remember the day I was drawing the plan for our house, this house. I had traced the rectangular structure in a trapezium, which represented the lot. And inside the rectangle I had outlined others where we were to live: front room here, kitchen there, bathroom, bedroom— One's house is an expansion of one's body, and, incidentally, that is why it cannot be so strictly functional as certain rationalistic architects now pretend. The uses to which the human body is put vary greatly during the course of life. It is with the same body that an individual who is today a cyclist on holiday will be a senator of the republic tomorrow. The body has a great plasticity and can adjust itself to the sportsmen's saddle and the parliamentarian's chair alike. Now the life of a house varies also; and in order that the house may not be too logical for one situation and absurd for another, its design must be sufficiently neutral to adapt itself to birth and death or whatever the days may bring. Architects must realize that a house has to be in some measure organic, and if a wing has to be added or a wall torn down, they must not regard it as an act of heresy.

Well, I was designing the rooms of our house, and I had just made an opening in a wall of one of the rectangles—"The door must be farther this way, or there'll not be room for the clothes closet."

It was Eunice. Leaning over my shoulder, she was pointing out the deficiency of that still abstract wall with a polished, rosy fingernail. I changed the location of the door, and she gave me a kiss. The plan was ready. The penciled lines were a forecast of our happiness. Here was the living room where we should talk together for hours. There was the bedroom. Here was the door, that same door— But that afternoon when Eunice slammed it with a bang, shouting that her life was a hell, and I, with clenched fists stood in the middle of the room, crazed with grief, which one of us remembered that the door was a door, that the floor was the floor? Which one of us still had any remembrance of the rectangles drawn with loving care?

Besides, even on peaceful days, I come in, I walk across the room, go up the stairs, and open the wardrobe, all without pausing for an instant's thought, without taking any courteous heed of things. Ah! how inattentive we can be!

Another time—there were so many such!—we had reached an intolerable degree of tension. The words of violence we uttered were disconnected, cut off, like the immature cells of my blood as it is today. Suddenly, as I was making a quick, angry gesture, I inadvertently struck the clock, which fell to the floor with a dull thud followed by a plaintive moan. I stooped to pick it up. The glass was shattered, the hand twisted, the pendulum caught, and the spring protruding like a rupture.

"Do you suppose it can be mended?"

"I don't know—probably—"

It was a birthday remembrance. We had bought it together at the antique dealer's. Eunice had been delighted with the pattern of the bronze, the good taste of the dial, and especially the pendulum's two tubes of mercury. I had tried to explain the principle of compensation, telling her about the center of gravity and thermal dilation; but Eunice grew bored. She preferred to think the mercury was there just for her pleasure. I conceded that she was right and put my scientific knowledge away.

When we got the clock home, we were uncertain about the best place to put it. Finally we left it in the living room, and for several days we enjoyed it. Sometimes we would stop talking, waiting for it to strike. It had a slightly minor key, reminiscent of an old harpsichord.

Then it withdrew into the background, as much as to say, "Don't mind me, I'll go right on attending to my business—"

"Do you suppose it can be mended?"

I was examining the disfigured clock. It seemed to rebuke me. "What harm have I ever done to you?" And around me, the table, the pictures, the Japanese vase, Mama's picture, all seemed to be looking at me with one accord. I was a criminal.

Do you suppose I have struck God? Whence comes to me now the acute sensation of having struck something innocent when I knocked over the clock? The clock was innocent. For years its pendulum had swung back and forth, with unvarying humility. For years it had repeated its modest little favor every half hour, inserting thus into the minutes' routine the poetry of correct time. It struck its simple music. If we cared to listen, well and good; if we did not, it would continue its obligatory tick-tock without sulking.

Raul, too, was innocent. He grew and wasted his futile little favors on the air of our tempestuous life. Ah! if only we could at all times be aware of the deep innocence of children and of things; yes, the innocence and humility of things. I ought to have kissed the clock that day, and every day I ought to have stooped to kiss the ground, the good ground that is the foundation of things—

I did kiss it just now. Perhaps too late. The house is empty— A moment ago I said that the echo of faith should be an awareness of a presence. And that awareness is all that is needed to modify the whole nature of our actions. There is an enormous difference between the attitude of a man who feels himself alone and that of him who is living in someone's presence. All our reactions are altered. The person does not have to be beside us, looking at us or holding our hand. He may be elsewhere in the house, speaking over the telephone or making arrangements with the cook. The person is there. "Elle est là," as the poet said of the Virgin.

The essential things about a presence is that it can be counted on and that it, in turn, counts on us. Even though it may go out shopping, the fact that it may come back any moment is a promise, and already a presence. The house is left empty, but not dead. Some part of the presence has remained to bespeak its return; its belongings, all the many things that bear its stamp, its dresses, its motionless shoes asleep in a corner of the room, awaiting the impatient little foot.

The truly empty house is quite another thing. It is dead.

Have I felt God's presence, I wonder? Shall I be able to comprehend a presence that puts infinite constraint upon me and yet leaves me infinitely free? I am beginning to think that I shall. For I can conceive also of a thing that digs deep into my soul: I can conceive of the terrible humility of a God wounded in his infinite innocence—

I see a God who makes himself small, a God fallen at my feet, who asks like the clock that fell, "What harm have I ever done to you?"

January 24th

The Duel with Sirius

The suffocating heat drove me from my room. I took a grass mat out to the back terrace and stretched out, with my arms flung wide and my eyes fixed on the starry sky. Away up high was the brilliant quadrilateral of Orion with its Three Marys in the center— Three Marys or the Warrior's Belt, according to whether one is inspired by Christian piety or pagan turbulence. Farther down, in the direction of the General's mansion, the one-eyed Bull was visible with its magnificent, blood-red Aldebaran; and not far from the celestial horns, still more to the west, glittered St. Peter's Chair, innocent bauble of crystal beads, partly twisted, but still intact, lying along the floor of the heavens, beside Taurus. It takes a long time to pick out the feet of that fragile chair.

And meanwhile all that is moving. I, myself, held fast to my microscopic terrace, am falling into a dark cavity. The earth, the sun, and the stars are moving, but like the rhythm of the roses, the rhythm of that great saraband is too slow for my heart. The figures traced by the stars have not changed since those far-off nights when the Chaldean shepherds filled the sky with dragons, bears, and legendary giants. Five thousand years ago the Bull was already there with its inflamed eye, and the fragile, twisted little chair was tossed there long before the time of Saint Peter. The Little Bear—that I can not see from here—was already wheeling like a Swiss clock, a sort of gigantic cuckoo-clock, around its wide-open polar eye when men of restless heart were beginning to roam the land and sail the sea, glancing occasionally at that plaything of the heavens in search of orientation and coordination for their uncertain feet.

And so has it always been: whenever man wants to know the ground he is treading, he looks to the sky; when he wants to direct his movements, he seeks something fixed.

The nebulous Milky Way looks like a great, frayed ribbon tied around the whole universe—a Christmas present that the angels have forgotten to open.

No. The Milky Way does not tie up the whole universe. It is only one spark of that immense explosion that we call the universe. It has the form of a lentil seed and it includes about a hundred billion stars in its domain. The other galaxies, at distances that cannot be measured with the minute base of our planetary orbit but are measured by the analysis of light, leave me with a feeling of strangeness as do houses and cities other than one's own and countries in which foreign tongues are spoken. The Milky Way is *ours*.

You who like to raise walls and mark boundaries, O human heart, see if you can find even a tiny haven in that galaxy that is yours and that encompasses a hundred billion stars. See if you can think of a flag for that corner of the universe.

It has been estimated that every earthling can consider himself the owner of thirty thousand stars. However, as only seven thousand are visible, the ordinary mortal's allotment cannot be seen. Who owns Aldebaran, I wonder? And to whom has Sirius been given? Not to me. I must be content with the more modest share of thirty thousand invisible stars that tomorrow or the day after no one will find on the executor's list of my goods and chattels.

Yesterday when I saw a streetcar go by I asked myself the poet's perplexed question: "Why so many legs? Today, going from legs to the stars, I am lost in the same useless quandary. Why so many stars?"

There is something cruel, a sort of imposition, in the fact of a thing's existence. The comfort that the intelligence experiences when it examines the properties of things and the connections by which they are related becomes anguish when it considers the thing from the mysterious and gratuitous side of its existence. No existence can be explained; none can be justified.

Aldebaron, once it exists, has distance, velocity, chemical composition, spectrum, and temperature. All that appears before my eyes in combination as a glittering celestial ruby. Yes, the star is all that, once that it exists. But why does it exist? Why so many legs on earth and so many stars in heaven? If the existence of one alone surpasses my comprehension, what, then, can be said of that profusion, that prodigious exuberance?

"The Southern Cross, which the beautiful Sophia would not gaze upon as Rubião begged her to do, is too high in the heavens to distinguish between man's laughter and tears." Then my stockholder's share in the universe—the thirty thousand invisible stars —must be a joke. They are too high. Indifferent. Any pretension to the crosses and bears of the heavens must be vanity on our part. They are inaccessible. Aloof. And I, a worm bound to that grain of sand that is our planet must be a microscopic monster of chance, with no ascendancy in that whitish, gaseous realm of which I was boasting but a moment ago.

I gaze at Sirius, and from here below, from this ground to which I am bound, despite my suffering, my leukemia, my unfinished memories—even more unfinished than my blood cells—I hurl defiance at the bright blue globe that looks down upon me from on high, from its abyss fifty light years deep.

"Oh sun, Oh diaphanous matter, Oh immensity lost in immensity, here am I where thou seest me, a Man. A conscious worm, *roseau pensant.* Which is the greater, Sirius or Pascal? Which of the two is of greater worth, the sun or the melancholy thinker?

"Oh star, Parsifal lost in the heavens, thou knowest not thy name. With thy excessive and a little ridiculous gases, thou dost go wandering about, Oh innocent, simple absolute. Thou dost stray as one blind, pass by as one deaf, and roam aimlessly as one who has lost his memory and whose eyes have a vacant stare. And see, notice that to humiliate thee it is even from man that I draw my images. In truth, thou art less than one blind, or deaf, or bereft of memory. The half of my table is richer than thy sphere of simplified atoms. Of what value is size? What nobility is there in distance? Thou art chained to thy equations; more truly bound than the constellation of Andromeda, portrayed as a woman in chains. Thou art Sirius, Alpha Canis Majoris, and thou hast right ascension and right descension. But we earthworms make use of thy splendor; we capture and tame it and inscribe it in the *Nautical Almanac.* Thou art no more than a colossal servant. I am a worm, but I am aware of it. I am wretched and I know it. I am ridiculous and I laugh. I am guilty and I weep."

"Alas! The race of Pascal is betrayed. There are many here, Oh star, who say that we, too, are in chains, that we, too, are only an agglomeration of atoms that for a certain time remain within our sphere, in the corner of an elbow, on the bridge of the nose, in the fleeting follicles of the hair. They say, too, that we are empty, that we live upon the shell that society lends us or upon the eructations of ill-digested experience. But let not those detractors deceive thee, Oh star. Ironically, their stupidity is the counterproof of our dignity. We have a great privilege, which is the underside of our royal mantle: we have the glory of error.

"But I shall not argue with thee, Oh star. I shall not dispute. I need only present myself for what I am—a man. The light that reaches my retina does not encounter an inert, passive thing, like a plate covered with bromate—a thing that receives the image, develops it in the liquid organic humors, fixes it in the hyposulphate of the mind, and then laughs, speaks, dances, and weeps in accordance with this impact of the photons. No. To think is not merely to receive. It is something more active, something that goes out to meet the object. When the star's light knocks at the door of my senses something within me rises from a throne, receives the messenger, examines the message, appropriates it, transforming and refining it and then says to its dazzling vassal in the sky: 'Thou art Sirius, Alpha Canis Majoris'."

I do not find it absurd to think that the whole of that sky is a spectacle for our eyes. Everything is ours. Before Pascal, the Apostle Paul expressed, in a different way, the paradox of our misery, and our greatness. "We, then, as poor—yet possessing all things." *Omnia possidentes.* I know, of course, that the apostle is referring to another plane, but why may I not apply his word to the realities of our own world?

Everything is ours. Now, with broader vision, I shall not insist upon partitioning the heavens in order to segregate the thirty thousand stars that have been allotted to me. Everything belongs to each and every one of us. Let us socialize the constellations.

The sky is a vast city park. The stars are roses that the good citizens must take care not to pull out—roses whose public duty it is to embellish the simple dreams of penniless lovers. What do I care about light years? What do I care about the figures that seek to bring panic to our thoughts, as though numbers had the power to cleave the universe in two? Everything is ours. The sky has come down to earth; the stars are the lights of our abode. Shine, shine on, Sirius, Canopus, Achernar; for down here below I am strolling slowly among the groves of thy brightly lighted park.

January 28th

The Universe à double face

As I think again of the starry sky and the streetcar jammed with legs, there comes to my mind the idea that the universe is an enormous contrivance *à double face.* I see two aspects, or two principles: one of order and economy, which governs the orbits of the stars with a precision nothing short of parsimoniousness; and the other of gay disorder and fantastic prodigality, which thrusts upon us the gratuitous existence of the stars and the flowers, of species and the individuals within the species.

When we study a phenomenon, seeking its explanation, the universal law that will surely lead us to the solution is the law of economy. Now, for example, I see the moon appearing on the low line of the horizon. I know that geometrically it is still below the horizon. It is the refraction of its light that announces its coming and that, so to speak, slants my visual beam. Does that mean that, under certain circumstances, a ray of light may relax its rectilinear rigidity and come to my retina obliquely? No. We know that light is refracted so that when it enters a new medium it may find the shortest distance. And so where caprice appears to intrude, discipline actually prevails.

If we calculate the earth's orbit and ask the reason for the curvature at each point, we shall have the same answer: the least distance. And it is thus in the entire physical universe; even in the bubbling, disconcerting intimacy of the atoms the same discipline is to be found—the law of chance ready to confirm the law of the minimum, the law of the least interval.

On the other hand, when we consider the mere fact of existence, and not the properties of things or their mode of generation, we are compelled to recognize that masculine aspect of the universe which is lavish and adventurous. Existence in itself cannot be explained. It is accepted. That is the limitless point of departure of every procedure of the intelligence. The universe, that well-ordered universe, appears to us then as a disordered spree, a bounty, a luxuriance born of freedom without restraint.

Men whose eyes are weary do not see the festive nature of existence. They look upon all things as routine. Hens lay eggs, and from the eggs emerge hens. The two marvels are neutralized by the regularity of the phenomenon, which is as routine and punctual as the eight-forty-five streetcar. That is the view of the Rationalist, the Determinist, I might even say the Essentialist.

But there is a madcap way of looking at the world which denies the intelligible, and denies causality and law. And that is the view of the Irrationalist, the Indeterminist, the Existentialist.

It is in the realm of human behavior, that other universe of freedom, however, that the twofold principles of economy and adventure acquires singular importance.

For the Rationalist, the history of man is fully explained by the law of least effort, that is, by economy. Printing, for example, was invented to spare effort—a truth only if one acknowledges the extravagant madness that impels man to read and, above all, to write. Navigation, according to the same theorist, developed only because of trade—a truth only if one admits the unreasonableness that prompts man to seek what is beyond his reach. If one takes as a starting point the quest for articles such as pepper, cloves, and cinnamon, the recklessness of the great voyagers becomes comprehensible and the spirit of adventure disappears. What then partakes of poetry and daring, what becomes obscure and half-mad is the desire that besets the human heart to mingle the condiments of another hemisphere with the cabbages from his own garden.

I am reminded at this point of a Marxist manual that has come into my hands. In order to combat what he calls spiritualism its author proves the nonexistence of freedom with this excellent argument: an orator has to drink water because prolonged eloquence dries the throat. He drinks it, therefore, out of physical and psychological necessity and not from free will.

Never, so far as I know, has there been a writer so senselessly spiritualistic that he has denied the existence of the throat. The orator does indeed drink water because his throat has become dry. This explanation fits well into any philosophical doctrine and into any religion. It is a clear, succinct explanation. But what is not so clear now, particularly for a Marxist, is the reason for the eloquence. And if to the Marxist preaching we add the fervor and pathos which are characteristic features of eloquence, the attitude of that individual who is now drinking his glass of water in a moment's bright rationality will become more and more mysterious.

Marxism, as everybody knows, is a great adventure whose objective is to purge human history of the spirit of adventure. It may be the final adventure to end all adventure, the final fervent impulse to kill all fervor, the final heroic effort to liquidate all heroism.

Moreover, to return to the glass of water, I must remark that the Determinist, for whom everything is as clear as water, begins to be troubled when he is confronted by the extravagant collection of liquids with which men have become accustomed to satisfy their physiological need. One has only to consider the poetry of multicolored bottles on the store shelves. The glass of water can be explained (though it is still harder to explain the frieze that ornaments, I believe, even Soviet glasses), but without poetry and adventure, without the creative instinct of man, it becomes difficult to explain the wine, the beer, the liqueurs, the Coca Cola, the guaraná,[1] the absinthe, the vodka, the cauim,[2] the fruit juices, and all the concoctions, the combinations, and the varieties of liquid that men are in the habit of serving in cups, goblets, and glasses.

Had anyone happened to be traveling on the southern seas in 1911, at a certain latitude and longitude he would have seen on the horizon a brig or a schooner with its prow turned toward the remote austral regions. He would have learned afterwards that he had seen the ship of the intrepid Norwegian Amundsen in search of the South Pole.

There he is on the bridge, the stubborn old lover of the Poles, talking with the ship's captain. What does he want of his ship and his captain? Obviously he wants to find the shortest way to the South Pole. But that legitimate and understandable desire was surpassed by Amundsen's desire for the Pole itself. And I find it difficult to deduce from human nature, even when the individual is a Norwegian, that irrepressible yearning for the point where the meridians converge.

What Amundsen wanted, as a man and as a geographer, was to study a part of the earth and take the result of his research to the Royal Geographical Institute of Christiania. What every scholar seeks is the joy of knowledge and the joy of communicating that knowledge to others. Of course, there were many goals,

[1] A beverage made from the berries of a Brazilian shrub (trans.).
[2] A beverage made from fermented manioc (trans.).

however, many routes to satisfy a geographer's hunger for knowledge and his thirst for communication. Amundsen chose the South Pole. He chose the longest possible distance between his study and the great hall of the Royal Institute.

And now, yes, now that he has once chosen the longest way, the geodetic folly of adventure, there he is on the bridge trying to economize time, distance, equipment, and fuel. There is the adventure-scientist looking for the shortest course on the longest route.

The evolutionary theory, too, sprang from that same incapacity to understand and to allow the aspect of adventure that set the history of the world aquiver. To that type of observer the variety of species presents an intolerable lack of order.

Though it is admissible to seek the explanation that best conforms to the criterion of casual economy, the Evolutionist carries that reasonable tendency to the point of madness with his senseless idea of stifling at birth what he considers a prurience for disorder. He endeavors to impose a boarding-school discipline on the universe and dreams of making all things march in file, from the crab to the discoverer of the South Pole.

The Existentialist, on the other hand, aspires to release man from the chains put upon him by the principle of economy, leaving him always at the threshold of an adventure. Man does not acquire human nature; he is always at the point of origin; he is always being born, still moist from the fluid of birth.

Is it, I wonder, in that message that so heightens the value of concreteness and individual experience that I must seek preparation for my journey into the abyss of death? I have come to think so. Struck with horror by the blithe air of the Rationalist, who confuses reality with the reticulate area illumined by a forty-watt bulb, I am turning to vertigo for shelter.

Yet now that I have defeated in challenge the brightest star in the heavens, I cannot despise the lance that brought me my victory.

Besides, I have just had a horrible vision, that of an adventure without any rules for guidance. I saw an Existentialist Amundsen smiling at me like a somnambulist and beckoning with disordered gestures from the gunwale of his galley, which was without helm or sextant and without maps or direction.

The solution, if there is one, must be in the synthesis suggested by the star-filled sky. Neither one thing nor the other, but both. I am reminded of what Plato said: "When I am obliged to choose between two alternatives, like a child, I choose both." But then—

I paused. The thought that I am a dying man, or rather, a man-who-knows-that-he-is-about-to-die, clutched at my throat. It threw me on the bed. It tossed with me and possessed me. It ravished me without shame. It defeated me—yes, though it was I who had just defeated a star.

February 2nd

Jandira's Carnival

Today, breaking her distrustful (I might even say hostile) reserve, my cook came to me about a highly important matter: her holiday during Carnival.

Indeed, that melancholy festivity that for a certain number of days will engross the attention of the people and their solicitous governors, is drawing near. There is talk of restoring the ancient splendor of the Carioca Carnival as though the country's honor were at stake. And the humble little people of the slums, though ever more impoverished and tortured, take up their drums and bemoan their simplified happiness.

There are ten days yet. Where shall I be on Mardi Gras? Jandira, my austere cook, cannot imagine the enormity that she is proposing, by forcing me to think, to foresee and plan that colossal ten-day future. She does not know that for me her request brings reverberations from the Millenium and the Apocalypse. She is not thinking about the end of the world. With the staunch unawareness of persons whose blood is for the moment normal, she is planning to undertake that most terrifying of all adventures—preparation. I believe she has already bought all the little things needful for her costume, and from what I could gather through the fog created by my eschatalogical considerations, my good cook is going to dress up as a Cossack.

She will go to the Carnival. It is indispensable that she go, indispensable that she spend these days in that suffocating costume, and that, despite the fact that she is no longer a young girl, she subject her corpulence to forced marches and drills that would knock out a Marine. Oh yes, she will go; she must go; she cannot fail to go.

Now, I do not believe that it is simply the attraction of a rest from work—time off, as they say—that prompts the sensible Jandira to exchange her casserole for a tambourine during a period of three days. Her motives are more profound. In the first place, we must consider her justifiable feeling that she has a right to the exuberance for which she can find neither opportunity nor spectators in the repressive atmosphere of the kitchen. There is something of the poet and of the madcap and the clown in us all. Now, dressed as a Cossack, Jandira will realize those three universal callings, which will not fail to have an appreciable result.

The principal motive, however, is, I believe, of another order. Like all of us, Jandira has to find some outward support in order to be freed from her metaphysical anguish. She has to flee from nothingness. She has to feel that she is alive. And for this there is nothing better than to become a part of collectivity, part of a conjunction that props us up, part of a group that increases the density of our being.

If she goes to the Carnival, Jandira will become an integral part of collectivity. The tambourines and the other fanciful costumes will serve to reinforce the shell, the crust of her personality. If she does not go, even though her legs may get a good rest, she will feel cast out, worse still, disembodied. Now, no one wants to be a spirit; so one must enter into the great corporeal symphony. One must parade and dance and, in short, do what everyone else is doing.

Then, too, it must be remarked that, like Pascal's traveler who travels so that he may talk about it later, Jandira wants to gain the right to say that she has gone and that she has paraded and danced.

The most important thing in life is to be present at whatever is taking place, and the next most important thing is to be entitled to exploit that simultaneity and concomitance of the body. More than bread, man needs something to talk about. And as the most imperceptible abstractions are invariably rooted in things visible and audible, one must from time to time let one's sleeping-self rub up against what is going on in the world, lest the soul become cramped.

A fire is a calamity; but to have seen a fire is a satisfaction. The man-who-saw-the-fire is a man who enjoys a heart-warming, if ephemeral, prestige. People will listen to what he has to say. In the circles in which the others have been discussing the deplorable event, the-man-who-saw-the-fire speaks from the chair to a temporarily inferior audience who have merely heard the news or seen a photograph, and can only conjecture or express banalities about firemen and burning buildings. It is quite different with him; having shared in the incident, he can savor it in all its concreteness, which is the prize drawn from the lottery of happenings.

It is for such transcendental reasons, I believe, that my austere cook is sewing on her Cossack's blouse, with the smile of a bride-to-be playing about her lips.

But what is true of a cook is equally true of the cook's mistress, though with different manifestations. Some time ago when Father Lebret was here preaching his Economy and Humanism, I had occasion to observe his audience. In it were a number of attentive ladies. They had gone to the Father's lectures, and there they were relishing the good, substantial prize offered by those two well-labeled hours (Father Lebret's Lecture). She who stayed home, when they told her next day that Dulce and Marta had attended, felt herself shrink in stature.

The lecturer is not deceived. He knows that the majority of people present want nothing more from his teaching than they want from a chair: contact, support, a remedy against loneliness. The lecturer, his theses, and his conclusions are like so many strips of clothing fluttering atop the mast of a lost raft. The preeminently important part of Father Lebret's lecture is the right it confers to say next day: "Yesterday, at Father Lebret's lecture—"

I remember Cerqueira. He used to like to tell how he had reached Paris in August, 1939, on the last train to run out of Berlin on a peacetime schedule. That coincidence had assumed the aspect of connivance in my friend's mind. For him the last train savored of participation in the great world events with which it had become associated, and permitted him to discourse on Hitler's policies and the armies' maneuvers in North Africa freely and with authority. From the facts he went on to philosophical ideas, and if any one of us disagreed with his principles the last train would always be brought into it as a sort of diploma that gave him entrée to the European drama with permission to predict the downfall of empires included.

And as for us who did not reach Paris by the last train, who did not witness the London fires, which one of us, in that same

August of 1939, when confronted by the terrible headlines that announced the War and foretold starvation and pestilence, which one of us, peaceful men and of exemplary habits, did not feel a strange and indefinable satisfaction lurking like a snake within his confusion and distressed perplexity?

I said a while ago that Pascal explains most travel by the desire to seek food for vanity and a theme for discourse. One travels to obtain a diploma, like that of the Bachelor, or to add to one's store of subjects for conversation. One travels to return with primitive drums in his trunk and volcanoes in his memory. I suspect that there may be an occasional traveler who has no thought of return, but I am sure that in general the chief reason for starting out is the wish to come back with broadened personality.

Yet that very idea, like everything pertaining to man, has two faces. That eagerness to bring wars and earthquakes and cyclones home and into the living room as subjects for discussion is, to my mind, very fine. On the other hand, I find regrettable that desire to enrich the fabric of one's personality from the outside with complete surrender of the greatest adventure of all, which is the conquest of one's self, the discovery of one's soul. There are two lightings upon the face of a Marco Polo: on one side the sunny brightness of good adventure; on the other, the green pallor of the man who is running away from himself.

At present, it is the somber aspect that impresses me more; and because of the state I am in it seems, indeed, worse than somber. What man looks for over the continents is the same thing that Eunice used to look for when she clicked along the street in her high heels, submitting to the elements of human geology, like the snowball that keeps getting bigger and bigger on the outside. And what is inside? A chance pebble, a circumstantial splinter, a mere nothing.

As for me, I shall stay here; I shall not go forth. Let everything, then, come to me: the Oriental isles seen from the gunwale of an incoming ship in the blue shadows of dusk, the galleries of dead geniuses in the quiet halls of museums, street scenes never witnessed, landscapes that appear to spring from nowhere like a joyous surprise, castles, forests, cathedrals—let them all come and let them fill me and surround me and give me protection and repose so that my consciousness may be lost like a bubble in the center of a mountain of glass.

I once knew a spiritualist who belied Pascal. He was a modest employee in the Judicial Section of the Ministry of Finance who dreamed of taking a trip to Europe. When I knew him all hope of realizing his dream had already been worn out by the daily routine of living, but he was seeking a source of consolation and a definitive ideal in the theories of Allan Kardec.

He would not go to Europe now; but he would go *afterwards*, that is, he would take his trip, which was to be for rest and relaxation, as a spirit-of-the-other-world. Disencumbered from the heavy fleshy wrapping that had bound him so humiliatingly to the job in the Ministry of Finance, his vacationing psyche would happily visit the museums in Paris and the Doges' Palace in Venice.

I really do not know, or at least I am unable to remember, whether my man, or rather, my phantom, was to fly over the seas or whether, despite his disembodiment, he would still need a ship. I subscribe to the latter supposition, since any good trip that is to be taken for rest and relaxation must begin with the so-called delights of life on shipboard.

From that supposition I draw the following conclusions. If the dead man had the advantage of invisibility over the ordinary passengers, which exempted him from the price of passage and the inconvenience of customs, because of that very invisibility he had the disadvantage of not being able to communicate. Agreeing with Pascal rather than with the functionary, I conclude that it would be very dismal to travel as a ghost. I can conceive of him leaning over the ship's gunwale all dejected and sad in his enveloping fluids; mortified in his invisibility. Or, worse still, I can imagine that, moved by a nostalgic urge, he might attempt some abnormal intercourse, which would only frighten those around him and increase his solitude.

Much more sensible than the spiritualist's dream is the ideal of my cook. Much more interesting than the psyche is the blue-satin blouse with which, in spite of her corpulence, color, age, and sex, she intends to masquerade as a Cossack.

I shall return to my former reflections, strengthened by that corroboration furnished by Jandira. The great trouble of our time is the sense of being cast out. Not feeling within himself an existence or activity of his own, man, with a desperate urgency far beyond the exigencies of his nature, requires an outward support. If he lacks a scaffolding, he feels deeply distressed, as one who, in a nightmare, finds himself in a room where everyone is having a good time in Chinese. He is like Papini's clock that runs only when the others condescend to join it and that stops dead when it is left behind by the gay throng of living clocks that goes on its way continuing the dance of the hours. Out of order, not understanding the Chinese in which the others are laughing and singing, the outcast has only one thing that he can do—the one thing that does not demand sociability. He can weep. And so he does.

And the result of all this is a society in panic that puts all its stakes on strident clamor and blatant show; a society of terrified men that trample upon the poor, the lowly, and the sick in their wild frenzy to attain a platform in the public square from which they can beckon to one another with feverish and meaningless signs.

For the young girl who bends anxiously over a fashion plate in order to know what she shall do with her own hair, for the poet who tries to find out what name is in vogue at the moment, what book is to be read and discussed, for the cook who is going to the Carnival, and for her mistress who is going to the lecture, what is of greater importance than the reality of hair, poetry, Humanism, and tambourine, is the fact of entering the great illumined theater and taking up the legacy of the other characters of the bewildering drama that for years upon years three billion poorly rehearsed actors have been enacting by the light of the scornful Aldebaran.

February 7th

A Priest Went By

Seeing a priest pass my window today, I was curiously reminded of the Carnival; the priest appeared to be disguised as Death. I do not know whether it is still the custom. When I was a little boy there was never a Carnival without someone masquerading as Death. The costume consisted of a sheet, a cardboard skull, and a scythe.

"Look at Death! Look at Death!"

The children would come running. With his face pressed to the iron grating, the little boy would watch that vague thing go by—that thing of which grownups spoke with sighs or mock laughter, and that would steal back at night through the portico of nightmare. Once the little fellow dreamed that Death carried him away. He was four years old. Death had picked him up and set him on his shoulder the way Uncle Afonso used to do. He had struck Death's head and shouted. But the skull seemed not to feel the chastisement of his tiny fists, and the thing continued to walk slowly, with shy solemnity and extreme circumspection, like the priest that I just now saw going by on the other side of the street.

February 8th

The Doctor's Visit[1]

I had a pleasant surprise today: a visit from Dr. Aquiles. I was reading Saint Augustine's *Soliloquies*, that I had found down on a lower shelf with its pages still uncut, when I heard three discreet knocks at the door. It was he. I do not know to what clever means he had had recourse in order to get around the strict Jandira. But there he was, framed in the doorway, deliberate, corpulent, with his shining bifocals, and his customary lack of tact, which was soon betrayed in the false pretext he offered for his unexpected visit.

"I've been to see a patient in the neighborhood and I thought I'd drop in for a few words. It's not a professional call. Or, if you like, it can be professional and friendly. How are you?"

"As you see, waiting—Lady Death's behind time. Isn't that just like a woman?"

Settled in the rocker, Dr. Aquiles was pretending to smile and was making an ill-concealed survey of my room. I had the impression that in order that I might not feel the pressure of professional curiosity, he was making an effort not to look at me; at my face and the emaciated chest revealed by my unbuttoned pajamas. I thought I should make some move and offered him a cigarette. As he stooped to light it he noticed the book that had remained open on the bed.

"Ah! Saint Augustine! I see that I have interrupted a most interesting *tête-à-tête*. You're in very good company. Saint Augustine is an extremely good writer; his message is highly pertinent

[1] In connection with this chapter it is interesting to remember that all his life Rilke, who rejected the suggestion that a mediator was necessary between God and man, was hostile to ecclesiastical Christianity (trans.).

to our time. I know only his *Confessions* and the *City of God.* I believe the *Soliloquies* is a youthful work."

"I hadn't read it either, though I bought it years ago. It was the title that enticed me today, for I, too, have been holding a long soliloquy. This is a dialogue between Augustine and Augustine, or rather, between Augustine and Reason. But I must confess that, despite the author's subtlety, I find him too clear; his debate with himself is too well disciplined. My own is quite different. It might better be called a multililoquy. It is a confused clamor. Reason, Memory, Imagination, and Blood all speak at once. And the poor José Maria who is presiding, becomes completely demoralized, and quite in vain rings the little bell demanding quiet and order. I conceived the idea of plunging into that reading to see if the individuals inside of me—the Prisoner included—might be put on their mettle and follow the good example of the learned scholar. I'm just at the point where Reason asks: "And what, finally, do you wish to know?" to which Augustine replies: "To know God and my own soul; that is all that I wish to know."

"Ah! That is the question!" exclaimed Dr. Aquiles.

And leaning back in his chair, more at ease now, he began to speak of the crisis of our time marked by man's evasion and by his aversion to an inner life and to a profound knowledge of self. In the Middle Ages, to the contrary, that preoccupation with the discovery of the soul was so predominant that one great philosopher and historian did not hesitate to say that the characteristic feature of medieval civilization is its Christian Socratism.

"Look at someone like Saint Bernard, Saint Thomas, Saint Catherine of Siena—do you know Saint Catherine?"

"I read her a long time ago. I believe that on those lower shelves I have her *Dialogues* or her *Epistolary.* I recall the insistence with which she speaks of knowing oneself—in God—yes, and I recall now the other theme of her sermon: Blood. She was the ardent propagandist of the great Donor. It's curious—"

Dr. Aquiles' kindly brown eyes looked into mine. Apparently

he was considering whether he should make capital of the similarity that had accidentally arisen between my medical case and Saint Catherine's spiritual prescription. But either he feared that it might be inopportune, or he was not adept at improvisation, for he resumed the thread of his reflections on the medieval mind.

He went on to say that that mind might be said to have lacked a certain extroversion, a dually proportioned interest in the physical world. In compensation for that deficiency, or rather, in opposition to it, is the modern mind, which, turned completely toward the physical and intoxicated still from its easy rewards, has become more efficient in deed than proficient in consciousness. The soul and God have been forgotten. Augustine's day came to an end. The men of the Renaissance ran away from themselves and set out in their caravels to seek gold and conquer the world. The epitome of that deflective trend can be found in the semantic history of the word fortune: the time came when that word which had meant destiny, happiness, and hence had designated something superlatively intimate, began to signify the possession of external wealth. The world is traveling swiftly toward the empty forms of an implacable economy and a tyrannical socialization. The individual has become an abstraction and society the only true reality.

"These last years, however," continued Dr. Aquiles, "there has been a notable reaction, a desire to get back to the mystery of man. Since Freud, in spite of his mistakes, the whole world has taken a feverish interest in psychology—"

I do not share the Doctor's sympathetic attitude toward that feverish interest in psychology. I have my reservations. I believe, moreover, that he himself said that just to please me and to throw up a bridge of understanding between us lest I think his Catholicism of the conventional sort, inimical to modernism and contemptuous of science.

I do not find in psychoanalysis that resumed interest in the human soul that he pointed out. Indeed, to the contrary, I see in that psychological interpretation the same extroversion to which he alluded. The curious thing about Freud's work, in my opinion, is his utter lack of interest in the core of man. His admirable discoveries disclosed the diversity, the mysterious wealth of our pyschic organism. Then he concluded that man is a poor lacerated creature, without any unity. Now to me this seems illogical. To my mind the more varied and positive our psychism may be, the more definitely will be asserted the principle of unification, which, despite the odds, achieves a victory, more painful, to be sure, but for that very reason all the more precious, since it represents a domination over many and scattered elements. In Freud's theory, however, the illogical conclusion to which he comes, or at least the one that he urges us to accept, is that of the weakening of our center of gravity. As a modern psychologist has observed, in the structure that Freud proposes for our psychism, the main part of the drama takes place between the *id* and the *super-ego.* The whole interest of the plot lies in the obscure intrigues between the unconscious and the categorical restraint that proceeds from the outer zone of the *super-ego,* while the conscious ego is a minor character that waves its hands helplessly in the middle of the stage. It becomes obvious then that that psychology and its derivatives are characterized by a marked extrinsicality, disguised because of its proximity to the center, but becoming only the more marked and positive the greater its effort to resist that proximity's powerful attraction. To my mind, that psychology, notwithstanding its respectable contribution, tends to disintegrate the human soul rather than establish the principle whereby the ego is the most single, separate, cruelly lonely thing in the universe. Through its insistence upon analysis and disintegration it contradicts the primary fact of soul-experience. Ah! If I were at the beginning of life I might seek a wise psychologist to dissuade me from taking up a military career in a moment of ardent patriotism or a naval career, like my unfortunate cousin Anísio. If I were going to get married I might endeavor to give my unconscious a prenuptial upbraiding. But seeing that I am going to die, I must try to discover the full, absolute meaning of life, I must try to know myself for what I am, what I really am—

"No, Dr. Aquiles, psychoanalysis is not for a dying man, precisely because, more than anyone else, the man who is dying must know the absolute meaning of life. Freud is farther from me and Saint Augustine than the most extroverted of the adventurers who set out to gain the most extrinsic of fortunes. Today's psychologists come nearer because they deliberately turn their backs on the problem. For me it is a question of finding an active, synthesizing principle, a salubrious enlightenment that will enable me to assimilate the idea of God and the idea I have of my own soul. For me the problem is one of bringing the aspects of truth together and transforming them into the substance of my blood. I must swallow my Creator; I must have him in my blood. You'll say that is easy because He became Flesh that He might be eaten; but my answer will be that first I shall have to swallow that word, and I think it will be hard—"

I was preparing to develop my theory of assimilation, when I perceived that in the pleasure of talking I had failed to notice the expression on Dr. Aquiles' face. He was looking at me with a mixture of respect and surprise as if, on the one hand, he were just beginning to understand and, on the other, understood less than before. I believe that my accusation against the Freudian doctrine had been to his liking, perhaps unduly so, for actually it might better have come from him, a doctor and a Catholic.

We remained silent for a moment. In Dr. Aquiles' quiet presence I sensed the prelude to a friendship that would be both long and good, were I, like Saint Augustine after his *Soliloquies,* to have twenty years in which to get to know myself and find God.

At the moment, I felt I had entered into that imaginary future, and I foresaw the strengthening of our sympathy, and the subsequent discussions, difficulties, and misunderstandings that we should share. Yes, we should have many serious misunderstandings, because Dr. Aquiles is a man of preconceived ideas, a man without improvisations or nuances. I foresaw the weariness he would cause me, and the vexations that could not fail to come from that good, rectangular person who was there to catechize me and who now was embarrassed.

Yes, he was embarrassed. For the apostolic purpose that had brought him he would have preferred to find me less familiar with the works of the saints and the Church. Above all more innocent. Then he could have resorted to the surprise that moves the innocent and have used one of the ordinary formulas with which men express that theological hope—so often prescribed for cases like mine—convinced that at least it would seem new and fresh to me, as did the great words of the Apostle to the ears of the idolators, the very words that to the hardened members of the synagogue seemed but the fantastic subversion of their law and prophecies.

I was to be the little boy who asks stupid questions, or raises objections, one of those classic objections that the students of apologetics crush easily with the ready-made secular answers they have memorized with eyes staring at the ceiling. And thus, a child led by an older brother, punctuating my journey with wondering whys, I was to enter the Kingdom of God with docility.

But now the good teacher was hesitating, disappointed to find that I was very much grown-up and that I was close, very close, but with my back turned. Why does he not say to me the same thing about myself that I said about Freud? Come, Dr. Aquiles, why don't you push me? Why don't you convince me?

Then I noticed the package he was holding.

"That package is in your way. Do you want to put it on the table?"

He got up to unburden himself of it, and when he was close to the table, he saw the sheets of paper on which I had written the day before.

"You're keeping a record?"

"Yes. I don't know why. I may show it to you—I may tear it up."
Still with his back toward me, Dr. Aquiles said quickly:
"Eunice was in to see me yesterday."
"Yes?"

We were once again sitting opposite each other, I, on the edge of the bed, tense with curiosity, he, on the edge of the rocker, leaning toward me, making for my sake the small sacrifice of relinquishing the comfort the rest of the chair could have afforded him.

"Yes, she was in. I don't know how she found out. I think she had met Pedreira. At any rate, she had learned of your illness. She didn't know any of the details, though, so I thought it my duty to inform her of your actual condition. She was very much upset, and appeared to want a reconciliation. But I wish to give you my word of honor that's not why I've come. I came rather out of sympathy, or friendship, if you prefer— I'd have come anyway one of these days. Only your wife's visit brought me a little sooner, I admit."

"She's not my wife, Dr. Aquiles. We're not a married couple, or rather, we're just a musical-comedy pair. Our certificate bears the seal of Uruguay. Eunice is my heresy, Doctor. I'm sorry to see you mixed up in this affair. I ought to have warned you, but I never imagined that Eunice would show up in your office. I supposed she was in São Paulo."

More embarrassed than ever, Dr. Aquiles made a move to rise. He looked at the package on the table and consulted his wrist watch, but remained seated.

"Does the obstacle to your marriage still exist?"

"The obstacle's name is André and he still exists, or, at least, he was existing up until last month. He's as unhappy a person as I. I don't even know for certain which one of us wronged the other. First, it was I, afterwards it was he. Besides, he himself proposed that charade one afternoon when I opened a door, breathing thoughts of vengeance. After that we suffered together. It's an old story—and now the ghosts have come back. Tomorrow it will probably be Raul who will come to see you in your office, so you should know that Raul isn't my son, either."

"How's that? The marriage may have been a musical-comedy affair, as you said, but that doesn't mean that your son's not yours."

I looked at the Doctor pityingly. How can an intelligent man be so stupid at times? I explained that it was not because of the Uruguayan seal that Raul was not my son.

"I learned that fact only shortly before we separated. It was Eunice, herself, who, in a moment's anger, flung the imposture in my face. The scene took place in the next room (our bedroom). She told me to consult a doctor if I had any doubt. I called the boy who was playing outside. He ran in, laughing and with flushed face, but when he looked at me, he stopped short with fear. I grasped his shoulders and held him, I don't know how long, analyzing his face, his nose, his eyes, seeing his fear become terror. He kept shouting: 'Let go of me, Papa! Let go!' And I, feeling the world spinning around me, kept shaking him like a madman. He was the image of André. How had I not seen it before? How had so sharp a resemblance escaped me? Losing my head, I began to slap the boy, while Eunice tugged at my hair and clothing, and called me a brute— Later I consulted a doctor. He made humiliating examinations. Raul couldn't be my son; no little boy in the world could be my son. And there I was: with a pseudo wife and now a pseudo son. And everything else would be the same, a pseudo house, a pseudo life. And I, myself, what was I? A shadow, an unhappy puppet, who was taking the pantomine seriously; and, mistaken as I was, for apparently the world is a circus, I was weeping pseudo tears."

The Doctor was listening, motionless, impenetrable. Only the mouth of his square symmetrical face was alive, contracting more than usual as much as to tell him that it was not to be relied upon.

"But that wasn't the day we separated. Violence has a sort of dynamic equilibrium. We were still to know hours of ecstasy, such as we had known years before in the vacant house on Ipiranga Street. It was later, two years later, I believe, in a moment of insipid boredom, that Eunice announced she was leaving and I wondered that she hadn't already left a long time ago. I gave her half of what I had, and I kept Raul. Yes, I kept the boy. Explain that as you will. The fact is, I kept Raul. At first, after she deserted me, I would go through crises of solicitous affection, which made me get up at night to see whether the child was sleeping well and to arrange his covers. Occasionally, I would stand and look at him for a long time. I felt that I should be lost if I didn't have Raul. But I went through crises of exactly the opposite nature, also, when I missed Eunice. The period of Raul's adolescence was torture for me—I don't think he knows yet, even today— It'll be better if he doesn't—besides, we're strangers now. He married a big, quiet girl from Belo Horizonte, who presents him with a child every year. They're my pseudo grandchildren—"

He remained silent for a long time. The heat was stifling. I got up to open the window because the sun was hidden now by the General's house. It was probably around five o'clock. A light breeze raised the curtain and stirred ever so slightly my red rose, a very full-blown rose, with a broad, open face like that of a sunburned country girl. I put a paper weight on my diary, and sat down again opposite the doctor.

"I am beginning to understand," he said then, bearing down heavily on each syllable. "I am beginning to understand. God is a chiaroscuro."

He settled back a little more comfortably as though he had finally found the solution to a theoretical problem, which he would proceed to explain. Seeing that I was trying to anticipate, he made a gesture of constraint as if to beg me not to interrupt.

"God is a chiaroscuro. His will is at one and the same time infinitely clear and infinitely obscure. When it's a question of His ends, of what He wants of us definitely, there can't be the shadow of a doubt. He wants us to be just and irreprehensible in His sight. He wants us to love Him with all our heart and all our understanding. But how? With what concrete means? That is where His will becomes obscure. And we lose our way in the labyrinths, often seeking to force His silence, His holy obscurity. Ah! my dear fellow, there's nothing more disconcerting than the concrete instance."

The Doctor held up his finger as if to say, "Take note of this," and shifted his position in the chair. I was lost in a maze that was not wholly disagreeable. His intention escaped me. Where was he leading?

"Occasionally," continued the Doctor, "we have a little glimmer of that *how* that is generally so obscure. But we are contrary creatures. Precisely when we have one of those rare signs we refuse to heed them. We think them useless. We should like them to be different, just as people in trouble seek a counselor and then seldom follow his advice. We prefer to follow our own will—"

He was coming down to a lower level. Ah! Dr. Aquiles, I see now, where you are leading, and I am saddened by the smothering predestination that poisons my life and determines my death. Can it be that you, too, are an automaton?

"In your case—"

Here he comes. Look out! He is going to speak of the spiritual profit that I must derive from my illness and pain.

"In your case, which I'm beginning to understand, your life has been a tissue of falsifications. Lying, deceit, discrepancy, sham—those are the threads with which you have woven your days. You were too discerning for such a fabrication, a specialist if I may say so, and that, I think, is why God has hidden His visible Church from your eyes. You couldn't have borne the sad spectacle that we offer; you couldn't have seen the Blood that flows from that mysterious body, for being too attentive to the ugliness of the feet.[2]

[2] According to Nora Wydenbruck, one of the factors that determined Rilke's revolt against Christianity was "his artistic sensibility, his passionate preoccupation with the perfection of form." In one of his letters he says: "If

The world is never free from an admixture of baser substances. The Church, being in the world, temporarily embraces that admixture. And you could not have borne it. There is a certain morbidness and a great weakness in your mad outbursts of sincerity. Forgive me. God has conceded you confusion, even heresy, pseudo heresy, and now He is granting you this retreat, this vacant period when you will come before Him without our being there to encumber His presence with our density and obtuseness. Right now I've stayed too long myself—no, no, don't protest! It's true. I've brought you a good sample of our colossal dull-wittedness."

The Doctor became silent and in his congested face I saw signs of the effort it had cost him to break his habitual reserve. He wiped his forehead with a white handkerchief on which his initials were embroidered in blue thread. What was his wife like, I wondered? How could that ponderous person perform the graceful exigencies of love?

In the dim light of the room, his massive face, which was slowly swaying back and forth in the rocker, began to yield its secret. I saw his weariness; I saw the weight of God upon his bitter soul. Thirty years of Catholic Action, of timid, disillusioning apostleship, of polemics with the taste of straw, of meetings with the taste of ashes! Ah! and the subscriptions to Catholic papers with photographs of illustrious prelates, and the parochial conferences to convince the superconvinced, to explain the horror of Communism to the superhorrified, to point out the disadvantages of divorce to the superindissolubly married.

"What corrupts everything is petty complacency," said the doc-

---

I were to become a practicing Catholic today, where would I find the church where I would not be offended by the *mesquinerie* of the pictures and representations?—to come into contact with the Church today is equivalent to condoning bad art, mawkish phrases, the entire and immense lack of expression in her pictures, prayers and sermons." Here, of course, the implication is much broader. Corçãos' protagonist is seeking not only esthetic perfection; he is seeking the Absolute—the sublimity of Rilke's Angel (trans.).

tor sententiously. And he added in a low, deliberate tone, "It is vanity—"

Apparently he had penetrated my thoughts, or, perhaps, he was concluding his own, which meanwhile had taken the same course. Our roles were reversed now, and it was I who must comfort the weary doctor or instruct the bewildered apostle. So I sat down on the bed and took up his ideas:

"Vanity!—shall I tell you what I think? There's too much talk these days of economic and sexual maladjustments, but the basic maladjustment, which pursues mankind to the brink of death, is in the focus of pride. That is where everything is falsified. And do you want me to tell you where, in what milieu, in what group of men, vanity is most evident? I'll tell you; it's in the groups of virtuous, well-meaning men of good conduct who unite to safeguard sound doctrine and good morals. It's in your Catholic Action, in religious congregations, and ecclesiastical assemblies. The rest of mankind, on the outside, is without guidance; and vice flourishes. Money and Sex predominate. Sin is fat and ruddy; it is sportive, comprehensive, tolerant, sympathetic, and one might almost say that it has the beauty of things that have thrived. Look at the man who vitalizes industries, who gives generously to charity, and has breadth of vision and amenity of manner. It is said that he keeps two or three women. Whence the moralists and reformers conclude that Money and Sex are the two great forces that must be rectified with new social structures and new psychological methods. They fail to see beneath the gross fat the essential root of pride, which is the thing that makes sin ridiculous as well as odious. But in the ecclesiastical assemblies, in the cloisters, and in the parochial gatherings men are stripped of the fat and ruddy vices. It is then that the root stands out and can be seen in all its sorry integrity, in all its starved ugliness, that pale, twisted, puny little thing that is pride. From the poor layman who bustles about his duties in the Catholic Action to the monk who walks in the garb of a penitent, those are the men who are the true specialists. There you have them unadulterated. Without the guise of frivolity. Without the show of prestige. Without the dramatic interest of the discrepancies of love. Essential vanity. Pride with its nerve exposed—"

"How does it happen that you know that?" the Doctor asked with ill-concealed emotion. "This is our secret!"

"And mine as well, though from a different point of view."

"In what way?"

I lay back on the bed, closed my eyes, and confessed:

"The story of my omissions, indeed my whole story can be put into these few words—a senseless horror of admixture. It was you, yourself, who discovered that. Actually, I dreamed of a world of crystal purity—I wanted my blood to be flawless as Burmese rubies!"

"Such rubies really do exist!" exclaimed the Doctor.

"I know."

"Genuineness and truth do exist, but one must look for them in an admixture; for a time one must accept the dross with the jewel and the chaff with the wheat. God has spared you my thirty years of delusion and mediocrity. He has spared you the heat of midday that wearied even Him when He sat down on Jacob's well and announced to the young woman from Samaria that the time had come to worship God in spirit and in truth. God has spared you all that, but now let me tell you something very important. He doesn't exempt anyone from a minimum that, if explored to its depths, may become a maximum. He doesn't exempt anyone from one particular minimum even at the eleventh hour—"

"Yesterday, from this window, I saw that Minimum going by."

"What do you mean?"

"It was a priest."

Dr. Aquiles looked at me closely. He made a gesture and apparently was about to say something more but refrained. He was even more excited and constrained than before. Then, abruptly, he rose and picked up the package from the table.

"I brought you this."

"Intrigued, I opened the parcel. It was a crucifix. Or, rather, the crucifix, the same one that I had seen before in his consultation room. And I had not guessed! The cross whose form is more widely known than any other in the world had been but partially concealed in that revealing parcel. And I had not guessed.

"It's a remembrance—if you don't mind, we'll nail it to the wall there, and then I'll be going so my Catholic obesity may not be an obstacle between you and your Savior. He didn't have a horror of admixture— Will you get me a nail and a hammer?"

And while Dr. Aquiles, like a good centurian, attired in Irish linen, was nailing the figure of Christ to my wall with rather clumsy blows of the hammer, I was thinking of Eunice, Raul, and the broken clock. "Do you suppose it can be mended?"

February 10th

Blood Wedding Anniversary

Today I am completing my third month of agony, my Blood Wedding Anniversary, shall we say. I should invite my friends and ask Jandira to make a cake wtih three red candles on it. Pedreira would come, and Alice, and a group of students, and the last to arrive would be Dr. Aquiles, hiding the donor behind him, just as good old Dodo used to hide her Jules Verne.

"Guess! Guess what the doctor's present is."

"Blood."

"Bravo! Bravo! What a clever dying man!"

February 15th

The Depths of Subjectivity

"The discovery of the *ego*"—I read today in the pages of a philosopher—"is completed in the depths of subjectivity." That is the document, written in secret runic characters, that fell into my hands by chance and that so concisely shows me the way to the center of the earth. Well, the time has come, Axel. Say good-by to your beautiful Gräuben, and let us go down into the depths.

First I repeated to myself the words of the good Englishman that it is more remarkable to have a nose than to have a remarkable nose. When I was a schoolboy and was interested in astronomy I used to derive great satisfaction from being able to see the star of sixth magnitude with my naked eye. I could see also quite clearly the binary of the Alpha of Centaurus. I prided myself on having unusually keen sight. To be sure, my vision was remarkable, but at that time in my life I did not yet know that the truly remarkable thing was the possession of vision. I was impressed by adjectives but failed to be impressed by substantives. I was vain of the gifts that singled me out from the others, because I had not yet considered the substantive reality of my soul, which distinguishes me so much more markedly, yet at the same time places me with the others in a startlingly wonderful equality.

The experiment that I now propose is to leave the adjectives behind; they are but the trappings that superficially differentiate me from others. Will it be possible, I wonder, to say of my entire self, my *ego*, what I have said of my nose and my eyes? Will it be possible to consider that substantiveness, that essentiality, to which my glittering adjectives cling like so many parasites?

The first attempt was lamentable.

That is what happens when man tries to discover that nuclear reality that is within himself, that entity that is so strongly attached, that source of life, that center of being, that substance of the soul: that is what happens when man tries to descend with his ropes and lanterns—why may it not be a descending as well as an ascending?—in search of the ultimate point to which he tapers. And when he bends down and leans over—or if he rises on tiptoe—why not?—in search of the ancient name by which Herzeleide called him and that only Kundry knows; or goes in search of the eye that sees without being seen unless it be in others, in the enigma, in the mirror of others; when, finally, he explores the place where is condensed in all of its marvelous and rich substance that entity that stands out and away from everything that is objective, everything that is scattered in picturesque and disorderly profusion like the superfluous exuberance of an ornamental frame—that is what happens, that is what the daring adventurer encounters: "Silence, darkness, and nothing more."

I had hung my outward titles away on invisible hangers. On that decisive expedition, what did it matter to me that I am a professor of the Philosophy Department? Of what importance to me was the whole series of petty conquests and great failures that constitute my life's outward appearance? I am a Brazilian, a voter, I have been vaccinated, I am the author of a work on Bessel's integrals, a member of the Engineering Club, property owner, poetaster, and now a victim of cancer. Yet all those predicates combined do not supply a subject. They surround it, hang themselves upon it, or rather, realize themselves in it. But the hidden subject, the subject that is sought, and that at times examines its externals with the melancholy eye of a half-doting nobleman who from the balcony of his ancestral estate surveys his domain overrun with weeds and ruined by neglect—where is it, that subject? Yesterday I hurt my finger. Yet, with all its live connective tissue, that finger seems a remote, external thing, like a broken fencerail that the unhappy owner of the dilapidated estate considers how and when he shall repair.

Withdrawing and descending ever deeper, opening up a way among the disparate externals, I give voice to the question: "Where is the throne room in the enchanted castle of myself?" From darkness to darkness, from silence to silence I traverse fearfully the recesses of my being.

This room with the soft yellow light is memory's study. But I am not my memory. Though it enables me to have a clear notion of my own continuity and to carry out today what I promised yesterday, and though, in short, it enables my *ego* to move forward in time, my memory does not constitute my soul. Memory is a register; a passive receptivity. One may break into its museum of old, battered things and, like a burglar, suddenly throw his flashlight on a forgotten chest. Or, one may be held there, like an unhappy prisoner, forever turning the pages of an album. And then, too, it has its involuntary, cameralike manifestations that may bring from our inner stirrings many things we should like to forget; there are certain recollections that thrust themselves upon the burglar unsought after. Its museum is a place of enchantment, a fairy-tale antique shop where everything whirls around in a kaleidoscopic dance of shifting colors and shapes to which the proprietor cannot give any semblance of order for even a moment. In mine, for instance, there are some thirty-odd telephone numbers, anniversary dates, addresses, algebraic formulas, authors' names—all there in plain view to deride me; but where have they put my mother's smile?

No, memory is not the center of my being; I am not my memory. Nor am I my imagination; despite the activity and inventive spontaneity of that stereoscopic camera that combines such divergent images as volcanoes, stars, and roses, it is not the core of my personality. I am not my imagination.

Retreating still farther, and turning out the lights of memory and imagination, I grope in the dark with desperation; but I cannot find my way. In that instant's nightmare, I lose my footing and totter between *all* and *nothing*. The extraordinary contiguity that in his cryptogram the philosopher called *être-avec néant* makes me giddy. And I fall. I tumble into the void. I awaken screaming. And I clutch whatever may be at hand, a waterspout, a lightning rod, the ledge of a window left open; actually I clutch my title of professor, and I plant my feet securely on the good tangible externals that sustain me and assure me in the language of mute contact, that I exist, at least, outwardly.

Then running and screaming, I start to flee from the darkness of myself. Hereafter, though it will be for only a little while, I shall be objective, extroverted, collective, social.

Why not? Would it not be more noble than to die with only the roses for company? It seems that I still have about two weeks. Now in two weeks I can become useful if I pick up my leukemia and go forth to show the world that amazing thing that Voltaire found so normal and Goethe so abnormal: the-man-who-knows-that-he-is-about-to-die. The newspapers would be full of me. The President of the Republic, of whom I should seek audience for an important philanthropic project, would rise from his presidential chair at the entrance of so noteworthy a personage as I, who am axiomatic death, an incarnate example of a syllogism, the certainty toward which everyone is hastening. I should be granted extraordinary allowances, so extraordinary is the fact of being mortal, and I could render great services to the community: manufacture tricycles that would be within everyone's reach; improve the living conditions of young girls who stand and serve coffee all day, *de marré, marré, marré*. My death would be the farewell of a great benefactor. I should depart in my phantom ship, watching the world slowly fade into the distance, and there would be a dock with many grateful people and many handkerchiefs—

The world is dying from its endeavor to run away from itself. It is dying from being riven in two. So am I. And in these few days that remain, the error that has manifested itself variously throughout my life still persists within me. I am the unhappy coachman of the second-rate melodrama, who, in a closed coach, is driving the Iron Mask, the pallid prisoner whom no one has ever seen. The grim coach is passing over the stones of an immense, deserted street with the doleful clatter of an ill-spent life in an ill-paved world.

Tomorrow or the next day—tell me more exactly, Dr. Aquiles—from my place on the driver's seat I shall hear muffled thuds on the sides of the coach, and for the first time my prisoner's hoarse voice will reach my ears:

"Here we are—"

February 16th

The Man Who Says Farewell

The plan that came to me yesterday in the guise of fancy has come back today, and I am considering it seriously. Who knows if I might not actually do something with those fifteen or twenty days that are left instead of staying here in this room recording the vertigo of my soul? Who knows if I might not inform two or three people of the "supereminent existence" that controls our explosive elements with a firm hand? I should tell Pedreira how I defeated in challenge the brightest star in the heavens. I should tell Gertrude the story about the innocent clock, victim of my blind passion. To the gentle Luciana I should speak of the depths of hope. And who knows if, by speaking to these others, I may not gain what I myself need?

I decided to start out after lunch. First I should go to Dr. Aquiles' office to arrange for a transfusion, and, especially, to continue our conversation of the other day. Then I should go to see the waitress. Also I should hop over to the flower market for three roses to take the place of those that have withered, and, then, depending on how I felt, I should take a taxi to Pedreira's laboratory.

Hearing my footsteps on the stairs, Jandira was startled and came to the living-room door. She was making a cake, and her hands were white with flour.

"I'll be back before dinner, Jandira."

She looked at me with shy deference and smiled as though she had something to say but did not dare. I thought I ought to initiate with her my resolve to be sociable and to show a sympathetic interest in others; so I asked: "How's your costume coming along?"

Jandira laughed, shaking her plump shoulders. She suspected, of course, that I was just pretending to be interested or that I was making fun of her. But she was wrong. I was genuinely interested; for I was no longer content with the abstract, artificial preoccupations of the past week. The stout Jandira, with her floury hands, is more complex and much richer in mystery than my futile philosophy.

Dr. Aquiles was not at his office today. The nurse told me that he has the flu. And I found myself out in the street again, rather upset by that small annoyance.

It was a blazing day. The extreme heat lent the passers-by an air of informality and extroversion. I was not so tired as usual. It seemed to me that the whole city was on holiday and that the surge of people coming toward me was benevolent and friendly. At a certain moment the street scene—why that particular one I do not know—engraved itself on my mind with singular vividness. In the foreground, a pink-cheeked, elderly gentleman in light gray was raising his right arm with a grave statuesque gesture while with his left, bureaucratically and methodically pressed against his body, he held a yellow-leather portfolio. His companion was showing his very fine teeth in a respectful smile. The surrounding crowd was less clear. A silk-crepe dress with a leaf-pattern in shades of light green. Two laughing young girls. An urchin. Hundreds of secondary silhouettes. And in the distance, as far as the eye could see, a confused mass of shoulders and heads, the perspective of the narrow street with its irregular facades, and far away, a scrap of intensely blue sky.

It recalled one of Rembrandt's pictures in whose foreground likewise there is an important figure with eloquently outstretched hand and in which a wonderful perspective breaks the bounds of the canvass— What is the name of it? I believe that it is the *Night Watch.*

But the scene had shifted. Perpetual motion had consumed my Rembrandt. The old man and the young man had gone on their way. "Sur le pont d'Avignon tout le monde passe." And now, letting my eyes linger with no effort to catch the bird on the wing, I could see the movement itself as a concrete reality—the constant flowing movement, the continual flux of all things. That picture had existed only an instant; the faces, the smiles, the swaying shoulders, the barely glimpsed neckties, the unfinished words—only an instant. And the poet in me whispered that I should look well at those rounded backs that were hurrying away.

> Qui nous a ainsi retournés que nous,
> quoique nous fassions, nous avons cette allure
> de celui qui s' en va? Et comme, sur la dernière colline,
> d' où sa vallée entière se montre à lui,
> une fois encore, il se retourne, s' arrête, s' attarde–
> ainsi nous vivous et toujours prenons congé.[1]

[1] "Who is it that thus turns us round, that we must always
Whatever we may do, assume the bearing
Of one who goes away? As does the wanderer
Who, halting on the hill from which he sees
His native valley the last time, turns round and lingers–
We spend our lives, forever taking leave."

These are the closing lines of Rilke's Eighth Elegy.

"The main argument of the Eighth Elegy is the division between man and the life he lives within the conventions of time, conscious simultaneously of his beginning and his end" Nora Wydenbruck, *Rilke: Man and Poet*–(trans.).

Oh consuming motion! I am not the only one who is taking my leave. I am not the only one who is seeing these things for the last time. Everyone is seeing everything for the last time. I am not the only one who, because of my blood, am dying. Everything is dying. The whole universe is a great, hurried leave-taking. Hastily closed trunks are stacked in the porticoes of the ages; white handkerchiefs flutter at the threshold of instants.

"Farewell, O Sun, we're moving on! Hurry, O laughing young girl, we're just passing through! Farewell, farewell, good journey, O streets, O people, O stubborn stones that loiter in the illusion of permanency!" Restlessness—impermanence—that is the meaning of everything."

All the tales of fiction that I have imagined—and there have been many—ended with a man walking at twilight along a road that wound away into a gray landscape. His back was toward me, and he would grow smaller and smaller until he fused with the dusk and became lost in the distance. And whether he had just begun his tortuous and futile departure or whether he was already nearing its end, that was invariably the close of the story.

Without thinking, I found myself in front of the coffee bar. I looked inside and saw at once that Gertrude was not there. I hesitated, but, taking advantage of a lull at the counter, I went up to the blond, freckled youth, the one who had made the girl laugh a few days before. I was embarrassed because I did not know her name; I fumbled for words in a blundering attempt to describe her, sensing the ridiculousness of the situation and guessing what the boy must be thinking of me.

"She's left the place. I think she got sick. I don't know."

I do know. Of course she got sick, and, yes, of course, she has left the place. What relation can there be between a profitable business and a girl who spits blood?

Walking more slowly now, I started in the direction of the flower market. The heat had tightened its grip. The genial expressions on people's faces appeared to have given way to a general congestion. Everyone was hot, perspiring, with shirt open at the neck. From the asphalt rose a furnace blast, and the sky had become a metallic lid painted blue.

In the doorway of a dry-goods shop, waiting for her husband, perhaps, was a young woman with a Raphael *bambino* in her arms. His serious blue eyes were staring a little sleepily into space. I paused, trying to capture the child's attention. I waggled a finger at him and was about to touch his little face lightly, but the mother drew back quickly and I saw a look of fear and indefinable repugnance in her eyes. Ah! of course, my thinness, and my pallor! I could have explained to her that there is no danger of contagion—she could ask Dr. Aquiles and Dr. Rosalvo—

It was at the corner of Uruguaiana that I felt the first dizziness. I stopped a moment. Indeed, there seemed to be no ground under me. I looked around. It would be better to take a taxi and return home.

I took a few more steps. An old lady in black talking animatedly to a boy with his arm in a sling was coming toward me. She wavered in front of my eyes, and the blackness of her dress expanded and engulfed me. Instinctively I held out my hands—

When I regained consciousness I was seated in a chair in front of an apparel shop. A stout, dark girl was offering me a glass of water.

"Drink a little more. Are you better?"

There were some people standing around in a circle. They had stopped, curious to see that livid, emaciated fellow who was there at their mercy, sitting in a chair on the street, like a peddler who had invented an original trick to attract his public.

"Are you better now?"

It was a robust, good-looking young man in a pink Palm Beach suit who was smiling at me—his teeth sparkling behind a neat, shiny little black mustache. Was he a doctor, I wondered? No.

More likely he was in business, a simple, light-hearted salesman. I asked him to get me a taxi.

He insisted on going with me. He said he had the time and that it would be better, because if I should feel anything on the way—but, of course, I wouldn't feel anything— It was the heat. It was suffocating. Perhaps it was going to rain.

At Marques de Abrantes Street there was a traffic jam. A streetcar had collided with a truck loaded with bottles. There were pieces of green glass strewn about and puddles of beer, and people were making observations about the accident and proffering solutions. My young Samaritan jumped to the conclusion that it was Light's fault, and used the spilled-beer episode as a springboard for an indignant peroration on American imperialism. He was a Communist.

"Just look at the atrocities they're committing in Korea!"

I maintained a constrained silence. Not daring to contradict him, I let the good youth instruct me and hold forth the promise of happiness based on historic materialism.

"That's it—Number Thirty-Four."

We were nearly there, and with no thought for class struggle or American imperialism I could only say to the Communist youth who was supporting my arm:

"May God reward you."

When Jandira saw me being almost carried in and saw my state of collapse, her forebodings were confirmed. She had seen well enough how weak I was and had wanted to say something.

"It's nothing, Jandira. It's just the heat."

"You should call the doctor who was here the other day."

"Later, Jandira. After the Carnival—"

February 20th

Rosa, Rosae

I was lying down. Outside, from the far-off streets where it was at its height, the Carnival was filling the night with a great, vague, raucous sound that might have been a roar of perversity or a moan of pain. I had put out the light, and a torpor had come over me that was more like an anesthetic than sleep. When it increased, even though my eyes were open, the sound seemed to draw nearer. It was as though Rio de Janeiro were snorting its Carnival madness directly into my ear, almost directly into my most intimate being. Then I thrust the torpor away once again; the sound became scattered in space, now here, now there, now with one variation, now with another.

But in a little while the torpor came back, and then the sound drew near again and compressed itself, and once again the streetcars and noisy merrymakers, the drums and tambourines were all inside of me.

Space is destroyed in the same way on certain nights when the atmosphere is heavy and merges all things into a close, compact mass. Then the sky comes down and lies upon the earth; the mountains move and become walls; the whole universe seems to be a cramped prison. But the dawn that follows such a night is one of wonderful spaciousness and translucence. Veil-like the sky is wafted upward with the lightness of a feather; the heights return to their comfortable distance and cease to be a thing of terror; little white houses are born in the morning light, and men breathe freely because the universe has expanded.

Now what I felt as I lay stretched out on the bed, without the courage to move, was a heavy night that was pressing down upon me and into me. What was happening? Could it be day? Should I resist, turn on the light, arrange the flowers, drink a glass of water? Should I call someone?

The torpor returned— At the threshold of sleep or faintness, but still conscious, I saw images that rose up before me—strange faces that I did not know. I heard voices. A youth, enveloped in a dark cloak, hurried by and, almost as though the voice were inside of me, I heard him say, "He has come!"

"Who?"

But the youth sped away into the air in zigzag flight, like a great bat. The sound waxed louder. The confusion inside of me waxed greater.

"Say good-bye, Axel! Come take your leave. Let us be on our way!"

It was my uncle's voice. We were at the mouth of the volcano and were beginning to go down a natural spiral stairway in the crater's walls. The sound that came now from the bottom of the well was different; it was disconcertingly grotesque, as if turned inside out. There were cries, laughter, and groans, and back of it all the roar of a Wagnerian whirlwind, colossally out of tune. Where was my uncle? Now I was descending alone, clinging to the rock projections. The swift messenger, wrapped in the dark cloak, went by again, shouting: "He has come!"

"Who?"

Unanswered, I continued to descend. I plunged into the amorphous sonority as if sinking into a quagmire. Exhausted, I felt horrible pains in my arms and legs. Might it not be better to release my grip on the rock and let myself fall?

"Go ahead, Axel! We're late!" said Professor Leidenbrock's voice in the same tone with which Dr. Rosalvo had questioned me about the atypic cells. I continued to descend, faster, faster, bumping against the rock, bruising myself as I fell, hearing all the while the voices that rose from the bottom of the well, the sighs, complaints, and recriminations that passed me in the form of great nocturnal birds spiraling up to the mouth of the volcano. "Hurry! You can't stay—"

"Stay, there's a verb that has no meaning," said the poet's shade that went by at that moment, holding a rose between its fingers.

"José Maria, stay!" sang out a woman's voice, light and pure and remarkably clear.

José Maria? Who had called me thus, as in my dreams I had heard my mother name me? Who is that, of such wisdom that she knows my name and my secret? Ah! In vain had I sought the woman who might tell me who I was. I had wandered through lands of error and suffering in quest of corporeal love, the encompassing love that might encircle and define me, the love that was solicitous and adaptable because of my desire to express the hue of the moment—golden in Eunice, white in Luciana, ruby red in Gertrude—and that was intolerant because of my contrary desire not to let the moments consume me. How can anyone live without the mirror of a woman's face? How could I find salvation outside a protective lap?

And I went on and on, running away from myself, or, if not from myself, from what, then?—but running away. I could not stay. I could not stop. I could not find the meaning of my existence, so long as there was no place to offer me shelter. Who will detain me? Who will find me, if I cannot find myself? Who is it who is hiding there and ordering that I stay; I who with drooping shoulders am going away down the winding road to make my farewells? Woman, woman hidden in the night—

"In the rock!"

In the rock or in the night, Kundry of guileless voice, tell me the story of my birth. The story of Herzeleide. Once upon a time—O woman hidden in the rock—

"In the night!"

"In the night and in the stone. Tell me the legend of the little boy who went far astray into the night. Ah! and don't forget the laughter, yes, the great loving laughter when the happy woman found him! Come! Speak! Tell me just one thing: that I was waited for. How can anyone live if he is not waited for? Tell me that she waited through days and nights, until her lamentations were stilled, and sorrow consumed her. Until there came the longing for a silent death and sorrow broke her heart. Tell me that Herzeleide died—"

"Herzeleide did not die. With seven daggers in her breast Herzeleide lives!"

"Who are thou? Art thou, too, a flower?"

"Rose! Rose! sang a chorus of light, white voices.

"Rose, oh pure contradiction, O sweetness of being no one's sleep under so many lids," whispered the sad, solemn voice of the poet.[1]

"*Rosa, Rosae, Rosae, Rosam, Rosa*!" declined another invisible chorus to the tune of a children's carol.

"Sweetness of being no one's sleep—" I repeated to myself amid the darkness and clamor. I should have liked to fall asleep gradually, vicariously, through the closing of the roses' eyelids one by one.

I was falling softly now, like a feather. The rock tunnel was widening and becoming suffused with a tinge of dull gold.

I am seated now. I cannot recall the transition, or perhaps I should say, rather, that there is no transition in the tinted images that slowly revolve in the album of one's dreams.

Dressed in black velvet with gold embroidery, like a melancholy king of Spain, I am seated on a rock throne ornamented with exotic relief. I believe even that I have a painfully heavy crown on my head. Then I notice the place where I am. It is a large cave, roughly hexagonal, and illumined with a dim yellow light. There are galleries, three, I believe, that wind into the darkness and merge with it. I guessed the presence of a multitude hidden in those tentaclelike labyrinths, for I heard whisperings and restless

[1] Rilke asked that these lines be inscribed on his tombstone:
"Rose, oh reiner Widerspruch, Lust
Niemanders Schlaf zu sein unter so viel Lidern" (trans.).

footsteps. It was then, just when I was beginning to despise myself, that there entered the crypt from the central tunnel a rather odd person who made me a most complex and ceremonious bow.

Short, stout, bilious, with hard, level-set eyes, a retreating chin, a dainty mouth in the form of a V, a hooked nose, that curved even more when he laughed, as though it were looking to see where the chin had been hidden—my man combined a great deal of circumspection with an extraordinary air of mischief. He was attired with the sobriety and outmoded distinction of a church dignitary on holiday: correctly buttoned dark jacket, crimson tie, and well-fitting well-creased striped trousers that came down to the tops of his small, shiny leather shoes of impeccable polish.

He came into the cave, as I have said, and after two elaborate salaams he began to execute on tiptoe, arching his short arms and bending his body, a mincing dance, half-classical, half-grotesque, which allowed me to get a good look first at his bilious face with its prominent nose flushed from dissipation and then at his enormous buttocks accentuated by the tautness of the too-tight jacket.

When these preliminaries had been accomplished he placed himself very correctly in the middle of the cave, blinking his eyes methodically, and drew a whistle from his pocket. The commotion in the dark corridors increased, and when the signal was given there started to emerge from each labyrinth a procession of new figures, while in the air thundered the pealing bells of Monte Salvat. In contrast to the mischievous circumspection of the master of ceremonies, I saw filing before me the most solemn and astounding collection of trappings imaginable. Crowns, mantles, diadems, republican sashes, high silk hats, medals, cravats, plumes, symbolical rings, regalia, scepters, maces, togas, plus an infinite number of insignia of unknown meaning. It was as though the inmates of an enormous hospice had escaped and rifled a museum. But the faces beneath that diversity of trappings were all alike in expression; all had the same staring eyes, the same frozen laugh, the same complacency of one who is standing before a mirror to examine how his jacket or his showy uniform becomes him.

The master of ceremonies informed me then that they were all important people. Very *important*! He stressed the word so that its significance might be impressed on my mind, and he went on to explain more fully:

"Not all of them were successful up there. Doubtless some were. The one over there to the left, the one with the sash, is the President of the Republic. But the one beside him is an employee of the government. Like the king's shirt, his importance is invisible up there and is known only to himself. Here, however, we have a perfect wardrobe so that everyone can array himself in accordance with his fancy."

While the puppets continued to march gravely by with the same staring eyes and the same paralyzed smile, the master of ceremonies sat down on a stool at my side and leaned against my arm with a shocking familiarity.

"You haven't asked me yet where we are—"

It was quite true. The question had not yet occurred to me. I looked more closely at the bedecked madmen. Each had an elaborate heraldry of exceedingly bad taste embroidered in gold and silver on his back. It was surmounted by a huge scarlet *I*. Then I began to discover in the faces certain signs that had escaped me before, and the more carefully I examined them the more transparent they became. I was able to guess the secret thoughts and the past of each face as it went by. I wanted to avert my eyes in revulsion, but my curiosity was greater than my disgust. And so I saw—in every face I saw a set story, an explanatory chart. Then a dreadful thought struck me, and I looked at the master of ceremonies, who was awaiting my answer with patient and amused good humor. He understood my terror and began to laugh.

"No! Oh, no! Oh! Oh! Ah! Ah! Ah! Ih! Ih! Ih! No."

And wiping his eyes, he added, seriously now, "It's very different there."

"What place is this then?"

"This is a theater, or a school if you prefer. A place for rehearsal or for training—this is the fifth act of a play that I thought up. The hero's about to enter now; watch closely."

Drawing the whistle from his pocket, he blew three long signals. The extraordinary figures divided into two groups, some to the right, others to the left, leaving the middle gallery free. Through it even more circumspect characters began to enter, dressed in black. It was a funeral procession. The wrought-ebony casket with gold and silver ornamentation and incrustations of precious stones was carried by four dapper gentlemen with graying hair and much-bemedaled chests. At a gesture from the master, they set the casket in front of me on a small rise of ground, while other characters, who were issuing endlessly from the dark gallery, placed enormous wreaths on and around the coffin. "The cenotaph is a ship— Only it has too many anchors, too many life preservers, and its crew of one is dead."

"Do you know who it is?"

I nodded. It was André. I could not refrain from telling about André's unhappy past, our friendship, Eunice, the first kiss of betrayal and love—

"Speak louder."

"What about them?"

"They can't hear; they're absorbed in self-contemplation and hear only the voice of their desire and the blowing of the whistle. Do you want proof?"

He began to shout horrible insults, but the characters did not lose their placid gravity.

"You see? This fellow's dead, the others are sleeping—we can talk as we like."

And daintily pulling up his trousers in order not to spoil the crease, he drew nearer with a show of profound attention. One might have thought him a doctor, listening to a patient's babble and reserving the right to separate the important points from the general confusion. In spite of an intense loathing, I continued my narration of André's story—my story. I recounted everything in detail. I told about the house on Ipiranga Street, the marriage in Montevideo, the birth of Raul, my jealousy, Apartment 402— My man became more and more interested. Occasionally he would smile understandingly and nod his head as if to say, "A word to the wise is sufficient." Now and again he laughed.

His laugh started with soundless spasms in his abdomen, then rose in a gurgle, swelled, remained a moment in his larynx, from which it spilled out like water from a sieve; then mounted to his oily face and ended at the tip of his flexible nose, which bent under its weight until it rested in the cleft of the obscene, red mouth.

Observing that he laughed at the wrong moments, I was vexed; but I went on with my tale, redoubling my effort to make the obsequious person understand, while at the back of the cave the others kept up their fantastic round of Importance. When I came to Gertrude's story the man suddenly grew serious, one might almost say startled.

"How's that? How's that?"

He had not understood. I repeated the episode, and he redoubled his attention. All of a sudden, thinking that he had caught what he was looking for in my story, he slapped his thigh gleefully.

"That's good! That's a good one!" and the abdominal spasms began.

That made me angry; I said sharply that the story did not call for laughter and that evidently he had not been paying due attention. Thereupon he became properly serious, replied that he had understood everything perfectly, that he had given all the attention that the matter deserved, and that he could repeat everything I had said, word for word.

And, thereupon, he proceeded to retell my story. I was amazed at its accuracy. It was my own story down to the very slightest detail. Yet, at the same time, it was monstrously false, as though he had dehydrated it, burned its flesh, destroyed its joints, emptied its arteries, diluted its color and was showing me only the fibers of my deplorable story—the same fibers but reduced to a cinder. It was not that he omitted facts or circumstances, not that he mutilated them; the story was intact, but no longer was it alive. So, though I could not point out where the falsity and error lay, it turned out to be unsurpassingly grotesque.

I was aquiver with impatience. The stony ornamentation of my throne was a torture to my arms and legs; the crown was a crushing weight. Never under the worst circumstances had I been so carefully imitated and so monstrously misunderstood. Shall I say that the man was unfair? No. What I can truly say is that he had an essential inability to see the other part, which was the sap, the blood of my story.

I began to plead my cause, going into minute details, making reflections, distinctions, and analyses, all of which came up against the oily, faintly amused face—if they did not fall into the sieve of vile laughter that emanated from the stomach and terminated at the tip of the hooked, dissipation-flushed nose.

Occasionally in the upper world I had felt that anguished need to convince and ingratiate an interlocutor whom I despised. Though they were more worthy, the others, those who agreed with me or understood me, they failed to elicit my interest. The one whom I wanted to capture was, precisely, the one who was trying to get away from me; and I wanted him with an absurd and distressing intensity even if I were to abandon him and relegate him to everlasting contempt as soon as I had conquered him.

What I felt now was that same desire, heightened to the point of frenzy. At all costs, I must make that repulsive person understand me. I humiliated myself. I urged him to make an effort. I implored him. And exhausted, clenching my fists, stamping my feet, and sobbing with rage and despair, I began a repetition of my story, but this time it was more like the one my tormentor had told me.

Just as I was on the point of losing consciousness, I looked up and saw a red star away up high at the narrow opening of the rocky funnel. It was Aldebaran. I summoned my strength and turned toward the man.

"Now I know what is lacking in your story. It's lo—"

With a leap, he was on top of me, clutching my throat and covering my mouth with his cold, fat hand.

"Can't you see that you'll set fire to all that straw?" he said angrily.

He pointed to the puppets, the casket, the wreaths.

I made a violent effort to cry out, and in my struggle I bruised myself on my rock throne. But finally I managed to articulate and, in a strangled voice, screamed to Aldebaran, "Love! Love! Love!"

Then the star fell down from the sky, and the bright red glow of a great fire lighted the cave. Ah! now I saw in the faces, arms, and legs that were fluttering in the air, like leaves dancing in the flames, a thing whose presence I had missed in that sepulcher until then. I saw pain, living pain, the living pain of love. The volcano had become active.

"Axel! Axel!"

Standing on a teetering plank, I was rising in a spew of incandescent matter between columns of basalt. Where was my uncle? The clear voices that had been declining the rose petals had faded away. I was alone. I was still rising amid the lava from the star. And then, gathering my strength and holding tight to my shaky raft, I questioned heaven and earth: "Who, who, if I cry out, will hear me among the ranks of the angels?"

My arms and legs are hurting horribly. I open my eyes. Where am I? Apparently I am in my own room, back in my own poor body once again. But I have the impression that space is different—submarine, non-Euclidian. The crack of light is there under the door, but bent like a blazing iron tossed into the corner of a forge. I do not see my mother's shadow nor do I hear footsteps—the house is empty, the house has died. And the roses? I look for them. There they are, two white ones and a golden yellow one. But how different they are! They appear to be leaning forward, offering themselves— Then I look in the direction of the roses' offering, and I see before me a sublime Rouault of such size that it covers one entire wall. There is the twisted crown, the matted hair, the suffering eyes, all in somber tones of emerald green and ultramarine; and on the uncovered breast long, slanting furrows of red. How long did I remain with bated breath and outstretched neck seeking the light of those eyes hidden in the shadow? I cannot say. The Figure was immobile, but I was aware that from that blood-streaked breast came a gentle warmth, a warmth as from a hearth that made my bones molten. And it was then that I remarked the hands held out to me and that I saw the two luminous wounds in the open palms— No! Dear God! what did I see in the two open palms? Two rubies of wondrous beauty: my Burmese rubies—

February 23rd

The End of the World

The first thing that attracted my attention when I finally managed to get my eyes open and while they were still blinking against the daylight, was the dazzling blue of a huge, vaguely oval shape that was slowly moving about in the middle of the room. In an effort to arrange my thoughts, I closed my eyes again for an instant. When I reopened them, there was the curious meteorite, even bluer and more brilliant than before, because now the sun was shining full upon one of its rounded hemispheres. It took me a long time to realize that it was Jandira dressed as a Cossack.

There were other people in the room, talking in a low tone. Dr. Aquiles, with his back partially turned, was over by the window, conversing with a tall, thin gentleman who was slowly shaking his gray, haggard head. In the wide open doorway a swarthy youth in shirt sleeves was holding a sort of lance or iron crowbar. He appeared to be there as sentry, though he offered no resistance when the scarlet woman entered and went over to Dr. Aquiles with a bottle.

"He's awake—"

It was Eunice! The scarlet woman was Eunice, little changed, almost not at all, and still pretty. What could have happened? How was one to understand that strange scene in which Eunice, the eternal Eunice and the ephemeral Jandira merged in a momentary blending of complementary tones? And the man with the crowbar? The wide open door?

"He's awake."

Bending down over my chest, which the unbuttoned pajamas left exposed, Dr. Aquiles made a sign to the other man, who then came over. And running his finger over my chest, Dr. Aquiles said:

"Petechiae."

I, too, looked and saw that my chest was dotted with dark spots of extravasated blood. They were reddish at the edges and purplish in the center.

"Look, they're rubies, real rubies," said my father, running his finger over the breast of the image.

It was an image of Christ, three palm-spans high, ablaze with silver and rubies encrusted in the body. It had come from his grandfather. The visitor gazed in awed admiration, and as my father replaced the Christ on the wall, said sententiously, "What fine craftsmen there used to be! They wouldn't make crucifixes like that today."

"Petechiae."

The doctors looked at each other. I thought to myself that my rubies were not real; they looked more like amethysts. Eunice, too, bent down to see, and the reflection from her dress imparted to my chest a rosy glow, a glow that was but a loan of health. Our eyes met, and all the absurdity of our life together seemed to be concentrated now in my utter inability to say three words. How could I put together in those few minutes what I had devoted twenty years of passionate anger to destroying? I felt that my reason was wavering between awareness and a kind of somnolence in which memories came and went, one superimposed upon the other. Raul! Raul! Eunice, in front of the mirror, was dressing to go out, and I, unable to move, my whole body wracked with pain, was watching her get ready, making herself beautiful to say good-by to me— She slammed the door, went down the stairs, clickety, click, click, and disappeared on the street where she became dispersed in the crowd. And my thoughts, too, scattered to pursue a thousand silhouettes of many hues, living roses, the blood from my opened veins that was flowing through the streets. Eunice went up in an elevator as in a glorious ascension, leaving me clutching a lifeless telephone while the barber, whose face was André's, a mortally sad face, shook his head and urged me to desist— I closed my eyes. I felt that the rosy glow was going away. Eunice's dress was robbing me of my health. I tried to call, to cry out, and tell Eunice that there was no hope for us—*

Six characters who meet; six chance characters. Only the two of us, Eunice and I, have a certain logic. The rest have none; they invaded the stage; they broke down the door on Ipiranga Street. They made my fifth act absurd. Six characters of a drama without beginning or end. "Life is but a walking shadow." And what must I do now? What conclusion can I devise with those improvised characters, those unrehearsed actors?

. . . .

Whence came that idea, at once so clear and so abrupt that it pierced my soul with a sudden blaze of proof? Whence came that strange certainty that I shall be the second one to die?

. . . .

* Here the manuscript becomes almost illegible.

I opened my eyes. The scene was almost unchanged, with the same characters. But where was the sixth? How long had they been there watching me? The room had grown dark— Should I keep still? Should I say something? An odd feeling of responsibility made me feel like the head of that small city of six that had set itself up in my room. I am the commander of my ship. It is up to me to save them. But where is the sixth? I motioned to Dr. Aquiles and asked:

"And the priest? Did he stay downstairs?"

Dr. Aquiles looked at me in astonishment. He explained that when he had learned through Jandira's phone call that my room was locked from the inside and that I did not respond to the knocking on my door, he had in fact gone to get Father Lucas. But he had not found him in, as Father Lucas was conducting a Carnival retreat in Juiz de Fora. So he had brought a priest who had happened to be passing on the street, one whom he did not know, one still young. Poor Dr. Aquiles! He is wasting time with that sly cunning. Have him come up, Dr. Aquiles, it is well that a priest be here to hear the highly important communication that I have come to make.

They are all in the room. Eunice is conversing very respectfully with the priest. The doctors are talking about the Carnival and the heat. The man with the crowbar has come closer to get a better look at me, and he seems impressed. But where was Jandira? Just as I was about to ask for her, I heard a faint sound that made me shake with terror. The cups! the cups!

It was Jandira coming with the coffee tray. Eunice asked the priest how much sugar he wanted.

"A little, just a little—"

Evidently it would not be becoming for the priest, poor man. to say that he wanted a great deal, a very great deal of sugar. Dr. Ramas, the other doctor, was not so modest, but he dissembled his greed as a joke:

"I drink coffee for the sugar."

I, too, took a cup served by Jandira, who had not yet had time to remove her glaring costume. I learned through her that it was Mardi Gras.

"I've spoiled your Carnival, Jandira."

The tray shook, and a blue tremor zigzagged across the Cossack's ample bosom.

Shall I speak or not? They are all around my bed, like devoted sons awaiting their dying old father's final wishes. The priest, a tall, blond young man with a slow, artless manner, showed the trace of an embarrassed smile. He could really be my son—that is, because of his age; arithmetically he could, but not physiologically. In the physiological plane, more concrete than that of numbers, no one could be my son. However, I feel a strange tenderness for those five persons as though I were their foster father or the commander of a ship that is going down. Yes, they are my first and last disciples, they are the heirs, the depositaries of a wearying, fruitful old age of which I had dreamed. I must be content with that handful of recruits, those chance characters for the epilogue of my story. I feel that the responsibility is essentially mine. Shall I speak or not? Which one of them will be the first?

I spoke. At first they did not understand me or thought that I was delirious. I had to repeat, and explain myself with mathematical precision. The first to understand was the Crowbar-man.

"You're all looking at me as though I were a being apart. You are vertical; I am horizontal. You are living for an indefinite time; I have ten days. Isn't that right, Dr. Aquiles? And that is what establishes an essential difference between us. I, alone, am truly mortal, like Socrates and Caius. I, alone, partake of death-dealing logic. You don't, for you're still in the sphere of life's absurdity. You have a compassion for me, but at the same time a great inner tranquility. You're saying: "He's done for." I used to do the same thing. Vertical, alive, happy, I used to go into the room of one classified as mortal, and I felt the same good compassion and the same easy tranquility. Now, what I have to say to you— Eunice, close the door! Thank you. Apparently there's a change coming in the weather. What was I saying? Ah! yes, I was saying that all six of us in this room are done for. Don't you feel the ground swaying, Jandira? Does no one feel it? Well, we're on a raft, castaways from the galley *Chancelor.* Father, have you ever read Jules Verne? No? But you've read the story of the Ark. Well, what I mean is that for the six of us in this small asteroid, the deluge has already begun—"

At that moment there was a loud clap of thunder and a heavy summer shower began to fall. Eunice stifled a cry. Jandira crossed herself. The Crowbar-man was livid.

"No! I'm not alone on the raft; I'm not the only castaway; I'm not an exception. I am the rule. See how the rule operates and how these blood spots punctuate the conclusion of the syllogism. Close the window, Jandira! The sea is high. Poor unhappy raft! It is done for. Now listen to the secret I have to tell you. Come closer."

They all drew nearer. Eunice was nervously twisting a handkerchief. The Crowbar-man was looking at me with fascinated attention. And then I disclosed to them the certainty that had struck me with the impact of a blow: the certainty that of the six of us there I should be the *second* one to die.

There was silence. The idea came up against the pride of the living, or percolated slowly into their hearts without their faces betraying any emotion. No one smiled. No one believed or disbelieved. And no one asked how I knew. The idea had been released into the air like a bolt of electricity. The priest blinked his blue eyes. He appeared to be about to say something, but he refrained. The situation lent itself admirably to sermonizing, but its undercurrent of superstition made him reluctant to speak. On the one hand it was explorable, on the other forbidden, and the priest did not know how to extract himself from the difficulty.

Again I told them that I should be the second one. Who would be the first? Then I explained the need to rehearse the scene with its six characters. I pointed out that my previous situation, my three months' secular experience had given me certain privileges and a certain right to leadership. I suggested that they should crown me Emperor of the Asteroid, and in exchange for the fealty of my subjects I should allow them an apprenticeship in death— I should be the master who would give them lessons in how to descend into its depths— Who would be the first to go? I was more sure than ever now. More sure than all the living, because I had a sign.

The priest made a gesture of impatience or incredulity and Dr. Ramos, who had finally managed to achieve a worldly smile, was on the point of saying something when the scene suddenly burst into activity. There was a terrifying peal of thunder followed by a shrill scream, the thud of a heavy body, a strident sound of metal and shattered glass. A gust of wind blew the rain into the middle of the room where the Crowbar-man lay as though dead.

"Jandira, close the window!"

The two doctors were kneeling beside the Crowbar-man. The priest, too, knelt on one knee and drew a book from his pocket. Eunice was running from one side of the room to the other, making useless and irrelevant suggestions. But Dr. Ramos, who had just used the stethoscope, got up with a dubious smile which was at once one of relief and one of deception.

"It was nothing—just a shock. Jandira get a glass of water."

Confused and trembling, the Crowbar-man was regaining consciousness and sipping a little water. The priest was encouraging him with words of comfort.

"Father, I should like to confess."

"So should I," said Jandira.

The priest rose to his feet and explained that since he was outside this parish, he did not have the right to hear regular confession; he could only attend to the sick. In vain I tried to make him understand that there was no one in my asteroid more intensely alive than I; in vain I endeavored to shake his hackneyed notion of sickness and health. The priest apologized and suggested that Jandira and the Crowbar-man go to their parish as soon as the rain was over, adding without a spark of humor, that Jandira should take off her gaucho costume—

"It's a Cossack costume, Father."

But the rain was streaming down as if it were a waterfall, and Eunice, who had gone over to the window, informed us, "The water's rising. The street is impassable now—*

They are extremely nervous. Dr. Ramos, the skeptical Dr. Ramos, telephones three times a day to inquire about Antonio, the Crowbar-man, who disappeared day before yesterday. It seems that he has gone to Minas, but it is not known for certain. The others are well. Dr. Aquiles promised to come back today or tomorrow.

I am taking advantage of the early morning hour. I believe this is the last page I shall write. I have already asked Dr. Aquiles to collect these notes and give them to Father Lucas. They are my incoherent testament. Let the man of God censure it and let him who can, or will, profit from its lessons. And you, unknown reader, if you find no value in this, my sad legacy, do then what I have suggested elsewhere: add to it the thirty thousand invisible stars. And pray for me.

I cannot coordinate my thoughts. I feel as though I have grown very small, and, above all, very much exposed. I cannot lock the door because the lock has not yet been repaired. They can come in at any moment. I am dying in a public square in plain view of everybody, like one who has been run over. So different from what I had imagined!—

Today some students from the University were here. They were cautious and courteous, and when they left they said they hoped I would feel better. Pedreira was here, too. He was reserved and

* The next two and a half pages completely illegible.

hypocritical and tried to amuse me, but when he was at the head of the stairs saying good-by to Eunice I saw the grimace he made and I could easily interpret it even without resorting to my dictionary of unsaid words. He promised to come again. It seems that Raul is coming today with his family—

I hear voices. They are waking up.

"Quick, Gertrude, give me your apron and cap. I'm on duty—here they come!"

I lie down and look around my room, whose sanctity they have violated. I look at the bookcase which has been hastily put in order and at the opaline vase, which has been set aside and which is empty—

"Alas! you haven't even left me my three roses!"

Milton Keynes UK
Ingram Content Group UK Ltd.
UKHW030835020824
446414UK00001B/13